"There are rules about kissing,"

Chase said. "Don't kiss before the first date."

"I suppose that's a good policy," Nettie agreed. "Is that it?"

He shook his head. "No. Rule number two— never kiss a small-town girl if you know you're not planning to stay."

Nettie's eyes narrowed. "Well, you got the wrong girl." *Forever* was no longer a part of her vocabulary. "I'm not a woman who follows rules," she said. The lie tasted so good on her lips she followed it immediately with another. "Never have been. Never will be."

In a decidedly un-Nettie-like move, she traced an index finger slowly up the middle of his chest. "But if I were, I would remind you about rule number three—always consult the woman in question before making executive decisions."

Dear Reader,

April may bring showers, but it also brings in a fabulous new batch of books from Silhouette Special Edition! This month treat yourself to the beginning of a brand-new exciting royal continuity, CROWN AND GLORY. We get the regal ball rolling with Laurie Paige's delightful tale *The Princess Is Pregnant!* This romance is fair to bursting with passion and other temptations.

I'm pleased to offer *The Groom's Stand-In* by Gina Wilkins— a fascinating story that is sure to keep readers on the edge of their seats…and warm their hearts in the process. Peggy Webb is no stranger herself to heartwarming romance with the next installment of her miniseries THE WESTMORELAND DIARIES. In *Force of Nature,* a beautiful photojournalist encounters a primitive man in the wilderness and must find a way to tame his oh-so-wild heart.

In *The Man in Charge*, Judith Lyons gives us a tender reunion romance where an endangered chancellor's daughter finds herself being guarded by the man she's never been able to forget—a rugged mercenary who's about to learn he's the father of their child! And in Wendy Warren's new sensation *Dakota Bride,* readers will relish the theme of learning to love again, as a young widow dreams of love and marriage with a handsome stranger. In addition, you'll find an intriguing case of mistaken identity in Jane Toombs's *Trouble in Tourmaline*, where a world-weary lawyer takes a breather from his fast-paced life and finds his sights brightened by a lovely psychologist, who takes him for a gardener. You won't want to put this story down!

So kick back and enjoy the fantasy of falling in love, and be sure to return next month for another winning selection of emotionally satisfying and uplifting stories of love, life and family!

Best,

Karen Taylor Richman
Senior Editor

Please address questions and book requests to:
Silhouette Reader Service
U.S.: 3010 Walden Ave., P.O. Box 1325, Buffalo, NY 14269
Canadian: P.O. Box 609, Fort Erie, Ont. L2A 5X3

Dakota Bride

WENDY WARREN

SPECIAL EDITION™

Published by Silhouette Books

America's Publisher of Contemporary Romance

For Gail Springer, dear friend,
who never let me give her a book, but rather bought
every one I wrote and then mailed them to me to
autograph—SASE enclosed! Your humor, support and
encouragement was unfailing and will cheer me always.

And for Brandi, Shawn and Jeremy Springer,
Gail's true loves.

SILHOUETTE BOOKS

ISBN 0-373-24463-0

DAKOTA BRIDE

Copyright © 2002 by Wendy Warren

Visit Silhouette at www.eHarlequin.com

Printed in U.S.A.

Books by Wendy Warren

Silhouette Special Edition

Dakota Bride #1463

Previously written under the name Lauryn Chandler

Silhouette Romance

Mr. Wright #936
Romantics Anonymous #981
Oh, Baby! #1033
Her Very Own Husband #1148
Just Say I Do #1236
The Drifter's Gift #1268

WENDY WARREN

lives with her husband, Tim, and their dog, Chauncie, near the Pacific Northwest's beautiful Willamette River, in an area surrounded by giant elms, bookstores with cushy chairs and great theater. Their house was previously owned by a woman named Cinderella, who bequeathed them a gardenful of flowers they try desperately (and occasionally successfully) not to kill, and a pink General Electric oven, circa 1948, that makes the kitchen look like an *I Love Lucy* rerun.

A two-time recipient of Romance Writers of America's RITA® Award for Best Traditional Romance, Wendy loves to read and write the kind of books that remind her of the old movies she grew up watching with her mom— stories about decent people looking for the love that can make an ordinary life heroic. When not writing, she likes to take long walks with her dog, settle in for cozy chats with good friends and sneak tofu into her husband's dinner. She always enjoys hearing from readers, and may be reached at P.O. Box 82131 Portland, OR 97282-0131.

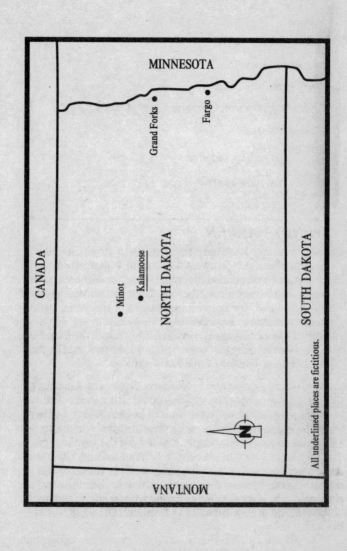

CANADA

MINNESOTA

Grand Forks •

Fargo •

• Minot

• Kalamoose

NORTH DAKOTA

SOUTH DAKOTA

MONTANA

N

All underlined places are fictitious.

Chapter One

Clouds hovered above the North Dakota prairie like a hand-me-down quilt—cozy and welcome at first, oppressively weighty if you'd been under them awhile.

Annette Owens lifted her face to the gunmetal sky and dared it to *do* something. Almost immediately, a brash wind rose in reply, whipping the dark curls back from her face.

Unclipping the barrette at the nape of her neck, Nettie shook her hair free and laughed. "Touché," she commended, filling her lungs with the crisp, rushing air.

So often lately she felt just like this sky—heavy and stuck. There were times when the desire to change, to…*burst free* became almost unbearable.

Gazing across farmland as achingly endless as the unpatterned sky, Nettie frowned. What would happen, she wondered, if she mentioned the keen restlessness she'd been feeling to anyone she knew—to a friend in town, perhaps, or to one of her sisters?

A smile—wry, self-effacing and just a bit naughty—curved her lips.

"They'd call up Doc Brody, and he'd prescribe enough tranquilizers to sedate the World Wrestling Federation."

A woman with her recent history could not go wild and crazy, after all, without the neighbors starting a phone tree. Not in Kalamoose, North Dakota, anyhow.

And that was, she supposed, understandable. For the past two years, she hadn't stepped foot outside the city limits of her small town, and the city limits of Kalamoose were, to say the least, cramped. For a year before that, she had barely stepped foot outside the clapboard house that stood as a stalwart haven behind her.

Agoraphobia—secondary to post-traumatic stress—that was the official diagnosis of her "condition." In layman's terms, that meant she was afraid. Of everything.

Taking several steps forward, Nettie watched her feet make imprints in the tall grass and pondered the facts.

Everything. Yeah, that about covered it.

She was afraid of what had already happened and might happen again and of things that had never happened and probably never would. She worried about her sisters and herself. She worried about her friends and their farms and about what would happen if the price of wheat fell. She worried about hurricanes in the east and earthquakes on the west coast.

And lately, she'd been worrying that she worried *too damn much.*

She hadn't always been this way. Once, she had been more like her sisters, with Sara's courage and Lilah's daring. There had been a time when the world beyond Kalamoose had seemed as tempting as an ice cream in the middle of summer, and Nettie had been ravenous for every delicious bite.

The wind stirred around her, its boldness invigorating. Nettie stood still, spreading her arms to the gathering gusts. When the first drops of rain pelted the ready earth, she began to run.

Her feet were bare, the grass was cool and tender and her summer skirt swirled around her legs as they pumped. She jogged the first steps, then picked up speed until all she could hear was the wind rushing against her ears and the echo-y pounding of her feet against the hard ground.

The rain began falling in slashes, mingling with her perspiration, and Nettie felt her skin cool even as her body continued to heat. She ran like a wild thing, like one of the antelope that roamed the Dakota prairie, refusing to stop even when the toll on her body became uncomfortable, slowing only as she approached the rutted dirt road that marked the end of her property.

Bending forward, she put her hands on her knees. Her shoulders heaved; her breath came in staccato gasps that burned the back of her throat. Her heart pounded the way it did when she had one of those episodes her doctors in Chicago had told her were panic attacks.

For three years, if anyone had asked her what she wanted, Nettie would have answered, "to stop being afraid."

But life, she had learned since, refused to be purchased so cheaply—with the absence of something. And that's what she wanted again: Life. The rain on her face and the wind all around, and her body on fire.

She had no idea, anymore, how to make it happen, or if she even could. It had been so long....

As the rain softened to a drizzle, Nettie straightened and looked up. A pocket of sky was beginning to clear. Shimmying through the clouds were twin arcs of translucent color, as if someone had taken a paintbrush and slashed watercolor across the sky.

A wondering smile curved Nettie's lips. Well, what do you know?

She laughed. A double rainbow. Now, who could ignore a sign like that?

Coffee and grease. Those were the first two aromas Chase Reynolds noticed when he entered the small country diner at quarter past eight Thursday evening...or was it Friday?

Having been on the road, driving, for most of the last three days, Chase was beginning to lose track of time and distance. At the moment all he knew was that he was in North Dakota, and he was starving.

The half-lit neon sign he'd spied from the road said Good Eats. If he'd learned one thing on his impromptu flight across the back roads of America, it was never to eat anyplace with "Grandma's" or "Good" in its name. "Grandma" inevitably turned out to be an ex-mess-hall cook in a love affair with white gravy. Unfortunately, five cups of coffee and a stale chocolate muffin from a gas station mini-mart outside Fargo had carried Chase as far as they were going to.

"Hi, honey. You want the counter or a booth?" A middle-aged blond waitress, whose breast pocket read Gloria in three-inch-tall embroidered white letters, approached him with a menu in one hand and a glass coffee pot in the other.

Falling into habit, Chase took quick note of all entrances and exits off the dining area, pinpointing where he could sit to maintain a view of the door without being immediately noticeable himself. When he realized what he was doing, a wry quirk curled his lips. The art of defensive dining. It came automatically these days—a swift, clever assessment of his surroundings. It hardly seemed necessary in a backwater burg like this, however, which was, after all, why he had chosen to drive through backwater burgs: the blessed anonymity. Most of the tiny towns through which he'd passed hadn't seen a major newspaper since Reagan beat Mondale.

Turning his smile on the waitress, he requested a booth, then followed her to a spot by the window. There was only one other party present, a pair of men who were, at the moment, studying the Porsche Chase had parked out front. Harmless. They could look at the car all they wanted as long as they didn't recognize him. Choosing the side of the booth that faced the door, he sat with his back to the other men.

Accepting the laminated pink menu Gloria handed him, he ordered the first thing he saw, requested a cup of coffee and hunkered over it as the waitress moved off to place his order.

What he needed, aside from a hot meal, was about a week's worth of uninterrupted sleep.

With the desire for sanctuary uppermost in his mind, he had decided to take an old friend up on a long-standing offer to visit a two-hundred-acre barley farm in the "wilds" of central North Dakota.

A wry smile quirked Chase's lips. As hideouts went, the farm ought to do; so far even *he* couldn't find it.

Selecting a package of soda crackers from a wicker basket on the table, he opened it neatly and ate. Once he fueled up—body and vehicle—he'd get back on the road. When he arrived at his destination, he'd sleep as long as his racing mind allowed, and then, God willing, he'd be able to figure out the next step in a game plan he was, after all, making up as he went along.

"Hello!" Stepping over the threshold of the Kalamoose County Jail, Nettie attempted to close the heavy door while she balanced a china dessert dish, a steaming mug with The Fuzz written across it in gold lettering, and a bundle of newly laundered sheets that were folded and tucked under her arm. She glanced around. It was after suppertime on Friday evening, but the sheriff, who'd been at work since early that morning, was nowhere in sight.

"Anybody home?" Nettie called as she stepped farther into the room.

After a few seconds, a figure emerged from the storeroom. Arms full of files, the sheriff greeted Nettie with a pleased smile and a bald, "What did you bring me?"

Nettie shook her head. "No one will ever be able to accuse you of standing on ceremony."

"Ain't it the truth?" The files hit the desk with a thunk and slid atop other papers already obscuring the wood surface. "Everyone knows you got all the manners in the family."

Clearing a space atop the desk, Nettie deposited the hot coffee and a healthy serving of peach pie. She grinned as Sara grabbed the dessert and took an unabashedly hearty bite, leaning against the edge of the desk to eat.

"Yum."

Annette Owens's eldest sister, Sara, had been the sheriff of Kalamoose, North Dakota, since their uncle Harmon Owens had passed away two years ago. Being Uncle Harm's deputy had given their neighbors plenty of time to get used to Sara wearing a badge, and though she was only thirty—and a woman—no one in the otherwise conservative town seemed to have any complaints.

"Heaven," Sara murmured, savoring the dessert. "Net, your baking is getting as good as Mama's ever was."

"Thanks." Nettie accepted the compliment with a smile and a rueful shrug. She baked when she felt tense or blue. Since moving back to Kalamoose, she'd spent so much time with her hands in flour, she felt like the Pillsbury Doughboy.

Nettie was five years younger than Sara, but eons different from her sister in both appearance and manner. While Nettie had inherited her grandmother O'Malley's fall of black curls, fair skin and round curves, Sara took after the Owens side of the family. She was tall and reed-thin, with an approach toward life and people that was as bold and unabashed as her fiery-red hair.

Watching Sara purr over the dessert like a cat lapping cream, Nettie shook her head. "How is it you never gain weight?"

Sara's slim shoulders lifted inside her khaki uniform. "Pact with the devil. Hey!" She stabbed the air with her fork as Nettie idly began stacking the lose pages scattered across the desk. "Don't mess up those papers."

Nettie raised the thin sheaf she'd collected. "These were in order?"

"Well, I know what's there. I'm looking for something."

"What?"

Sara reached for her coffee, blew and took a big swallow. "An all-points bulletin I got last week about— Wait a sec." She cut her explanation short as a police radio crackled to life.

"Watchdog One to Red Sheriff. Come in, Red Sheriff. Over."

The reedy voice of Ernie Karpoun, owner of Good Eats, the local diner, sputtered over the radio.

Nettie arched a brow. "Watchdog One?" Ernie was five-feet-four inches when he wore his lifts, and in all his seventy-two years he'd never weighed more than a hundred and fifteen pounds. Gazing pointedly at the copper hair Sara usually slicked into a low bun, she said, "And what did he call you? Red Sheriff?" She grinned. "Catchy."

"Oh, knock it off! I told him a dozen times not to do that," Sara grumbled. Taking her plate with her, she sat down in front of the radio and pressed a button. "What is it, Ernie?" No response. She rolled her eyes and hit the button again. "Ten-four, Watchdog, what have you got?"

Nettie laughed. She'd been back in town three years now, but there were still times when she forgot how small this place really was.

"What I've got is a pack of trouble ready to happen. I think you'd better warm up the squad car, Sheriff. Over."

"Oh, yeah?" Meeting her sister's eyes, Sara shook her head.

Trouble at the Good Eats generally meant someone had discovered the french fries came frozen. "What's up?"

"You know that fella who's been robbing banks out toward Fargo? Over."

Nettie sat on the edge of the desk, glad she'd decided to venture over to the jail tonight. It beat hanging around an empty house. With Lilah in California and Sara at work most nights since her deputy moved to Minot, evenings gave Nettie too much time to think.

Sara leaned over to scoop up another bite of pie. "Yeah?"

"Our bank could be hit next. Over."

"Really?" A tiny smile curved Sara's lips.

Nettie swung her legs as she listened to the exchange. This was far more interesting than a rerun of "Law and Order."

For the past several weeks, the evening news had been peppered with stories about a man the media had dubbed the "Gentleman Caller," a tall, well-spoken male between thirty and forty who robbed no fewer than twelve branches of the Bank of North Dakota, relieving them of hefty five-figure sums each time. According to eyewitnesses, the Gentleman Caller was polite, worked alone and never resorted to violence, at least not yet.

"What makes you think he's interested in us, Ernie?" Sara asked, lining up another big spoonful of pie. "Far as I know, the Gentleman Caller prefers savings and loans in bigger cities. We've got a tiny branch of the Bank of North Dakota. I doubt he's interested in us."

"Yeah? Then what's he doing in Kalamoose? Over."

Sara nearly choked. "Explain that," she ordered when she stopped coughing.

"That fella is sitting here in my diner right now!" Ernie's excitement came through loud and clear. "He come in about thirty minutes ago. I wasn't sure it was him at first, but... Uh-oh. Gloria just waved to me. That's our signal for when he's gettin' ready to leave. He ordered the chicken fried steak platter. It comes with mashed potatoes and corn—it's a lot of food, you know—but he's a quick eater, I noticed that right off the bat. Probably got used to eatin' fast because he's always on the run and lookin' over his shoulder. Bet he swallows a lot of air—"

"Ernie!" Sara snapped. Nettie had one hand over her mouth,

trying to contain her laughter. "Tell me exactly why you think your customer could be the Gentleman Caller. What does he look like?"

"He looks like that drawing they had in the paper a couple weeks back. Kinda normally-like, you know. Gloria says he's good lookin'. Got a few days' growth on his face, probably for a disguise."

Nettie was surprised to see Sara actually taking notes. "You're not seriously considering this?" She shook her head. "Sara, that composite in the paper was so generic it could have been you."

Sara waved at her to hush. Nettie rolled her eyes. None of the eyewitness accounts about the Gentleman Caller jived. Several frightened bank employees swore he'd flashed a gun; others said he'd merely claimed to have one. He'd been described variously as suave, dangerous, unflappable and, by one particularly whimsical teller, sweet.

"And," Ernie's voice crackled across the Kalamoose airwaves again, this time with ominous portent. "He's wearing a Ducks' cap."

"Ducks' cap?" Sara repeated, scribbling again.

"Anaheim Ducks."

"I don't remember that from the bulletin."

"It weren't in the bulletin. But tell me this—what kinda fella roots for a hockey team in a city that wouldn't recognize snow if they stepped on it? Anaheim. Shee-oot!"

Nettie rocked with laughter. Sara shot her a dirty look, then growled tightly into the radio, "Ernie, I can't question somebody because you don't like the Ducks."

"I don't like Anaheim."

Flinging herself against the back of the chair, Sara hurled her pencil at the CB. "Aw, for crying out loud!"

"Okay, Sheriff, how 'bout this: You know how when Gloria puts the food down, she sets the check down, too? Well, this fella paid right away, and when he reached into his pocket, he took out a wad of cash big enough to choke a horse. Smallest bill he had was a C-note. I gotta go into the safe to make change. And he started askin' Gloria about the layout of the town, too. Where's the market and how late does it stay open? And he's been real polite like they say, but he talks quiet, unnatural soft, like he's disguisin' his voice. And he don't make eye contact if he can help it.'' There was a slight pause. ''Over.''

The sudden tensing of Sara's shoulders telegraphed her alertness. Nettie's grin faded. She sat motionless, watching her sister's reaction.

''Oh, boy! Gloria just signaled me again. He finished the potatoes. You better get here, Sheriff, and I mean quick-like. Over.''

Leaning forward, Sara spoke calmly but firmly. ''I'll be at the diner in a few minutes. Keep him there if you can, Ernie.''

''Well, sure we can!'' There was a brief pause. ''How? Over.''

Sara was already on her feet. ''Give him free pie, coffee... Have Gloria spill lemonade on his trousers... You'll think of something. But don't try to detain him against his will or do anything to make him suspicious, you hear?''

''Roger, Sheriff, you can count on us.'' Ernie sounded like a radio spot for the United States Marine Corps. ''Over and out.''

As Sara prepared to leave, her hands moved automatically to her gun belt, checking to make sure everything was in place.

Nettie's eyes widened as an eerie chill skittered up her spine. ''You're serious about this?''

Sara was too preoccupied to reply. She reached for her hat.

Hopping off the desk, Nettie moved swiftly toward her sister. ''Sara, do you honestly think this man is the bank robber?''

Sara answered vaguely, her mind on the business ahead. ''I don't know. Could be.''

Despite her initial disbelief, Nettie's heart began to pound. ''You're not going to go over there alone then?''

''What?'' Sara plucked her jacket off a wooden rack by the door. '''Course I am. What are you talking about?''

Nettie began chewing on a thumbnail, realized what she was doing and whipped her hand down and behind her back. Scarcely two hours earlier she'd promised herself she would stop worrying and start living.

She'd always had rotten timing when it came to resolutions.

''If this man is the Gentleman Caller,'' she began, knowing she would not win a battle against fear when the safety of someone she loved was at stake, ''then he's a hunted felon. When

hunted felons feel cornered, they strike out. You could be walking into a potentially explosive situation. Call for backup.''

Sara looked at her sister. ''Have you been watching 'Dragnet'
again?'' She headed for the door.

''That's not funny.'' Nettie followed after her. ''Why can't
you wait until—''

''Fifty thousand dollars in reward money if this is the guy,
Nettie.'' It was all Sara had to say. Opening the door, she strode
to a squad car parked by the curb out front.

Nettie rushed outside, alarm bells ringing in her head like a
Sunday call to church. She knew exactly what her sister was
thinking. Kalamoose was in financial distress, nearly bankrupt,
a state of affairs that had become a fact of life for the struggling
farming community. Years ago, Sara had gotten it into her head
that she was going to do more than protect and serve; she was
hell-bent on saving the town she loved. Fifty thousand dollars
in reward money would be a good start.

When Sara wanted something badly enough, she could be
single-minded, unafraid and, too often, downright reckless.

''Don't go!'' Nettie blurted as Sara got in the squad car. ''You
know how Ernie likes to exaggerate. This man probably isn't a
thief at all.'' She endeavored to sound reasonable. ''He's probably a tourist who forgot to buy traveler's checks. You'll be
wasting your time.''

Sara made a face. ''A tourist in Kalamoose?'' She started the
car.

Good point. Kalamoose wasn't even on the way to anyplace.
''A lost tourist.'' Nettie groped for a logical argument, but time
was an issue so she settled for a highly emotional plea. ''Sara,
please don't go there alone. I'll be worried sick.''

The headlights came on, but out of respect for her sister, Sara
took a moment to lean out the window. ''I'm the sheriff, Net,
this is my job. Go home, will you, please? And try to relax.
Play one of those California mood music tapes Lilah sent you.
I'll be home soon.'' She backed away from the curb while she
was still speaking, turned the car and sped down the block.

Nettie stood at the curb, feeling chastened, damned ridiculous—and scared.

She walked back to the jail and opened the door, but changed her mind about going inside. It was cooler on the street, easier to breathe.

All right, so she was a coward. But she'd learned some things about life that Sara hadn't yet...Lilah, either. Like about how even when you were absolutely certain there were no more low cards in the deck, Fate could pull another one out of her sleeve. If she was overly cautious, it was only because she had learned the hard way to grab whatever control she could in life; there wasn't much.

Still, as she stood on the deserted street the bitter taste of shame filled her mouth. Her sister was willing to march into the lion's den, and her own grand contribution to the situation was to stay home and fret.

Leaning back against the cold brick of the building, she gritted her teeth in sheer frustration. Oh, how she had come to loathe feeling alone and afraid.

It was pitch black with a multitude of visible stars in the sky when Chase walked into the Kalamoose jail with his hands cuffed behind his back and his eyes narrowed into two angry slits.

If anyone had told him that his first arrest would come at the hands of a skinny girl sheriff in a town so small you could spit and overshoot the city limits, he never would have believed it. Over the past years, he'd gotten himself into some pretty close calls—pelted by gunfire, detained by officials in three foreign countries and interrogated by the best agents the FBI had to offer. He'd managed to emerge every time without a scratch.

Less than an hour after arriving in Kalamoose, North Dakota, however, he was handcuffed; and that was only after he'd been force-fed pie and soaked to the skin by a flying pitcher of lemonade. He just didn't get it.

"Keep moving!" Snapping the order, the foul-tempered sheriff gave him another in a series of small shoves. Chase clenched his jaw. If she did that just one more time, he would not be responsible for his actions.

As his eyes adjusted to the dim light of the jail, he glanced around, amazed by what he saw. Curtains, cute curtains with ruffled edges, framed every window. The building was old, a squat brick-and-wood structure that looked like it hadn't seen many updates through the years, but there was a vase with flowers perched on a small wood table, and pictures, mostly pastoral scenes of grazing sheep, dotted the walls.

Aw, hell, he thought, stopping dead in his tracks, I've been arrested by the sheriff of Mayberry, RFD.

Irritated by his abrupt halt, the sheriff jabbed him again, "I said—" she began, but Chase spun around before she could finish.

"Do not," he growled, enunciating each word clearly through gritted teeth, "do that again."

To her credit, the gangly sheriff glared back at him, hesitating only a fraction despite the fact that she was a good four inches shorter than his six-foot one.

"Don't tell me what to do, smart mouth," she shot back, "you're the one wearing the bracelets." With a decided lack of subtlety, her right hand moved to rest on her gun. "Your room's on the left." She hitched her chin. "Head over. Continental breakfast is at eight."

Giving her a long, malevolent glare, Chase ultimately complied with the order, largely because he was too damned tired to argue anymore tonight. For some reason, the yokels in this misbegotten haystack had it in for him, and he'd sealed his own fate for the night by failing to provide identification for the good sheriff. He complied with her command s-l-o-w-l-y, though, strolling to the cell as if he was on a nature walk and couldn't be troubled to rush.

If his right to a phone call was granted, he'd ring his lawyer, who was probably tired of hearing from him this month, and then Nick, who expected him to arrive at the ranch, wherever it was, sometime tomorrow. In the meantime all he could do was get some sleep and try not to imagine the publicity this arrest would generate if the AP picked up on it. And that really irritated him, because publicity, good or bad, could only interfere with what he needed to do right now.

His approach came to a halt several feet in front of the cell. Chased blinked, wondering if his tired eyes deceived him: It appeared that the cell on his left was already occupied.

Lying on her side on the narrow cot, eyes closed, hands tucked beneath her cheek, was a woman whose lush beauty

seemed almost cherubic. Chase's brows rose. Her ebony curls
were glossy and thick; escaping from a loosely gathered pony-
tail, they tumbled across the blue pillow and against her silky
cheek. She wore a round-necked white T-shirt; a thin, waist-
length sweater; and a skirt that skimmed a pair of wondrously
round hips and long legs. There was nothing intentionally pro-
vocative about the way she was dressed; she possessed an inherent sensuality, and Chase felt his body react immediately. The
response surprised him. Women had been the furthest thing from
his mind of late...though he'd always considered himself a man
with an open mind.

"Nettie!"

Behind him, the sheriff's exclamation held surprise and agitation. As Chase took a step closer to the cell, the sleeping
beauty stirred. Long lashes fluttered, the cupid's lips twitched.
When she opened her eyes, she looked directly at him.

"Well, well," he murmured, a slow smile curving his mouth
as if he were flirting at a nightclub bar, not standing in a tiny
town jail with his hands cuffed behind his back. "Tell me again,
sheriff...what time is the continental breakfast?"

Chapter Two

Nettie popped up on the cot as if her spine were a spring. Hands braced on either side of her, fingers curled over the edge of the mattress, she gazed at the man standing outside the cell.

From beneath the bill of his cap, his shadowed eyes seemed to gleam, like animal eyes staring out from a cave. Nettie caught a flash of white teeth when he smiled, and her heart skittered with a shot of adrenaline. Frantically, she struggled to shake off the lingering effects of sleep. She had decided there was no way she was going to go home and stew while the action happened someplace else. Unfortunately, exhaustion had overtaken her while she was tidying the jail and she'd dozed off waiting for the action to begin. When the man spoke again, his voice came to her like a slow rolling tide.

"Hello, Sleeping Beauty. Are you always here to greet the inmates or did I get lucky tonight?"

The last syllable had barely rolled off his tongue before he was lurching forward—shoved from behind.

"You keep your nasty thoughts to yourself!"

Sara's ringing growl cut through the fog in Nettie's brain. As the man stumbled and caught himself, Nettie saw the flash of silver binding his wrists. Her breath stopped. Sara had returned with the Gentleman Caller!

Tall, imposing and angry, the bank robber took a deep breath and turned with deliberate slowness to face Sara. He spoke through clenched teeth. "I asked you not to push me again." His tone shifted with such subtlety from the silky drawl he'd used with Nettie that one could almost miss the threat—almost. "Didn't I?"

"Yeah." One corner of Sara's mouth curled derisively. "But you forgot to say please."

Sara! Nettie wanted to wave her arms, stop her sister from saying or doing anything more.

Nettie realized already that this "Gentleman Caller" was not the benign anti-hero the press made him out to be. Tension enlivened his every muscle. There was a final-straw grimness to the line of his lips. Also, he was unpredictable, smiling one moment, growling the next. Moreover, he was large. Even with his hands cuffed behind his back, he would be stronger than Sara. And Sara hadn't yet learned fear.

When he took a step in Sara's direction, Nettie's response was swift and unpremeditated. She jumped from the cot and rushed to the open cell door.

"Leave her alone!" Her throat clutched at the words.

Chase turned at the choked order. His eyes widened when he saw the beautiful woman—Nettie—standing at the cell door like an avenging angel, her lips parted, blue eyes blazing, escaped black curls wild about her face. She grasped the bars of the cell door in such a white-knuckled grip, he was sure the steel longed to cry out for mercy.

His brows swooped into a frown. Why was she afraid? Other than telling Olive Oyl not to shove him, he'd been pretty damn nice so far. What did she think he was going to do? Chase held her gaze, questioning her. It was strange, but everything else faded away in that moment—the jail, the sheriff, his predicament—until he saw only the brave, frightened beauty before him and felt only the tightness in his own chest as he realized that for her, fear was nothing new.

Don't be afraid, angel, not of me.

Lost in the silent communication, he took a step toward her, intending to reach up, forgetting the handcuffs on his wrists. He felt the slice of the steel rings at the same time that he saw her jerk back. A second later, he heard the sheriff's gun being whisked from its leather holster.

"Hold it! Take one more step, and you'll walk bowlegged the rest of your days." The sheriff's voice was low and deadly serious. "My gun's aimed behind your knee."

Chase froze. He sucked in a breath, then spoke with forced control. "Really. Which one?"

"That's your guess, smart mouth. Nettie, come out of there." Obviously surprised by the sheriff's threat to shoot, Nettie complied, moving carefully.

It may have been his anger over having a loaded pistol pointed his way, or the stress that had been mounting inside him for weeks... It could have been his frustration over frightening the fragile beauty or all three factors combined, but something inside Chase started to feel like a geyser held too long in check.

He released a startlingly rude word and then bit it off with hard-won control. Turning slowly in the hope she wouldn't shoot him before he could insult her some more, he said, "Let me spell it out for you— I've had all the country hospitality I'm going to take for one night. If there is anyone in this town who isn't one can short of a six-pack, get him over here and tell him to call my lawyer."

"Get in that cell right now, mister! You're making me lose my patience."

Chase responded to her order with a bark of laughter. "That's priceless! I'm being held at gunpoint—probably illegally—and you're losing your patience? Let me guess: That's a toy gun and Barney Fife is your favorite action-adventure hero."

"*Get...in...the...cell.*" Raising the gun, Sara spat the words through gritted teeth, her expression suggesting she'd just as soon put a hole in him and toss his carcass in the alley as lock him safely behind bars.

Standing to the side of the cell, Nettie shook her head. If they kept baiting each other, someone was sure to snap. Sara looked like steam might shoot out of her ears at any moment, and the stranger seemed poised to pounce.

When Sara issued another order, to which the man growled, "Make me," Nettie's heart began to palpitate. The desire to flee was almost overpowering. This time, however, she shut her mind against the fear. She could not, would not, allow her anxiety to paralyze her, not when a member of her family was in danger.

Raised voices buzzed in her ears as she used the adrenaline shooting through her veins to move with a purpose. Praying her rubbery legs would continue to hold her, she fled to the store-room where Sara kept the guns.

It didn't take long to grab the rifle she knew Sara kept loaded. Raising it, Nettie checked and then released the safety lock the way her father and Uncle Harm had taught all three of the Owens girls years ago. Taking a deep, determined breath, she turned and raced back to the cell.

When she arrived, the Gentleman Caller was in mid threat, leaning forward as if he no longer cared a bit about the gun pointed his way. He smiled evilly. "I sincerely hope you know of a good paper route, because when I'm through suing you for false arrest you can kiss your current job good-bye."

Nettie winced. Unbeknownst to him, he'd just hit Sara where it hurt the most. "Is that so?" Sara snarled back. "Let me tell you something. Not only will I have a job after your trial, I'll send you a thank-you note. I wouldn't be surprised if someone named a city—or maybe a bank—after me."

He scowled. "You're delusional."

"No, just happy. In case you haven't been reading the papers lately, there's a fifty-thousand-dollar reward for your arrogant hide—"

"What?"

"—and I'm going to collect it!"

"The only thing you're going to collect is dust while your sanity hearing is pending, you nutcase. Now take these damn handcuffs off me!" His roar shook the rafters.

"Stop it, both of you!" Punctuating the order, Nettie cocked the Winchester. A bullet slid loudly into the chamber.

Chase and the sheriff each gave a jolt and then froze.

Chase turned his head slowly. The other woman, Nettie, stood ten feet away, a wood-stocked rifle hoisted in her thin arms. Her face was flushed and her arms shook so badly it looked like she was dancing a jig with the rifle, but the expression in her eyes was fierce and determined.

"Stop it, I said," she repeated, though no one had moved a pinky since she'd cocked the gun. "You ought to be ashamed, acting like this," she admonished in a voice that telegraphed her strain. "Why can't you behave like a normal sheriff and bank robber?"

"Bank rob—" Chase's stunned protest was abbreviated by the rifle being raised a notch. Figuring he'd tempted fate enough for the time being, he nodded in what he hoped was a conciliatory manner. "Okay. You're absolutely right. We should all calm down." He smiled. "I'm sure we can work out whatever misunderstanding has brought us all here."

"Oh, gag me," Sara muttered.

"I'd love to," Chase growled back.

"That's enough! *I want quiet!*" Nettie shouted the command with more force than anyone including her, thought she possessed.

"Okay!" Chase and Sara answered in unison and each backed up a step.

"I have a problem with tension," Nettie shared with them.

"Okay," they answered again.

"So no more arguing."

They nodded, and she released a long, slow breath. "All right. Now you—" Indicating Chase, she directed him with the gun barrel. "Please step into the cell as my sister asked."

Sister? Chase glanced between the two women. This whole situation was starting to seem more and more surreal, like a Robert Altman movie. Or *Nightmare on Elm Street*. Maybe if he fell asleep on the cot, he'd awaken to find this was all a bizarre dream, induced by stress and a very greasy chicken-fried steak.

He studied Nettie, her eyes wide and glowing blue, like a sea on fire. Wielding a rifle and fighting to be brave only made her seem more vulnerable. Illogically, he had the impulse to comply with her request—for now, at least.

"All right." Slowly, he moved, demonstrating how cooperative he intended to be. "I'll step into the cell." He flicked a quick, sour glance at the sheriff. "But only because you said please."

He was halfway across the cell's threshold when he felt a boot pressed firmly to the seat of his jeans. Caught off guard and unbalanced by his bound hands, he stumbled headlong onto the cot as the boot shoved him forward. Angry as a bull, he let loose a string of oaths as he fell onto the narrow cot and his shoulder smacked into the brick wall.

"Sara! What's the matter with you? I told you to behave."

"I don't have to behave. I'm the sheriff." She pointed to Chase. "And I don't like his attitude."

Chase had never before hit a woman. Fortunately, he thought he could make a pretty good case that this sheriff was no woman.

Lowering the rifle, Nettie took a few steps toward a wood chair. "I can't take anymore. I have to sit down," she muttered. As she collapsed onto the hard seat, her exhausted muscles shook and the rifle slipped from her grasp. The butt of the gun thunked onto the hardwood floor.

KA-BLAM!

The blast that echoed through the jail jolted them all. Nettie heard a shriek, which turned out to be her own, a loud curse— Sara's—and a series of sharp pings as the discharged bullet ricocheted first off the iron cell bars, then the light fixture above the cot, imbedding itself finally in the brick wall behind Chase.

There was a moment of stunned silence from the dazed trio, punctuated only by a tinny creak as the light fixture swayed.

Heart pounding, Nettie looked at Sara, who for once seemed incapable of immediate speech. With his hands still bound behind his back, the Gentleman Caller lowered his head, shaking it. It took Nettie only a moment to realize the man was laughing. The low chuckle was rich with irony and seemed to blend perfectly with the creak-creak of the light fixture.

Nettie looked up. She tilted her head, realizing that the short chain suspending the fixture from the ceiling had been sliced through. The severed link struggled to hang on, but with each rusty creak the connection grew more and more tenuous, and then—

"Oh! Look—" Nettie started a warning she had no time to finish before the hanging light cracked loose, plummeting. It might have landed harmlessly on the cot—if the Gentleman Caller's head hadn't gotten in the way. "—out," she finished.

With his arms behind his back, he had no way to protect himself, even if there had been time. Unfortunately his thin canvas cap offered no protection against the thunk of steel against skull.

A moment's surprise crossed his whiskered face. He blinked and wagged his head as if to clear it.

Nettie and Sara watched open-mouthed as he teetered, looked curiously at the light, then back at them.

"When," he asked, working hard to make his lips and tongue form letters, "do I get my free phone call?"

With that, their Gentleman Caller fell soundly, face-first onto the cot.

"Do you see any blood?"

"A little." Gingerly, Nettie parted the man's dark hair to examine his scalp. "His hair is so thick."

"To cover his thick skull, I suppose."

"Sara, stop it! You're making everything worse. Haven't we got enough trouble?"

"What trouble?" Sara waved a hand at the figure lying on the cot. "He hit his head and got a boo-boo." But she didn't look altogether confident right now, and Nettie was glad to see it.

"He's out cold, and we're responsible," she countered firmly. "If we haven't already killed him, we'd better hope he wakes up with amnesia."

Reaching into her sweater pocket, Nettie withdrew a clean tissue and pressed it gently but firmly against the wound, wincing in sympathy. Though she could never figure out why, the fears that had governed her life the past few years would sometimes abate at the oddest times—when she was in the midst of an actual crisis, for instance. Efficiently, she placed two fingers beneath the man's unshaven jaw to check for a pulse. His skin was warm, alive. He didn't feel unconscious at all.

"Is he still kickin'?"

It took Nettie a moment to register Sara's question. She pulled her hand away quickly. "Yes—" Her mouth felt dry and her tongue thick. She swallowed and tried again. "Yes, his...his pulse is steady. Strong." Like the rest of him.

"Good. So he'll come to and— What do you mean 'we're responsible'?" Sara jumped back to Nettie's previous comment. "This was an accident."

Nettie spared her sister a look that said *puh-lease.* "Is it standard practice to boot your prisoners into the cell?'' She shook her head. ''And I had no business handling that rifle.''

Sara frowned. ''Yeah. I almost had a heart attack. I haven't seen you pick up a gun in years. What got into you?''

''I was afraid the two of you were going to kill each other. And I do know how to handle a gun,'' she reminded her sister for the record. Of herself, Lilah and Sara, she'd always been the best shot, but popping soda cans at fifty paces was different from pointing a rifle at another human being. Still, she refused to take all the responsibility for the trouble they were currently in. And she did sense trouble. Studying the man's features, peaceful and handsome in repose, she said, ''Sara, are you sure he's the Gentleman Caller?''

''What? Of course!'' Sara put both hands on her gun belt. ''Although, I don't have to be positive, you know. I had a reasonable suspicion. And he wasn't carrying ID.''

''Did he say why?''

Sara snorted. ''Yeah. He said he thinks he lost his wallet at a taco place somewhere in Nebraska. I should have arrested him just for being a lousy liar. Plus he's got that wad of cash in his pocket.''

''But if he really did lose his wallet—''

''Oh, come on! He resisted arrest. Why are you defending him?''

''I'm not defending him. I'm concerned. He said he was going to sue you for false arrest.''

''He was bluffing.''

''You shouldn't have bickered and sniped at him.''

''Me?'' Sara gestured angrily. ''He—''

''There's something familiar about him. Without his cap, I mean. He reminds me of someone. Who does he look like?''

Sara crossed her arms. ''He looks like the composite sketch of the Gentleman Caller.''

''Do you have the composite sketch? I haven't seen it since it was in the paper. Where is it?''

Sara hesitated a bit too long. ''I was looking for it when you came in tonight.''

Nettie thought it prudent, for the time being at least, not to comment on her sister's organizational skills. She folded the tissue. ''He stopped bleeding.'' She checked her watch, biting her bottom lip. "He's been out for four minutes now. Maybe we ought to call Doc Brody."

Mere mention of the elderly physician evoked an expression of sheer horror from Sara. "What for?" She gestured to the man lying unconscious on the cot. "You said his pulse is strong." Leaning forward, she gave him a shake. "Come on, buddy. Get up." She jiggled him again. "Come on."

Nettie wagged her head. Doc Brody had mended every broken limb Sara had ever had, and there had been plenty of them. He thought she was an unladylike hooligan. He was also one of only two men who could make Sara feel like she was ten years old again, and she generally went to any length to avoid him.

"Hey, look," Sara said. "He moved!"

"Of course he moved, Sara, you're shaking him." Taking her sister's arm, Nettie directed her out of the cell. "You go get the first-aid kit. It has smelling salts. We'll try that, but if it doesn't work, we've got to get some help."

"All right," Sara said, but she hung back, reluctant to leave Nettie alone. "But if he comes to or even starts to, holler for me and get yourself out of that cell."

"Okay. Now go." Nettie shooed Sara away. "And I only hope you're right about him being the Gentleman Caller," she muttered, turning back toward their guest and studying his face.

Without the cap hiding his features, he seemed more coolly handsome and less dangerous than he had before. A tiny frown nestled between his brows, but otherwise all trace of anger was gone. The lips that had curved sometimes seductively, sometimes sardonically were now soft and neutral.

Ernie had described him as "normally-looking." Nettie thought his face deserved a more creative description than that. His features were refined, projecting intelligence even though his eyes were closed. Eyes open, his sheer physical presence had been unnerving.

She shivered, or maybe it was more of a tingle. He had stared at her, this man. Stared the way she hadn't been stared at in a long, long time.

"Who are you?" she whispered. And what was he doing in Kalamoose? Because something told her this situation was not as straightforward as Sara believed it to be.

When he'd fallen face-first onto the cot, she and Sara had

turned him right side up and straightened him out. Now, if Nettie wanted to, she could reach into the front pocket of his jeans to look for the identification he had either lost, as he claimed, or refused to produce.

Quickly, she glanced toward the storeroom. She could hear Sara rummaging around and swearing, looking for the first-aid kit she probably hadn't seen in months.

Beginning with one hand in front of her mouth, Nettie reached out tentatively with the other, patting the right front pocket of his jeans. She detected the outline of a set of keys. Nothing else. She could have stopped there. She should have stopped there. But something told her to press on, some hunch that he might be carrying I.D.

Gaining a bit more courage, she stretched across the man's body to reach his left side. The tip of her tongue came out to rest at the corner of her mouth as she investigated the pocket below his waistband. She felt something here…something sort of square, but not solid enough to be the wallet. Probably the wad of cash. His jacket had pockets, too. She moved there next.

Nothing on the right. Reaching over to the left side, she hunted around the area of his ribcage, trying to determine whether his jacket had an interior pocket.

As she patted him gently, feeling for a telltale corner or edge, he gave an unexpected jerk. Nettie's hand froze. Looking left, she glanced at his face.

His eyes were open and trained her way. "I'm ticklish," he announced, sounding as bleary as he looked. "Are you?"

Nettie's mouth dropped open. Bent over the cot, she was mere inches above him. "How…how long have you been awake?"

"I'm not sure I'm awake now." He frowned, scanning what he could see of her, beginning at her hairline and ending in the vicinity of her bosom, where her sweater opened to reveal a scoop-necked T-shirt. Gaze lingering, he drawled, "Did I miss any good stuff?"

Nettie whipped her hand from his chest, then felt like kicking herself for betraying her nervousness. Forcing herself to move more slowly, she straightened. "No," she answered as calmly as she could. "Most of the good stuff happened before you passed out."

The Gentleman Caller grunted. With effort, he raised himself to a sitting position, then seemed to remember something and grimaced. "Where's Belle Star?"

His tone conveyed such ominous foreboding, Nettie had to smile. "She's getting the first-aid kit."

"Awww." He groaned and lowered his voice. "You wouldn't let her touch a wounded man, would you?"

This time Nettie checked her answering grin to defend her flesh and blood. "Sara's only trying to do her job. She said you resisted arrest. And," she added, watching him closely, "you fit the description of the Gentleman Caller."

"I look like the Gentleman Caller," he repeated in a murmur, obviously bemused. He seemed to roll the information around in his brain a while, then raised his brows in perfect horror. "You mean that red-headed hellion arrests people she wants to date?" He was wide awake now. "Forget about it—"

"No, of course not!" Nettie interrupted. "What a ridiculous idea."

Relief flooded his face before his expression turned wry. "Yeah, I don't know what I was thinking. After all, everything's been so normal up until now."

Nettie conceded the point. Her concern mounted. As a thief, he could, of course, be an excellent actor, but she was increasingly inclined to believe that they had all made a terrible mistake.

Chase studied the woman before him. She nibbled at her full bottom lip, appearing worried, but no longer frightened of him.

With his hands bound behind his back, he pushed himself off the cot. The dull ache in his temples turned into a pulsing throb. His arms were beginning to feel sore, too. He wondered what time it was, how long he'd been out, but before he could ask, he caught the scent of the woman's hair. Flowers…no…clover. She smelled like the clover fields he'd passed on his way into town.

For more reasons than Chase cared to count, he had no business thinking what he was thinking in regard to this woman. If nothing else, the timing was absurd. Still, he couldn't help but notice that if they stood a few inches closer, the top of her head would tuck very neatly beneath his chin. A good fit…

For the first time, he felt almost grateful for the cuffs around his wrists. If his hands had been free, he might have brushed one of those wild black curls off of her cheek, might have tested her reaction.

His gaze moved where his hand could not. "You aren't afraid of me anymore," he stated softly, with male satisfaction.

Nettie's mouth opened and closed in protest. "I was never afraid of you. I'm just cautious."

Chase grinned. "Where you and I are concerned, angel, caution seems like a good rule of thumb." Leaning forward enough to be heard if he whispered, he couldn't help adding, "Then again, the next time we meet we won't be standing in a jail cell...and my hands won't be behind my back."

Nettie stared up at him, her mouth dry, her palms moist and the sound of the ocean at high tide roaring in her ears. Sara rushed in, saving her from a response, and Nettie had never been so glad for—or so irked by—her sister's timing.

Clutching the first-aid kit, Sara breathed, "Okay, I found it. Now what—" She stopped, realizing the Gentleman Caller was on his feet and that he and Nettie were standing only inches apart.

For a second, no one said anything, then Nettie, feeling as if she'd been caught with her hand in a till, pointed to the suspect. "He's awake."

"I see that." Sara's lips pulled back from her teeth, but it didn't look like she was smiling. "What is going on?" she asked her sister.

The Gentleman Caller answered, nodding toward Nettie. "She was tickling me." A slow smile curved his lips. "I liked it."

Sara stared at her sister.

"I was not!" Nettie denied, swiveling toward the man. "I was not tickling you! I was...conducting a frisk."

He coughed discreetly. "I don't mean to be rude, miss, but I've been searched before and from experience I can confirm that what you did was not at all frisk-like. Now if you feel you could improve, I'd be happy to let you practice." His eyes danced with pure devilish humor.

Nettie did something then that shocked her sister, surprised the man watching her, but most of all shocked herself: She giggled. As the absurdity of this whole situation struck her with increasing clarity, she clapped a hand over her mouth and laughed until her stomach ached and tears rolled down her cheeks. The harder she tried to stop, the more hysterical she felt.

"You should have seen...the look on your face..." Pointing at the Gentleman Caller, she struggled to speak intelligibly through gasps of laughter, "...when the lamp hit your head!"

Somehow it didn't seem to matter any more that this situation was almost as embarrassing as it was ridiculous, or that she usually embarrassed faster than flies found honey. Where pain typically resided, Nettie felt a long-forgotten giddiness, and she caught a glimpse of enjoyment and curiosity on the man's handsome face before tears blurred her eyes again.

"Nettie, what is the matter with you?"

Nettie shook her head. "I'm sorry, Sara, but you should have seen your face, too...when he passed out." She doubled up as the laughter made her stomach cramp. "You looked like you thought he was dead, and you saw your fifty thousand dollars flying right out the window!"

"I didn't think he was dead," Sara snapped, "but he'd be a lot less trouble if he were. And I'd still get my reward."

"Not if he's not the Gentleman Caller, you wouldn't," Nettie countered. "You'd just have a really good-looking dead guy." She dissolved into another round of giggles.

"Thank you." The guy in question grinned. "I think."

As Nettie continued to entertain them with her unusual response, the door to the jail opened and closed. Boot heels scuffed across the hardwood floor, halting at the cell. The three people inside turned toward the newcomer. Sara stiffened immediately. Nettie regained some control over herself, but slowly. "Hello, Nick," she said, grinning.

Nick Brady leaned against the iron post of the cell door, thumbs hooked casually in the belt loops of his denim jeans. Dense brows angled over dark eyes as he noted the hands cuffed behind the stranger's back.

Ignoring Sara completely, he shifted his gaze back to Nettie and nodded. "Good to see you enjoying yourself." Eyes narrowed, he stalked past Sara to stand face-to-face with her prisoner.

The two men were of similar height and build, with Nick perhaps a shade taller and stockier. What they shared was an aura of strength, masculine, arrogant and unequivocal. Nick noted again the suspect's bound arms and a small smear of blood in the upper right corner of the younger man's forehead. This time he turned toward Sara with a glare that was so frankly disapproving, Nettie saw her audacious, defiant sister actually blush.

Turning back to the other man, Nick nodded. "Chase," he greeted, "I see you've met the Owens sisters."

Chapter Three

Slouched at the kitchen table while Nettie chopped carrots at the sink, Sara ripped the head off a gingerbread man, her sixth casualty in an hour. "It's eleven-thirty," she growled, stuffing her mouth full of cookie. "Why are you doing that now?"

"I told you." Briefly, Nettie suspended the knife. *"Chopping...relaxes...me."* She brought the cleaver down, halving a carrot with a swift, ruthless *thwack.*

Food crimes were on the rise in the Owenses' kitchen tonight.

Nick's arrival at the jail had cleared up a few questions, most pertinently the identity of Sara's prisoner. On his way home from a buying trip, Nick had stopped in at Good Eats, heard from Ernie about the evening's activities and headed directly for the jail, where he informed the women that they had in their clutches—bloodied, verbally abused, handcuffed and nearly shot—Chase Reynolds, special reporter for a top cable news program and Nick's houseguest for the next two weeks.

Well, who knew?

Nettie whacked another carrot. Bad enough she'd nearly shot a man who'd once won a William Jay award for excellence in on-camera reporting; she'd also frisked one of *People* magazine's "Fifty Most Beautiful People." It didn't seem funny anymore.

"We should have recognized him," she muttered, not for the first time. "This is what comes from discontinuing cable. Although how you could arrest a man when you don't even have a composite sketch to ID him is really beyond—"

"I told you." Sara slapped her cookie onto the table. "I *had* it. I just couldn't *find* it. And as far as I'm concerned, he was just another suspect. I was following protocol."

Nettie paused in her chopping to lean one hand on the counter, the other on her hip. "When you were insulting him or when you were punting him into the cell?"

"That's it!" Sara shoved the glass of milk away from her, scraping her chair back from the table. "I don't have to listen to this." She stabbed a thumb at her own chest. "I had a reasonable suspicion."

"Really. What tipped the scales for you, Sherlock, the fact that he's a fast eater?"

Sara gaped at her sister. "What is the matter with you tonight? You've been sniping at me since we got home." She waved a hand. "I don't see what you're so upset about, anyway. He's not going to sue *you*."

"I'm sorry." Nettie put a hand over her eyes and shook her head. "It's just all so…humiliating! But don't worry, he won't sue. We're not important enough for him to sue." She resumed rapid dicing. "By the time he leaves here we'll be just another cocktail party anecdote. Something to entertain Barbara Walters with while he's stirring martinis: 'Did I ever tell you about the time I was held captive by two women in Kalamoose? One olive or two?'"

"Well if that's all we have to worry about, big deal. Who cares what he says to Barbara Walters as long as he doesn't cause trouble around here?"

I do. "What's someone like Chase Reynolds doing in Kalamoose, anyway?" Nettie tried to sound offhand, but her true interest felt almost raw in its intensity. "How do you suppose he met Nick?"

"I don't know, and I don't care," Sara replied unsatisfactorily. She took a last swallow of milk. "I'm going to bed. I've got a lot to do tomorrow." Crossing to the swinging door that led to the dining room, she paused. "Listen, about you grabbing that rifle tonight—"

Nettie groaned. "Don't remind me. I swear I will never again touch one of your guns, just please, *please* do not talk about it!"

"No, no, I wasn't going to… I mean I'm not upset. I—" Never one to speak easily about her feelings, Sara scratched her neck and shifted uneasily. "I just wanted to say, you know…thank you." She shrugged. "I know you were trying to protect me, and… I think you put the fear of God into him when you knocked off that shot." A smile nudged her freckled cheeks. "Put it into me." Hesitating a moment longer, she nodded toward the severed carrots. "Bet those would make a good cake." Wishing her sister a good-night, she left the kitchen and headed upstairs.

Nettie pressed her palms to her cheeks. She stood like that a moment, breathing, trying not to think at all. Then she dragged a plastic container out from one of the bottom cabinets and put the carrots in the refrigerator.

Twenty minutes later she was upstairs, a pink terry robe wrapped around her just-showered body, her mind still as active as a kitten with a ball of string. Forget sleep.

Tiptoeing past Sara's room, Nettie headed for a small attic work studio. Stepping inside, she closed the door softly behind her.

The room smelled pleasingly of canvas and paint and of the oil-based pastels she arranged by hue in old soup tins and plastic cups. This was her private aerie, the sanctum to which she escaped each day. When she flicked the light on, a soft yellow glow illuminated her easel and drawing board and a corner desk, where she wrote the children's stories that were winning a loyal and ever-growing audience. A bookshelf she'd hand-painted housed copies of her There I Go Again books, a series of illustrated tales featuring a little boy named Barnaby, whose incredible adventures took place at night while his parents were sleeping. Barnaby trotted the globe, engaging in acts of daring or heroism or simply having outlandish good fun and then returning home to a bed shaped like a racecar and to parents he trusted to keep him safe.

Crossing to the bookcase, Nettie ran her fingers across the

spines of several books, then touched the top of a small pewter frame. Her body stiffened as she awaited the customary catch in her throat.

Inside the flower-stamped border was a five-by-seven color snapshot of a man and woman barely out of their teens. The girl sported a purple maternity top with a big golden happy face over her protruding belly and the young man wore a smile that gave validity to the description "a mile wide."

She and Brian. Back in the days when they'd expected only good things to happen.

Nettie held the picture with both hands. Sweet longing filled her chest even as her stomach muscles clenched with a pain so bitter she thought she could taste it. They'd been so trusting— two children bringing a baby into the world.

Anger snaked up from her belly like a weed threatening to choke her. Falling in love and having a baby were acts of faith that should have been rewarded.

And they had been, she supposed, for a time. The photograph was evidence. Also on the bookshelf, propped on a small display easel, was a likeness of her son's face, sculpted from clay then cast into plaster. One of Brian's art projects. Smooth and perfect in illusionary 3-D, it seemed capable of coming to life. Brian had intended to sculpt their son's face every three years, beginning with age two and a half. This was the only sculpture Nettie had. She kept it on the shelf even though it was fragile, even though there was only one. And she was grateful that she had it. Although there were times when touching it—tracing the nose and the chin and the brow—served only to increase her loneliness.

Every day for three years she had tried to remember…and tried not to. What good, she sometimes wondered, were memories when the heart couldn't touch hair or skin, the heart couldn't hold hands with Brian or press kisses against Tucker's soft, soft cheek?

And she wanted that. God, there were times when she didn't think she could live another minute without it—one more chance to touch.

Returning her focus to the picture of herself and her husband, she flattened her fingers against the cold glass protecting the photo as tears began to run, salty and hot, over her lips. She'd been living in limbo, and she knew it. Couldn't go forward, couldn't back up. A quick, watery laugh escaped her lips. Brian would have hated that for her.

She had begun to hate it herself.

She closed her eyes and a man's smile—not Brian's—came into view. A smile so recent she could still see it without effort: Wry and searching, flirtatious and bold. And then, as if Chase Reynolds were there in the room, she felt again the deep-down tingle, the chord of anticipation his smile had struck.

Opening her eyes, she noticed that her hand was starting to shake. Holding the picture frame tightly against her stomach, Nettie turned toward her desk. Her legs felt so heavy and wooden she had to command them to move. When she reached her desk, she opened a bottom drawer.

The pain in her stomach rose to her throat and like the anger, it squeezed. She bit her lip as she placed the photo gently inside the drawer.

"Oh, God."

For an instant she thought she might stop breathing, honestly felt as if she'd pushed a red button that could destroy the whole world. She waited, feeling the pounding in her chest, the tightness of grief.

It was then, with a clarity that seemed brittle, that she understood more completely the awful price of choosing to go on.

Standing, she sent a brief, silent apology to heaven. She'd been a girl when she'd married, barely a woman when she'd lost everything she loved most. With all that had passed since then, she'd earned her womanhood. Chase Reynolds was the first man who made her want to explore it.

She didn't expect to have what she'd had before—the hopes, the dreams of a future. The innocence. Not with him or any other man. She didn't even want that. With a new relationship, one that was obviously impermanent from the start, she wouldn't have a whole thunderstorm to deal with. Just a little bit of lightning to say she was still alive.

Looking down at the drawer, Nettie drew a breath that felt like needles pricking her lungs. Then she made herself whisper what had to be the most difficult word in the whole English language. "Goodbye."

* * *

It was 10:30 a.m. when Nettie guided the Owenses' old wood-paneled Jeep Wagoneer up the long drive that led to Nick's farm. Patches of wild mustard splotched the bright emerald grass leading to the house. A gentle breeze snatched the echo of clover from fields across the road, scenting the air with a clean spicy freshness. As moderate as the temperature was outside the car, however, inside the vehicle it felt like high noon.

Perspiration bathed Nettie's forehead and upper lip. Her palms were sweating, her back felt clammy and her stomach whirred like a washing machine stuck on ''spin.''

She hadn't driven alone in years, not since she'd started having anxiety attacks in the car. The first time she had a panic attack while driving, she'd thought that surely she would lose control of the vehicle. For no reason at all, it had seemed, she had begun to feel hot and clammy, then nauseous, weak and scared. Her arms had started to shake, her vision had blurred and her heart had pounded and raced and skipped beats. The more she had fought the sensations, the worse they had become. By the time she'd reached home, she had been exhausted and utterly confused about what had just happened to her. When she had another attack two weeks later, she went to see her doctor. ''Post-traumatic stress,'' he had called it. It felt like impending death.

Eventually Nettie had stopped driving unless there was someone in the car with her, hoping to avoid the sudden attacks. She knew more now about anxiety attacks, what they were and what they weren't, but she hadn't yet overcome her fear of driving alone. Unfortunately Nick's farm was not within walking distance. If Nettie wanted to see Chase Reynolds again—without Sara in attendance—she had to get behind the wheel all by herself and drive. She'd spent half the morning convincing herself she could do it. She'd spent the other half getting ready.

For a jolt of confidence, she had chosen to wear a gauzy dress that Lilah had sent her from a chi-chi boutique in Los Angeles, but now the thin material glommed to her back in a decidedly less than chi-chi way.

Plus, a glance in the rearview mirror showed that her makeup was running south. ''Very seductive,'' she muttered, scrounging in her purse for a tissue to blot her damp forehead and cheeks.

At least focusing on her appearance allowed her anxiety to abate somewhat and by the time she pulled up to Nick's house, her body felt more pliable again.

For a minute she sat, taking in the realization that she'd done it—she'd driven!

The remaining jitteriness in her limbs began to turn into a feeling of excitement. "Oh, my gosh," Nettie whispered. To someone else it would have been a small thing, not an accomplishment at all. But she understood the importance of what she had just done—and the reason she had done it. Chase Reynolds was obviously a powerful prescription.

Peering through the windshield for signs of life, Nettie squared her shoulders and opened the car door. Her sandaled feet had barely touched the hard gravel when she heard the wet snuffle of an equine snort. Assuming Nick was out for a ride on King, she felt herself relax a bit more.

Nick was an old friend who knew about her anxiety attacks. Picturing his surprise when he saw her emerge from behind the driver's seat, Nettie allowed herself a taste of victory.

"Good morning." She smiled broadly as she turned. "I bet you didn't expect to see me here all by myself, but I— Oh." Her smile turned to stark surprise when she saw Chase Reynolds astride King.

Nettie stared at him. He stared back.

He'd shaved since last night. There was no mistaking his identity now. He looked exactly like his picture in *People* magazine—masculine, intelligent, hazardous to a woman's peace.

They each waited for the other person to speak.

Bringing his right leg over the saddle, Chase dropped to the ground. He was hatless, his eyes masked only by an unreadable expression.

"You were saying?"

Nettie blinked. Heat sizzled steadily through her body, and suddenly her brain seemed too full. She was saying...

Chase raised a brow. He walked forward, bringing the horse with him. "You bet I didn't expect to see you here all by yourself, but you..." he prompted.

Nettie licked her dry lips and mustered a smile. "Um, I thought you were Nick."

Black eyes narrowed. Tilting his head, he considered the admission. "You're not here to see me?"

"You? No." Caught off guard, Nettie squeaked the denial. "I…" She shook her head. "No."

"Hmm." He frowned, musing. "That's funny. Because actually, I *was* expecting you."

Nettie stared at him. Embarrassment crept up her neck as she imagined those night-dark eyes reading her thoughts. Okay, so she *had* arrived here this morning hoping to flirt with him, or rather, hoping he'd flirt with her. But even before anxiety, she had never been the kind of woman who could admit to such a thing.

"Actually, Mr. Reynolds, I didn't know you'd still be here."

He scratched his neck, obviously unmoved by the denial.

"If I had known," Nettie insisted, a distinct chill in her voice, "I certainly wouldn't have shown up unannounced."

He brushed at a fly that buzzed past.

"Right, I am here unannounced," she conceded. "But not to see you."

"I just thought you might want to apologize."

"Apologize?"

"It's the usual practice after you've nearly shot an innocent man, Ms. Owens." He shrugged. "Maybe that's a city custom."

He stood calmly, looking down at her.

It was his straight-faced irony that eventually penetrated her attempt to remain cool. A smile tugged at her mouth, urged her cheeks, and she relented, nodding. "You're right. I should have come here to apologize. How's your head?"

Chase rubbed the spot where the lamp had smacked him. "Not bad. Although my barber once told me I had a perfectly shaped head, so I never had to worry about going bald. I guess that's shot."

She laughed outright at that. "I really am sorry."

The breeze pulled a lock of her hair across her face. It caught between her lips, and she brushed it away. Chase watched her steadily, his gaze focused on her mouth.

Nettie felt her gaze drop to his mouth, too. It was closed, lips firm. When she looked back up, into his eyes, she felt her heart thump with adrenaline. They were like two animals on the prairie—circling, watching, testing. She waited as long as she could for him to make the next move, but the anticipation made her feel like a balloon ready to pop. Feeling her heart beat faster, she gathered her courage.

"Can I make it up to you?" she asked, her voice sounding as if she'd swallowed too much prairie dust. "How about dinner while you're here? As amends for all you've suffered. Nick's not much of a cook, but I'm pretty fair, so you could consider yourself safe. Not much chance of food poisoning or of offending the chef by having to rush out for a burger or anything." She smiled.

The wind whipped up again. This time he reached for the hair that blew in front of her face, pushing it back with a touch as subtle as a whisper. His knuckles brushed her cheek and even that slight touch sent a shiver through her. "I bet there isn't a burger joint within twenty miles of here," he said.

"That's true," she agreed, too breathlessly. "There's only Ernie's."

"Ernie's?"

"The diner."

"Ah." He nodded. "Pass."

Nettie wondered if he knew that a little groove appeared between his brows when he was thinking. Or that the laugh line on the right side of his mouth was deeper than the one on his left. His smile seemed to begin mostly on the right....

She was still lost in her study when Chase said quietly, "Well, Miss Nettie Owens, I thank you very much for your offer. Dinner isn't necessary, though. And you have nothing to make amends for."

Was he letting her know he wanted dinner to be her choice and not her obligation, Nettie wondered? The possibility made her feel flattered and satisfied, and some of the lightness of the morning seemed to enter her own spirit.

"Oh, sure, you say that now," she replied, engaging in some teasing of her own. "But one day I'll turn on the TV and there'll you'll be, telling Mike Wallace all about last night. I'll come out looking like the bad guy, and I can't have that. I'll have you know I won Miss Congeniality twelve years ago at the Kalamoose Founder's Day Fair." Her tone suggested he ought to be mightily impressed.

Chase smiled, the humor deepening in his eyes, and Nettie's courage took flight. "So now you'll have to come over, if only to preserve my reputation." She smiled more freely. "I'll make stew and soda bread. My mother's family was Irish. I have a great recipe—"

"I can't." The refusal was swift and decisive.

Chase's expression grew taut. Softness and humor vanished like mist, and his voice became a gravel-paved monotone. "I'm not going to be here very long, two weeks at the most. It's going to be a busy time. Thanks anyway. Is there anything you'd like me to tell Nick?"

Nick.

"He's not here. But I can give him a message."

Oh, that Nick.

Nettie frowned, trying to think. Chase's mood, his entire being, had altered so rapidly, she couldn't quite grasp what had just happened, other than the fact that she'd been rejected. Thoroughly. Utterly.

Swallowing hard, she decided that getting out of here with even a smidgeon of dignity was now her first order of business.

"Nick," she said, forcing her mind to work. "Yes, please do tell him…" *What?* She gave a small shake of her head. Chase Reynolds had a life filled with adventure and amazing people. *Come over…I'll make stew?* What had she been thinking?!

"Please tell Nick," she continued, "that I came by to pick up the eggs." The lie emerged in a voice too strained to sound wholly genuine. "He usually brings some to the house each week." That much was true. "He's been so busy lately, though, I thought I'd save him the trouble."

She should have let it go at that and left, but with no hint to suggest Chase believed her, Nettie felt the compulsive urge to try harder. "He always has extra. Eggs. Nick does. His chickens are such good liars—layers!" *Oh, my God.* Chase Reynolds gave no indication that he noticed the slip, but Nettie began to speak double-time to cover it up. "I use the extra to make cakes and muffins…" She pointed again. "There's a nursing home on Fifth and C Street. They love sweets. Of course, there is the cholesterol issue, but when you're pushing eighty, who's counting, right?" Smiling broadly, as if this were an actual conversation rather than one person's rambling attempt to sound convincing, she closed with a brisk nod. "Well, I can see you're not an egg man. So, I'll just come back another time. Oh! If you think about it, you can tell Nick I plan to make that stew sometime this week. He loves Irish stew.'' She nodded again. ''Well, so long.''

Taking a step toward the car, relief almost outweighed disappointment until she realized that now she was going to have to drive back, her efforts fruitless, feeling more alone than she had when she set out this morning.

Nick's absurdly long driveway loomed ahead of her like a broad jump. The nausea that had blessedly subsided rolled inside her again now and she knew she couldn't face another anxiety attack, not yet.

''If you don't mind,'' she said hoarsely, reluctantly glancing around, ''I think I'll—'' Chase was already heading toward the barn with King, oblivious to her dilemma.

''—sit on the porch and wait for Nick,'' she finished, speaking aloud to Chase's departing back. She watched him go, resentment beginning to edge out embarrassment.

Maybe she was no longer the calmest person in three counties, but at least she was polite and consistent. Chase Reynolds had just made Dr. Jekyll and Mr. Hyde seem predictable. Had she *completely* misread him last night? Her exhalation turned into a dismal sigh. She was so out of practice with this whole man-woman thing. Come to think of it, she hadn't had a first date since high school.

Trudging up the porch steps, she seated herself with a thunk on the blue-painted wood.

This was worse, far worse even than high school, when the boy you had a crush on ignored you and you spent your lunch hour in the girls' room crying into a wad of toilet paper. Pulling her legs toward her chest, Nettie lowered her forehead to her knees.

There was never a girls' room around when you needed one.

Chase paused outside the barn, his conscience and his ego taking turns pummeling him.

If the lovely Nettie had come to see him, then he probably ought to be shot for the way he'd treated her. If, on the other hand, she'd merely come to pick up eggs from Nick— Muscles bunched in Chase's jaw. He didn't like that possibility one little bit.

Whipping the reins over King's ears, Chase made the horse prance nervously and had to pause a moment to settle him down.

He doubted there was another woman in North America right now capable of making him rethink his moratorium on women, but something about this Midwest country girl got under his skin. *Everything* about this Midwest country girl was getting under his skin.

Chase shook his head. He'd had relationships with models, news reporters, a foreign head of state once. Sophisticated, fascinating women about whom he had never lost his objectivity. Maintaining emotional distance was one of his innate gifts.

That gift warned him clearly now: A hometown girl who hung curtains in a jail was not someone to add to his little black book.

His yearning in response to the simple offer *Come over...I'll make stew* had scared him, made him feel like he was standing in a minefield. Domesticity was not detectable in the Reynolds family's DNA pattern. As a rule, he only dated women who shared the same biological aberration.

That left Miss Nettie Owens clean out of the running. Which brought him back to the source of his present agitation: He'd had no business flirting with her. And *absolutely* no business wanting to hear her say she'd come to see him rather than Nick.

Shaking his head in disgust over his lack of mental discipline, Chase led King toward his stall. "I suppose I should have unsaddled you outside," he told the large gelding, trying not to listen for the sound of Nettie's station wagon pulling away, "but we can handle the cramped quarters."

Soon now he would have the results of the DNA tests he'd taken before he'd left New York. Maybe then he'd be the pilot of his own mind again. It was the damned living in limbo that bothered him the most.

Holding the reins in his right hand, Chase reached with his left for the door to the stall. A flash of movement caught his eye. Before he could investigate, King was rearing, pawing the air with his front hooves and neighing in distress. The horse nicked Chase's forearm on his descent, then reared again.

"Whoa! Hang on there." Confounded by the horse's behavior, Chase tugged the reins. "Settle down!" King was not re-assured by a stranger pulling on his bit and became more agitated.

Chase stood too close, crowding the large animal, and this time when King dropped to all fours, the big animal caught Chase's shoulder with enough force to off-balance them both. Falling into the stall, Chase let go of the reins and the horse took off like a shot.

Outside, Nettie saw King emerge from the barn in a near panic. She stood as the horse headed for the barley field, changed his mind and turned sharply toward the house.

She was down the porch steps in a flash. In years gone by she'd ridden King with great relish. She knew the horse well, and once she caught sight of Chester, Nick's cat, sitting calmly outside the barn door, cleaning his paws, she had a pretty good idea of what had spooked the sensitive gelding.

King snorted and stamped the ground as Nettie approached. "Shh-shh," she soothed. "Shh, you're all right." Carefully, she reached for King's bridle. "Did that big old cat scare you again? Hmm?" Stroking the bridge of his nose, she guided him gently as he calmed, so that he was facing the barn again as the cat strolled leisurely toward the side of the house. She continued her ministrations as Chase reached them.

"I don't know what happened in there." Without preamble, he described the scene in the barn. "I was trying to get him into the stall, and he took off."

Nettie sent a sidelong glance to the man at her side. Bits of straw stuck to his crisp jeans and shirt. A larger piece of hay nestled in his mahogany hair. Rumpled and bemused, he seemed more approachable than he had earlier. Nettie felt her pulse increase—with interest, not nerves—but she pasted a cool expression on her face. "Mmm," she murmured, "maybe he didn't like your attitude, Mr. Reynolds."

Dark brows spiked in surprise. Nettie held his gaze. Slowly, a reluctant smile edged Chase's mouth. "You think that was it?"

Hesitating a moment, Nettie shrugged. "No. Actually," she nodded toward Chester, "there's your culprit."

Following her gaze, Chase squinted, then brought his hands to his hips and craned his neck forward. "A cat?"

"Mm-hmm. King and Chester have a long and complicated history."

"Is that so?" Chase massaged his sore shoulder, eyeing King with displeasure. "So the cat was in the barn." He shook his head. "You're not going to tell me a big animal like that is afraid of a stupid little cat?"

"Chester isn't stupid." Nettie countered. "And King is perfectly comfortable around an average barn cat. He's only afraid of Chester."

"What the devil for?" When Chase raised his voice, King danced unhappily again. Nettie cooed to him as if to a child before she explained.

"Chester is wily. He jumped on King's back years ago when they were both young and scared the heck out of him. Once he got that reaction, he dedicated himself to tormenting King every chance he got. Call it little-man syndrome. He's not allowed in the barn anymore. Usually Nick keeps Chester in the house when King is out."

"I let the cat out this morning," Chase confessed. "He was meowing."

"Ah." She smiled at his sheepishness. "Well, no real harm done. King just had a good fright, didn't you, boy?" Nettie pressed the length of her palm against King's forehead. He pushed back, nuzzling into her.

Chase stood to the side, watching her soothe the horse. She communicated with the big animal, no doubt about it, by look, by touch. "You're good with him."

Lightly, she ran her knuckles along the soft area of King's nose, ducking her head so that she was almost forehead to forehead with the horse. When finally she turned her head to glance shyly at Chase, he felt his stomach muscles clench. "This is something I know a bit about," she said.

Chase felt bewitched. "Horses?" he murmured.

Nettie meant fear, but didn't say so. Patting King's neck, she said, "I think he's calm enough to unsaddle now. I bet he'd enjoy a good rubdown, too, wouldn't you, fella?"

With one hand on the bridle and one holding the reins, she walked King to a post outside the barn. Chase followed, admiring the grace of her movements, noting and enjoying the quick glances she directed his way as she looped the reins around the wood.

With her hand on King's neck, she spoke to Chase, but it took him a moment to register the soft request: water. She wanted a bucket of water, a currycomb and a brush.

"Can you find all that in the barn?"

Chase nodded. He wouldn't be able to find his own head with two hands and a flashlight if he didn't stop staring at her.

He answered gruffly, "Right," then turned and strode into the barn.

Looking for a currycomb seemed like an innocuous activity, but then the fresh bedding in the stalls reminded him of all the Westerns he'd seen in which the hero and heroine eventually wound up lying in straw....

Picturing Nettie with straw in her long curly hair wasn't much of a mental leap.

Clenching his jaw, Chase concentrated on collecting the grooming supplies, but the image of her hands, gentle and feminine, and her amazing innocence as she awkwardly asked him to dinner refused to leave his mind.

He'd had a damned hard time not questioning Nick about her last night, trying hard to convince himself there was nothing he needed to know.

With a bucket of water in one hand, brush and currycomb in the other, he walked into the sunlight, frowning when he saw that Nettie had unbuckled the cinch and was attempting to drag the heavy saddle from King's back. The Western-style gear was cumbersome and though she didn't appear weak, unsaddling the tall horse was obviously an effort.

Immediately, he wanted to take over and wondered if she would care about the political incorrectness of his response. There were women in his circle who would throttle him for interfering.

While he hesitated, King shifted sideways toward Nettie. She murmured to him, balanced herself and repositioned her grip on the saddle. Chase heard her count, "One, two, three," then watched her heave the saddle up and off the animal's back just as Chester the Devil Cat strolled lazily—and deliberately—within view of the horse.

"I'll be damned—" Chase began in amazement, then forgot

about the cat as King fussed and bumped into Nettie, throwing her off balance. She began to teeter. Trying to calm King and save herself at the same time proved to be too much, and she stumbled, emitting a little yelp as she started to fall backward.

The yelp did it.

Chase dropped the bucket, tossed the grooming tools and was behind Nettie in a flash. She was slight enough that his arms circled her with ease as he reached for the saddle she clutched to her belly. Sandwiching her between himself and the saddle with a triumphant ''Gotcha!'' he felt her slender shoulders, the curve of her derriere and finally the back of her head as she stumbled against him. He'd have to be a mannequin not to react to the feel of her.

He hung onto the saddle more easily than he did his sanity while she steadied herself. Her sandaled feet danced around his borrowed cowboy boots, and the scent of flowers wafted up from her hair so that he barely registered pain when she ground her heel on his instep.

Chest to back, they breathed together. He felt her body expand and contract, felt his own breathing quicken in time with hers. His biceps bunched as he carried the weight of the saddle, but what he really noticed was the softness of her arms against the hardness of his. This was not an effective way to avoid thinking about her. Chase stayed very still, hoping she wouldn't notice that body parts other than his biceps had gone rather...solid. His mouth twisted wryly. He was reacting like a high-schooler with runaway hormones.

When she was balanced on her own two feet again, she pulled away slightly, tilted her head up and around and said, so softly that he had to read her lips to make out the words, ''Thank you.''

Chase nodded. And gritted his teeth. *Those lips.* Soft, lush, ripe. Cupid had drawn them to drive a man crazy.

Neutral, he reminded himself. *Think of Switzerland.*

Tensely, he waited for her to turn around again or to slip out from beneath his arms...something. But she stayed put, eyes so wide and so beautiful that he wanted to capture them on film.

He failed to come up with a single neutral thought that would stick as his gaze locked with hers, as the delicate, perfect parting of her lips made her look as if she were on the verge of saying something.

If his expression conveyed anything at all, she must be able to guess what he wanted. And yet she didn't turn away.

Directly under his gaze, her breasts rose and fell, and he thought—in fact, he could have sworn—he heard her sigh.

Switzerland. Capital city, Bern. Swiss…banks. Swiss…chocolate. Swiss…

"Ah, to hell with it—"

Forced between his teeth, the words hovered between them for a moment. Then Chase answered the mild surprise on Nettie's face by claiming that glorious mouth with his own.

Chapter Four

He meant it to last a moment; but her lips were soft and tasted like cherries, so he lingered a moment longer and then—

Chase stifled the groan that wanted to rise from his belly. Her lips parted—just a bit—but the temptation to press his mouth more firmly against hers became irresistible.

Holding the saddle in his hands was an exercise in frustration. He craved the freedom to turn her around, thread his fingers through her thick, curly hair and let his other hand roam where he knew it shouldn't.

Guilt made his muscles tighten. He had no business kissing her like this. She was trapped between the saddle and his chest. He hadn't asked if he could kiss her and he didn't want it to go any further.... He didn't.

Exerting more effort than it usually took to finish his last set of curls at the gym, Chase tensed his jaw, stopped kissing and lifted his head. Then he stared down at the beautiful woman before him.

Her eyes remained closed a while. When her lids fluttered, she looked up and Chase found himself staring into two huge blue pools of soft dreamy surprise.

He almost growled.

He didn't want innocence in a woman. Never had. Where there was innocence there was also expectation. The only expectations he ever wanted to live up to were his own.

"I need to put the saddle down." His voice was a disgustingly weak croak.

Nettie blinked at him dazedly, then nodded. "Yes." Smiling a little shyly—which, dammit, made him want to kiss her again—she glanced around, finally deciding to slip down under his arms.

Chase silently nodded his thanks. Walking past her, he slung the saddle over the tie-out and turned back. She looked uncertain, but full of anticipation and utterly beautiful. She looked—

As though she wanted to be kissed again.

Grimly, Chase shook his head. *Don't even think about it.* He walked toward her. Time to say good-bye.

Nettie watched Chase Reynolds with a curious blend of excitement and objectivity.

Brian had been handsome, but in a boyish way. Until a minute ago, he had been the only man she'd ever kissed.

Kissing Chase Reynolds was different. He kissed the way he looked: sleek and dangerous, vital and strong. Her lips were still tingling. There had been a moment there when she'd been sure he was going to kiss her again, and the sheer excitement of expecting it had been exhilarating.

Good grief, Annette Louise, you've barely stepped into the starting gate and already you want to race down the track!

"Slow down," she murmured under her breath, not even aware she'd spoken until Chase responded by holding up a hand.

"I'm sorry." His voice was low, gravelly and somber. "That was a mistake."

It took a moment to realize he was responding to her. "No!" she said. "I wasn't talking about the kiss. I meant… It was?"

Chase grimaced, looking like he wanted to kick himself. "Not a *mistake.* That wasn't the right…"

"Word. No. No, it didn't feel like a mistake." She blushed. *Pay attention. The man is telling you he's sorry he kissed you.*

"Maybe it was a bit precipitous." No way was she going to let him think he was the only one regretting this.

"Precipitous?" Ironic humor poked at the corner of his mouth. "Good word." He walked toward her, stopping when there was less than a foot between them. Even that short space seemed to be filled with something. An electric charge. A magnetic pull.

"There are rules about kisses," Chase said, his smile fading. His eyes grew dark and sober.

"Rules?"

"Don't kiss before the first date."

His closeness made it hard for Nettie to take a deep breath. "I suppose that's a good policy," she agreed, sounding, she thought, as if she'd just run a mile. "Is that it?"

He shook his head. "No. Rule number two: Never kiss a small-town girl if you know you're not planning to stay."

Nettie's lips thinned. To a man like Chase, *small-town* no doubt implied a certain naiveté, a husband-hungry woman who expected to hear the word *forever* every time she was kissed. Nettie's eyes narrowed. Well, you got the wrong girl. *Forever* was no longer a part of her vocabulary.

It occurred to her suddenly that she was sick and tired of other people's opinions. Fed up with following rules, about dating or anything else. She'd followed rules all her life, either other people's or the ones she'd made up for herself, the ones that were supposed to keep everyone safe and calm and happy. A lot of good that had done her.

What if, just this once, she did what she wanted and not what she thought she *ought* to do?

"I'm not a woman who follows rules," she said. The lie tasted so good on her lips she followed it immediately with another. "Never have been. Never will be." In a decidedly un-Nettie-like move, she traced an instructive index finger slowly up the middle of his chest from breast to collarbone. "But if I were, I would remind you about rule number three: Always consult the woman in question before making executive decisions."

Chase exhaled heavily. "Are you real?" he asked.

"If you're asking whether I mean what I say, there's only one way to find out."

For a moment there was only silence. Neither of them so much as twitched.

Nettie could have sworn Chase moved first, but when she thought about it later she couldn't be absolutely certain. In the long run, who cared? In an instant they were moving together, grabbing shoulders, tracing hands across backs, melding lips and clinging with an abandon that electrified her down to her toes.

She lost all track of time and her surroundings. They both seemed to. When tires crunched along the driveway, neither reacted. They didn't hear the sound of a truck parking in the driveway or of a door opening and closing. They weren't aware of a thing except each other, until Nick coughed loudly behind them. Even then, it took a moment to respond.

Chase reacted first, squeezing Nettie's arm before he broke off the kiss and lifted his head.

He cleared his throat. "Company," he murmured, holding and shielding her from Nick's view until she collected herself.

Nettie tuned into her surroundings slowly. She felt like she was quite literally melting, as if she were being filled right that very moment with drippy, delicious golden sunshine and couldn't be troubled to move or think or worry about a thing.

She moistened her lips. And smiled. "Hello, Nick." She giggled. Her voice sounded like she'd spent too much time on a hot beach.

Nick didn't seem to appreciate the perfection of the moment. He divided his scowl between Nettie and Chase, finally demanding tightly of the other man, "What's going on?"

Chase stiffened beside her. He let go of Nettie's arm and faced his host squarely. Tall, broad and appearing remarkably adversarial for two people who were supposed to be friends, the men held each other's gazes while Nick waited for an answer and Chase stubbornly refused to give one.

Finally, Nick broke the stare and turned toward Nettie. "Where's Sara?"

"Sara?" Nettie shrugged. "In town, I suppose."

Nick glanced toward the Wagoneer parked in front of his house. "How did you get out here?"

Since he was looking at the answer, there should have been no need for the question. But Nick was aware that Nettie hadn't driven anywhere all by herself for some time.

Their parents had been good friends. Nick had acted as a protective big brother through the years, and as appreciative as Nettie was for his steady presence in their lives, she did not want him blabbing about her fears in front of Chase.

Hurriedly stepping in front of Chase, she said, "I drove, of course," then gave Nick a don't-say-*anything* look. He didn't seem to get it.

"By yourself?"

"Well, of course!" Trying once more to communicate by expression alone, she winked and puckered her lips to mouth *shh.* "I came to pick up the eggs."

"The eggs?"

"Yes." She winked again, longer. "I know you usually bring *the eggs* over to our place, but I wanted to save you the bother since you've been so busy lately. Besides, you know how *I love to drive.*" She smiled over her shoulder at Chase. "I'm always out somewhere." She waved a hand. "Flying here, flying there."

Nick's brows shot up briefly. He glanced between the two of them without exercising any subtlety whatsoever before his expression filled with understanding.

Wishing she could kick Nick hard in the shins, Nettie said, "I'll get the eggs now."

She started toward the car, intending to get one of the boxes she'd thrown in the car to support her excuse for coming over. Nick's voice stopped her. "Nettie?"

She turned.

"I don't have chickens."

An awful heat crept up her neck. She focused on Nick, not even daring to glance Chase's way. She could have sworn…

Nick shook his head.

The heat moved into her face. "Well. My goodness, where did the chickens go?" Silently, she pleaded for Nick to help her out.

He scowled. Scratching his sideburns where they met his beard, he looked extremely uncomfortable as he improvised, "They…ran away."

Nettie affected dismayed surprise. "Again?"

Both men stared at her. Chase shook his head in utter disbelief, then laughed at his friend. "What kind of chickens run away from home?"

"The kind that don't want to get eaten!" Nick growled, glaring to say he didn't intend to discuss it any further. He looked at Nettie. "Did you come over for anything—" His quick glance at Chase told her he knew exactly why she'd braved the drive over today. "—besides eggs?"

"No." She prayed fervently that she wouldn't blush again. "That was all." Nettie nodded toward the horse still waiting to be attended to. "King needs to be rubbed down. And the cat is around here somewhere. I've got to get home." She began backing toward the car. "Nice seeing you again, Chase." He appeared a little off-kilter, which under the circumstances was probably a good way to leave him.

Hoping Nick wouldn't blow her cover once she left, Nettie nodded to her old friend. "Bye, Nick. Sorry to hear about your chickens." She turned and hustled to the car. Smiling as she started the vehicle, she turned it around and waved to the two men who watched her head down the driveway as if she didn't have a care in the world.

She was halfway down the road that led home before she had to pull over to the shoulder to catch her shaky breath.

In a single morning she, the self-confessed Miss Goody Two-Shoes of Kalamoose County, had turned into a liar, a flirt and—

She expelled a long noisy breath. "I'm a hussy."

She hadn't just made a date to get together for drinks or coffee; she hadn't climbed back in the saddle, as it were, by agreeing to go on a blind date. Nope. One minute she'd decided to reenter the dating scene and the next she'd locked lips with Chase Reynolds, the sexiest man on the planet.

When she decided to change, she *really* changed.

A smile, genuine this time, stretched across Nettie's lips. The sexiest man on the planet hadn't been exactly reluctant to kiss her, either. What would have happened, she wondered, if Nick hadn't shown up? How did you talk to a man you barely knew after kissing him like that?

Throwing the car into drive, she eased back onto the empty road. Sunlight relaxed her like a warm bath as it streamed through the window. The hot rays weren't nearly as toasty, though, as the memory of Chase's incredibly male, hungry lips.

Imagining the scene that might have ensued if Nick hadn't shown up kept Nettie occupied all the way home.

It wasn't yet noon when Nettie pulled the Wagoneer to the back of her house. A familiar patrol car was parked out front, and the door to the mud porch was wide open. Sara must have returned home for lunch.

Nettie had only reached the porch steps when Sara sailed through the open door. "You gave me the fright of my life, hang it all! I came home and you and Jezebel were both gone. Who's with you?" Craning her neck, she tried to look over Nettie's head toward the Wagoneer.

"No one is with me," Nettie said with enviable calm and poise. "I decided to go for a little drive. Alone." She edged past her sister into the house. The surprise and confusion on Sara's normally confident face was almost worth the panic Nettie had suffered when she'd first got into the car.

"You went alone?" Sara dogged her heels into the house. "All alone? How? I thought you couldn't drive since—" Sara stopped short of saying "the accident."

Nettie kept moving as she decided how to answer. She went to the refrigerator and pulled out cold chicken, mayonnaise and a tomato, crossed to the bread bin and took out two large potato rolls. As she reached for plates, she spoke quietly. "I couldn't. Or I *thought* I couldn't." She shrugged. "Now I can." Without looking in her sister's direction, Nettie could feel Sara watching her closely.

"Just like that?"

"Yes." Unwrapping the chicken, she amended, "Sort of. I've been listening to some audio tapes Lilah sent me."

"You mean those New Age voodoo hypnotist tapes?"

"They're not voodoo! They're part of a very practical, very common-sense program to heal agoraphobia. It was designed by a therapist. And I think it's helping."

Sara snorted grudgingly. "If they're so common-sense, I wonder how Lilah found them? Boy, leave it to her to handle a problem long-distance."

Nettie scrunched the foil into a tight ball. "When you say *problem*, just what *problem* are you talking about? Me? I certainly hope not, because I am not your problem or Lilah's!"

"I didn't say you were. Don't be so touchy. I just didn't expect to come home and find you gone, that's all."

"Well, expect it more often, because I may not be here a lot in the future." Yanking a knife from a wooden block on the counter, Nettie carved several pieces of chicken for sandwiches. "I drove all the way to Nick's place today, and I liked it."

Halfway into the act of snatching a piece of chicken, Sara paused. "Nick's place? Why would you go—?" Her mouth opened to form an O, or in this case, an Oh, no. "You went there to see him, didn't you?"

Nettie skirted around her uniformed sister on her way to the pantry. "You want lettuce on your sandwich? I'm going to put cranberry sauce on mine."

Sara attempted to block Nettie's path. "If there's something going on between the two of you, I think I should know."

"Really. Why?" Looping around Sara, she grabbed a can of cranberry sauce and looped around Sara again.

"This is a small town. People are going to talk."

Nettie bristled. "So what?" Deciding she was very hungry, Nettie piled chicken on the rolls. "It'll give them something to do between 'Golden Girls' reruns."

"This family has had enough gossip about it with Lilah dating anything that didn't walk on all fours!"

"Oh, stop exaggerating."

"I'm not exaggerating." Sara thumped her hand on the kitchen counter. "Hang it all! Are his intentions serious?"

"Sara, for heaven's sake, you sound like Uncle Harm." Beginning to see some humor in the situation, Nettie laughed. "No one has any intentions right now, serious or otherwise." She tossed the tomato once in the air before setting it on a plate. "All we did was kiss."

Wickedly enjoying the absolute shock on Sara's face, Nettie cut thick slices of tomato, laying them precisely atop the chicken as if sandwich assembly was the only thing on her mind right now. She couldn't decide which was more red—Sara's cheeks or the tomato.

"You kissed him." The tight line of her Sara's lips were pinched and disapproving.

"That's right."

"Was it the first time?"

Nettie paused in the act of spreading mayonnaise across the cut top halves of the rolls. "That is so none of your business. It's my life."

Sara obviously wanted to say more, but didn't know how. She opened and closed her mouth uselessly a couple of times. "Fine!" She strode to the door. "Do whatever you want!"

"Where are you going? Don't you want lunch?"

"I lost my appetite," Sara grumbled. "I'll eat at Ernie's."

"If you're going to eat at Ernie's, you haven't lost your appetite."

Swinging around, Sara aimed her thumb at her chest. "It's my appetite. I know when I've lost it."

Scooping the chicken off Sara's roll, Nettie transferred it to her own. "Fine."

Staring at her naked roll as if Nettie had just committed the ultimate act of betrayal, Sara nodded ominously. "Fine!" She marched out to the squad car.

As Sara drove off, Nettie slapped cranberry sauce on top of the mayonnaise and smooshed the huge sandwich together. "Fine back!"

Quashing guilt, she carried her plate to the living room. Aside from the fact that she'd just participated in the single most inane conversation she'd ever had, she thought she'd made her point fairly well: Things were going to be changing around the Owens household; *she* was changing.

Chewing with more force than necessary, she considered the choices that had brought her to this point.

For as long as she could remember, she'd been the family peacemaker, a veritable bottomless pit of nurturing and reliability.

"Couldn't get more boring than that as a teenager." She'd struck a bargain with God at an early age: She'd follow all the rules and He would keep everyone happy and safe forever and ever, amen.

She'd kept her part of the bargain.

It was high time that she considered the cost of such diligent obedience. She was twenty-five and if she thought about it, she wasn't sure she'd ever really asked herself what she wanted or what she liked. She rented the movies her family enjoyed. She cooked the food she knew other people preferred.

Frowning heavily, Nettie pulled the chicken out of her sandwich until all she had left was tomato, cranberry sauce and mayo on a fluffy white roll. She took a large, ferocious bite. *Yes.* A smile of satisfaction curved her lips. Limited nutritional value, but exactly what she wanted.

By being so *good* for so long, she'd given everyone else a chance to test their wings while her own had grown cramped from disuse. All right. It was time to find out what she wanted, what she liked... And with luck it would be more exciting than a tomato-and-cranberry-sauce sandwich.

Putting her feet on the coffee table, Nettie chewed and thought. She liked country music. And painting. She enjoyed an ice-cold beer on a hot summer day, but she didn't want to turn that into a hobby. She wiggled her foot. What else? What else did she like—

Kisses. Chase Reynolds' kisses.

Yep, if pure enjoyment were the goal, those kisses would go a long, long way.

"Goes without saying. But you can't run around kissing people for kicks." She set her sandwich on the plate.

Not people, a voice inside her responded, *just Chase.*

"That's not a hobby."

It could be.

"Please. Embrace reality. The man was featured in *People* magazine. He's probably kissed Madonna."

So? He kissed you. He liked it.

Her foot stopped wriggling. "Well, that's still not a hobby," she mumbled, setting her plate on the coffee table. "I need something I can do on a regular basis, like knitting."

Good choice. Why kiss a hunk when you can purl a scarf?

That settled it. Nettie plunked her elbows on her knees and rested her chin on her upturned palms. She was going to see Chase again. And not only because he made the ground shake when he kissed her. Not only because his hands made her feel warm through and through for the first time in years.

Not because she forgot the past and stopped wondering about the future when she looked into his eyes.

No, those weren't the reasons she was going to see him again. She was going to see Chase Reynolds again because if she didn't, she would spend the next ten years knitting scarves and wondering what could have come after the kisses.

Chapter Five

Nick's coffee tasted like mud with caffeine. It tasted angry, Chase mused, evidently reflecting the mood of the man who'd made it.

Sprawled in a tan suede easy chair, Nick was, at present, glaring at his houseguest.

Taking another sip, just to be social, Chase met the blatant disapproval in his friend's eyes and decided, *the heck with polite.* Setting his mug on the coffee table, he sat back and volleyed the glare.

With a pointed glance at the mug, Nick growled, "What's wrong?"

Chase felt his shoulders square as if he were preparing to fight, not chat. "It's a little strong, don't you think?"

"I like it strong."

As casually as he could, Chase shrugged.

Nick was on his feet in an instant. "What's that supposed to mean?"

"You need to get out more." Chase crossed an ankle over his knee. "Because if this is really about coffee, I'm scared for you, buddy."

Nick glowered a bit longer, then sat back down, elbows on knees, hands clasped.

Chase studied his former college roommate and suddenly knew what was coming. "This is about her—your friend—isn't it?"

"'Her?' 'My friend?'" Nick offered a disgusted snort. "You don't even know her name."

"Of course I know her name!"

"What is it?"

"Nettie!" Angry himself now, Chase swore. Some strong emotion bubbled beneath the anger. Disappointment? Frustration? His gaze narrowed as he demanded of Nick, "Why didn't you tell me yesterday that she was off limits?" *And why was she kissing me?*

"You've been in town one day and you spent part of that in a jail cell." Nick ran a hand over black wavy hair that was as thick as it had been in college. "I forgot what a fast mover you are."

"'Fast mover?'" Uncrossing his legs, Chase leaned forward, too. Fast mover. He despised that term. It implied instability, insincerity and a shallowness that was chronic—

Nick arched a coal-black brow.

"In college I might have—"

A corner of Nick's mouth joined the brow.

To work off some of his mounting irritation, Chase stood and crossed the wood floors of the old farmhouse. The view from the living-room windows was too peaceful; it irritated him further. "You're telling me to stay away from her?"

Nick nodded slowly, watching Chase carefully as he said, "You don't know her, so I'm going to tell you flat out— A relationship with you is not what she needs." He waited only long enough for Chase to narrow his eyes before he added, "Think about what you're doing here. You're hiding out from the press while you wait for a paternity test. If it's negative, you're out of here and off to where next? Wherever the next big story is, right?" Nick persisted. "Do you know what you're going to do if the boy turns out to be your son?"

Just hearing the words aloud made Chase's heart pound. Even his throat tightened. What did he know about being a father? Zilch. Less than zilch.

Nick paced to the fireplace. He reached for a carved wooden box, withdrew a piece of cigarette paper and a large pinch of tobacco and began rolling a cigarette.

Chase grimaced. "Haven't you given those up, yet? They'll kill you."

"I used to think the same thing about your career. I read that you were shot in the thigh last year while you were trying to run down a big drug story in Brazil."

"It was just a graze. I was back on the job in two days."

Nick nodded. "I read that, too. So what's the boy's name?"

Inhaling and exhaling deeply, Chase made a quarter turn toward the window. "Colin."

"And he's six, right?"

"Seven."

"How long had you known his mother? You never really said."

No, Chase thought, and he didn't want to say. He didn't want to think about this situation at all, not until he was forced to. Every time his mind moved in that direction, he felt a completely unsettling guilt, and he had nothing to feel guilty about. He hadn't even known about Colin until two weeks ago. Chase ran both hands over his head, from his forehead to his nape. "I met Julia in England."

"The supermodel, right? I read about the two of you. I was in line at the grocery at the time."

"Yeah." Chase acknowledged the gibe. "We were together four months, a record for me, as you've pointed out. And a record for Julia, too. We parted very happily. I had a job in the Middle East, and she went to France, where she fell head over heels for a Paris baker who wanted to be a performance artist. Using bread dough."

"Eclectic."

"Uh-huh. I spoke with her once, twice—who even remembers now? She could have contacted me anytime, though. Through the station, if nothing else."

"Does it bother you that she didn't?"

Chase rounded on his friend, fierce outrage in his golden-brown eyes. "If he's my son? Of course it 'bothers' me! What in hell kind of question—" He stopped, realizing the implication was completely fair. He hadn't planned to have a child. He hadn't called Nick, ecstatic over the possibility when the lawyers had phoned. He'd called looking for a place to hide out while he prayed his life would stay exactly as it was.

Nick licked the edge of the paper to seal his cigarette. "You and I are bachelors through and through."

"What are you talking about? You were married."

"According to Deborah, I was a bachelor then, too. She put up with me for three years. It hurt her pretty badly." Reaching for an old-fashioned silver lighter, he touched a flame to the end of his cigarette and snapped the lid. "Nettie's like Deborah. Home and family are everything to her. She doesn't move in your world. She couldn't."

Recalling Nettie's admonition about making decisions for women, Chase began to smile. "You sure about that?"

Nick exhaled a long stream of smoke. "I'm sure." His expression turned grim. "I understand what I saw. I know she was kissing you back. You're a celebrity, pal, and she grew up in a small town. You're glamorous."

Chase winced at the word. "Give her some credit."

"I am. She's a rare person, good through and through. I don't want her to be hurt. Not when I can see it coming and stop it."

Chase got the point. He was an old friend and a welcome guest as long as he played by the rules. It hovered on the tip of his tongue to point out that *People* magazine considered him a pretty good catch. Right up there with Sean Puffy Combs. Irony curved his lips. The qualities that made him successful in his career ruled him out as family material. He knew that, but it had never bothered him before.

It didn't bother him now.

Nick waited for an agreement. Chase let him wait a little longer while he turned the tables instead. "What are you doing these days, relationship-wise?"

"There's a woman in Minot I see every now and then. Nice lady, but she doesn't have a candle in the window for me, if you know what I mean. She's fine if I'm there and fine if I'm not. That's the only kind of woman you and I should have anything to with. The kind we can't hurt."

It was exactly what Chase had always said. It was the way he'd lived all of his adult life. But it ticked him off royally to hear it today.

In the absence of a verbal response, Nick persisted. "Nettie can be hurt."

"All right, I get the picture."

"She *is* the candle-in-the-window type."

"Got it." Chase was beginning to sound snappish.

"And you are *not* the candle-in-the-window type."

"All right, I said. I get it!" He stalked toward the entryway to the hall, intending to find some solace in the upstairs guest bedroom Nick had given him. "I hope this woman in Minot doesn't mind reruns," he said on a parting shot. "Because you are the most repetitive sonova—"

Nick pointed with the cigarette. "That temper of yours is another reason you ought to stay away from—"

"I said no problem!" Chase stormed out of the room and up the stairs.

Nick spoke quietly after him, but the sound carried. "Good. I'm glad we're in agreement."

Cloudless, the night sky looked like a billowing swatch of black velvet. Like a magic carpet, Nettie thought as she lay in the queen-size bed tucked beneath a double window in her second-story bedroom. She'd placed the bed under the window in lieu of a headboard so she could watch the stars glimmer and change on clear nights like this. In winter, before the harshest storms came, she scooched the bed over. Lightning and thunder were not as friendly as black velvet and stars.

The full moon was high and amazingly bright tonight. Wondering what time it was she lifted her head to look at the digital clock on her dresser. Only a little after midnight. Oh, brother. One more sleepless night, and her eyes would be as swollen as the moon. She'd spent the past two nights tossing and turning as she thought about Chase. Or as she tried not to think about him.

She hadn't seen him since the day she'd driven to Nick's, and that was three days ago. Despite her conviction that she *would* see him again, she had to admit she'd expected him to come to her this time. Or that they'd run into each other in town. There was only one tiny grocery in Kalamoose. If he intended to buy food in town, surely she would see him there. Working on that assumption, in three days she'd bought two heads of lettuce she hadn't needed, way too many canned goods and enough peanut butter to last half a year.

Sighing, Nettie flopped onto her side and pulled the quilt over her bare shoulder. The beloved wedding-ring quilt covering her bed had been in her family for three generations. In years gone by, it had made her feel cozy and happy simply to look at it and think about tradition—the tradition of handing down heirlooms, the tradition of marriage.

"That's your problem," she muttered, burrowing more deeply into her soft pillow. "You want to live a Courtney Love life, but you've got a Donna Reed brain. Women who live for the moment have silk sheets." She rolled onto her stomach. "And if you want to see Chase again, you're going to have to hang out where he hangs out." From her stomach, she moved to her other side and then her back. "I wonder where he's hanging out in Kalamoose?" By now the town should have been buzzing with news about his presence. Celebrities were rare in Kalamoose, but so far she hadn't heard a word.

A sharp tap made her open her eyes. When she heard it again, she sat up abruptly and looked around. "What—"

Ting!

Something hit her window. Nettie turned, leaning on her pillows to look out the window and down to the ground. Sara always left the porch light glowing because it deterred criminals (not that they were inundated with them way out here) and because as the sheriff she felt she was on-call twenty-four seven. The front porch was around the corner, but the light spilled over to softly illuminate the side of the house on which Nettie's bedroom was located.

She squinted. There was a man down there. And he was throwing something at her window.

Quickly she sat up, all but pressing her nose against the glass as she tried to see who was out there.

The man ran a hand over his head, searched the ground, picked something up and *ping!*

Nettie jerked back as another stone hit the window. With the man's face upturned, she recognized Chase.

Scuttling off the bed, she raced to the bedroom door, but realized an instant after she flung it open that her nightgown was

sheer wispy nylon, hardly adequate covering for running out of
the house in the middle of the night, so she hurried to the closet,
searched madly for a robe and wrestled herself into it as she ran
down the stairs.

"Don't leave, don't leave," she chanted, forcing herself to
slow down as she reached the front door. Sara slept like a rock,
but Nettie didn't want to take any chances. Opening and closing
the door carefully, she trotted barefoot down the porch steps and
around the side of the house.

Chase was there, winding up to pitch another stone at her
window. She smiled. Her heart skipped and a shiver that had
nothing to do with the chill night air skittered along her arms.
Suddenly she felt as young, as light and carefree as she had at
sixteen.

Silently, she crept up behind Chase and whispered, "Are you
sure that's her window?"

With his arm raised to throw the stone, he turned so quickly
he almost lost his balance.

His deep-brown hair was ruffled, and Nettie thought he must
have run his hands through it several times tonight. His expression conveyed first surprise, then chagrin and finally sheepishness.

"Caught throwing stones at the girl's window." She shook
her head and grinned. "That misdemeanor carries quite a fine
in Kalamoose."

It wouldn't have shocked her a bit to discover that her blood
had turned to golden honey; she felt so sweet and warm as his
face relaxed and his left eyebrow hitched with the same humor
that curled his masculine lips. His eyes said clearly that seeing
her made him very, very happy.

Chase cocked his head. "I committed the crime, I'll do the
time."

Amusement sparkled in Nettie's eyes and made dimples appear in her cheeks. The sight pleased Chase more than scooping
the collapse of a foreign syndicate. He didn't want her to be
awed or to find him "glamorous," as Nick suggested. He
wanted their interaction to be clean and unbiased, just one man
and one woman, on a prairie in the middle of North Dakota.

Tousled from bed, Nettie's wild black curls fell softly around
her cheeks and past her shoulders. Gently, carefully, he reached

out to release a section of her hair from beneath the collar of her silky robe. Her huge eyes blinked heavily, as if she were sleepy, or hypnotized.

Chase had been feted and flattered so often, he barely noticed it anymore. He'd seen so many exquisite women, he tended to take beauty for granted. Yet standing in front of this woman made him feel like a sixteen-year-old misfit who'd been granted a date with the homecoming queen.

He was in deep, deep trouble.

"I've been warned to stay away from you, Ms. Owens." His intention was to keep this light and amusing, but he didn't feel light or amused.

Her surprise was evident. "By who?"

"Nick. He thinks I'll hurt you." Again he had the urge to touch her hair. This time he resisted. The effort further tightened his tone. "He's probably right. I'm not…" Chase sighed, unsure of how to proceed. He didn't like being unsure.

"You're not 'serious.'" She finished his sentence with a startling matter-of-factness. "You're not staying in Kalamoose." The blue eyes rolled. "Duh." She used her fingers to tick off the next couple of facts. "You're not looking for anything permanent, and I'm a small-town girl who's not going anywhere—" About to continue in the same vein, she stopped and shifted gears. "What did Nick say about me?"

"He respects you. Admires you. He says you're good through and through. And that you're a home-and-hearth type." All complimentary stuff as far as Chase was concerned, but it made Nettie's teeth clench. She muttered something he didn't catch. "Beg your pardon?"

"Donna Reed," she growled. "He's making me sound like the mother in a nineteen-fifties sitcom."

"And that's not you?"

Her eyes narrowed, and she answered grimly. "No. On all counts."

He found himself wanting to believe her, because it would be easier. But Nick had also said, "Home and family were everything to her." *Were.* What did that mean? She'd had a family and now didn't? Chase had assumed Nick was talking about the loss of her parents.

"How did you know which bedroom was mine?" Nettie

asked, before Chase could pursue his line of thought. "Sara could be standing here right now."

He winced. "Not a chance. She'd have shot me from the window."

The smile returned to her face. Chase really didn't want to answer the question. The truth, the *whole* truth, was that he'd scoped the house out earlier this evening, which made him sound like either a high-school freshman or a total pervert. He settled for a partial truth.

"One bedroom has lace curtains, one has shutters and one has a hand-lettered sign that says This House Patrolled by N.D.P.D. stuck in the window. I took my best shot."

She laughed. "I'm glad."

"You're not angry? It's past midnight."

Nettie shook her head. Her eyes never left his. "I'm not angry."

The words emanated from some newborn place inside her. She felt herself grow calmer and more sure of herself by the minute. "I was warned away from you, too."

Chase frowned. "Nick gets around."

"He hasn't said anything to me. I warned myself." It was the truth, and amazingly she didn't feel a bit embarrassed saying it. "I told myself you've had relationships with some of the most beautiful women in the world. With exciting women. 'What could he possibly see in you?' I said."

"How did you answer that?"

"I didn't. You did. You threw stones at my window."

Nettie took a breath at the same time that she took a step forward. It made her appear both bold and nervous. Chase didn't want to wait another second. Desire coursed through his veins; he had wanted women in the past, of course. Wanted them physically, wanted them *now*. This was different, though he didn't know quite how, except that in the past his desire had seemed like a wind—swift and strong and fleeting. What he felt now was an uncontrolled burn, a fire that gained strength as it moved.

"You are so damn lovely." His hoarse whisper cloaked them like the night. "You should see what I see." The eyes of the women he typically dated would have smiled with satisfaction if he'd said the same words to them. Nettie's eyes widened happily, hungrily. Chase thought his self-control had never been so tested. "You should listen to Nick," he told her, his voice more a growl now than a whisper. "Or *I* should listen."

Because he didn't think he could stand not touching her a moment longer—yet didn't want to hold her in a passionate way—he grasped her upper arms and promised himself his hands would not wander.

"I travel all over the world," he told her. "I'm never in one place very long. I haven't slept in my apartment more than three nights in a row for the past five years. And I am lousy at relationships. Lousy. I can tell you who's who in the Middle East political scene, but if you want a shoulder to cry on or a comforting voice in the middle of the night, or someone who'll remember your birthday—"

Nettie's hands came up to hold his face, as firmly as he had taken her arms. "You talk way too much." She stepped closer, unmindful of the fingers that tightened unconsciously around her. As she raised her face, she felt energy, like a buzz, at the contact. When she touched her lips to his, a shudder of barely exerted control ran through him, and Nettie felt a surge of delicious power.

Last time, he'd controlled the kiss, and, dazed, she'd simply hung on for the ride. This time when their lips met, Nettie took control of the vehicle and wasn't about to let go for anything!

Still holding his face, she began the kiss softly, an explorer in uncharted country. One...two...three gentle touches, each lasting a bit longer than the one before. After the third kiss, she lingered, allowing herself to be excruciatingly aware—of his skin, of the infinitesimal beard he would have to shave tomorrow morning, of the aftershave she'd noticed that first night and which she decided she really loved. What she wanted, truly wanted, was to move along the outline of his lips to the corner of his mouth and then down, teasing that little nook between his lower lip and chin.

So she did it. She did exactly what she wanted, exactly the way she wanted and for at least forty seconds she paid no attention to the fact that she was standing in her side yard in the middle of the night, wearing only a thin, plain gown and robe, with a man *People* magazine had called "beautiful."

When she kissed his chin, Chase kissed her nose. Nettie had the blissful urge to snuggle into him like a cat. She lifted her face and again pressed her lips to his, this time allowing them to part slightly. It was a hesitant move, and Chase stayed absolutely still, letting her set the pace. She looked up. His eyes were shadowed by the silky night, but she could tell that they were open and watching her. In one electrified instant she felt everything...everything...the whisper of his breath, the thud of her own heart, cold grass beneath her bare feet and his warm, warm hands resting on her upper arms.

"What are you doing to me, Nettie Owens?" Chase's whispered question held a smile. His hands began to move down her arms, pulling her closer, settling on the curve of her lower back.

Nettie released his face reluctantly. Suddenly she felt self-conscious. Winding her arms around his neck seemed too intimate, somehow, a sensibility that smacked of the ridiculous in light of the kisses they were sharing. Still, he was fully clothed and she was pressed against him in a silk robe—no bra. Her bare feet, taking tiny steps toward him for balance, bumped into his leather boots, and that, too, seemed achingly intimate.

So what to do with her hands? She settled for lowering them, resting her palms on his shoulders.

Chase was still looking down into her face. "What now, Nettie?"

Good question. *What now?* He wasn't staying. A relationship would go nowhere, and she appreciated his honesty in saying so. She didn't even know how long he planned to stay. But he felt so warm and sturdy, holding her this way, closely but lightly, too, giving her the freedom to make a choice.

As for wanting a man who would provide a shoulder for her to cry on, tears were not what she was interested in. She'd cried enough already.

"October twenty-third," she said.

Bemused, Chase edged his head back a bit. "What's that?"

"My birthday. Think you can remember it?"

Chase's smile carried through the shadows. "I think so."

Unconsciously, Nettie sighed. Looking him square in the eye, she said, "Good enough."

Clearly he had no idea what she was talking about at first. Then understanding dawned. A gratifying look of wonder lit his face, punctuated swiftly by a frown. "Are you telling me you want a relationship given everything I've said?"

Was she? Nettie nodded.

Chase's arms stiffened around her. "Say it, Nettie. Out loud. I need to hear it, because when I look at you, I see babies and Christmas trees and dinners at home before the PTA meeting—"

"No." Swift and adamant, the denial left no room for doubt. His simple description was all she needed to hear to know that her decision was made. "Look again," she said. "I don't want…" Knowing she would choke up if she told him what she didn't want, she focused instead on what she did. "How long will you be in town?"

Chase grimaced. "Two weeks, maybe three. But I—"

She interrupted him. "Fine. A few weeks." Wrapped in his arms, feeling vulnerable but surprisingly strong, she raised a brow. "You'll miss my birthday, but we could celebrate early. Or not." She took a breath. "Do you want a girlfriend while you're here?"

"A girlfriend?"

She stood taller. He was smiling at her, gently and with a tinge of amusement. If he wanted to hear her say something sophisticated, like *lover,* she didn't think she could do it. There was only so much daring she could handle in one night. If he asked her what she meant by *girlfriend,* she wondered whether she could define her picture of the next two weeks in his company, for him and for herself, out loud.

He released her, bringing his hands up to her neck and cupping her jaw in his palms. Before she could speak, he rubbed a thumb lightly across her lips. "I'd like you to be my girlfriend. I would like it very much."

He didn't add, "while I'm here." He didn't need to. An agreement had been struck, an agreement that was rife with implications.

Nothing innocent about it, Nettie thought. And nothing ordinary. For a woman who played by the rules, she was bending quite a few of them tonight.

She'd had only one lover in her life. She had no complaints about her sex life with her late husband, but once she'd unearthed a copy of *The Women's Guide to Sexual Satisfaction* while cleaning out Lilah's old room and had laughed herself silly. Either half the things in that book were physically impossible or she and Brian had been as daring as Ozzie and Harriet.

Chase was an experienced man. No doubt he'd had experienced lovers.

When he brought one hand up to smooth the hair back from her temple, his fingers tangled in her long curls. He smiled and suddenly it was just the two of them. No other people, no pasts, no future beyond the next two weeks. Even the night seemed to fall away. The only thing Nettie saw was Chase's head lowering. All she felt was a bubbly, tingling anticipation as suddenly his mouth was less than a whisper away. "Nettie—"

A door clicked, a screen slammed, and whatever he had been about to say was lost to the sound of Sara's heel-heavy steps marching onto the porch.

"Nettie! Are you out here?"

Nettie jumped. Caught by surprise, she let out a little squeal. Grabbing fistfuls of Chase's sweater, she began pushing him toward the side of the house. "Shh."

Automatically, Chase held her more protectively, cupping the back of her head.

"Nettie?"

"It's my sister," she hissed.

"I know." He whispered back.

"If she sees us, this is going to be the longest two weeks of our lives. She thinks you're a playboy."

"Last night she thought I was a bank robber." His breath was warm in her ear. "We won't be able to hide from her for two weeks."

"I know. But for right now…" Nettie figured that if she sounded like she was pleading…well, she was. She didn't want to have to fight with Sara or to explain herself over and over. She didn't want to talk about Chase. Not now. Maybe not ever. "Please, you've got to go. I'll call you at Nick's tomorrow."

First Chase shook his head. Then he grinned. "I have a feeling this boyfriend gig isn't going to be as easy as it sounds." Repeating her promise as a command, he said, "Call me tomorrow," then kissed her temple at the corner of her eyebrow.

They heard Sara's footsteps, a bit softer now, heading in their direction. With a quick glance back toward the porch, Chase gave Nettie a brief salute and trotted around the corner of the house. When he was cleanly out of the light, Nettie heard him pick up speed and jog across the lawn.

"Wha— Who is that? Hey!" Sara rushed down the porch steps and along the side of the house.

"Sara!"

"Nettie?" The lanky redhead stopped and searched the shadows for her sister. Dressed in a pair of plaid pajama bottoms and an I Love Fargo T-shirt, her feet stuffed into leather-soled moccasins and her hair plaited into a single sleep-mussed braid, Sara looked as cranky as she sounded. "What the heck is going on out here? Who is that?" She pointed demandingly toward the road.

Nettie made a great show of peering into the yard, which at this time of night didn't look like anything more than a great black void. "Who's who?"

"That person!" Sara stabbed the air.

"Person?" Nettie blinked, managing a stunning show of bemusement for someone not used to lying. "What person?"

"The one who is running through our yard!" Sara's head swung dizzyingly from Nettie to the yard and back again— twice—as she obviously wrestled with an impulse to run after whoever was out there; the only thing stopping her was the fact that she wouldn't be able to see more than three feet in front of her. "What is going on out here?"

"Person?" Nettie murmured. "Person. Ohh, you mean the dog."

"Dog?"

"Yes." Nettie yawned. "A really big dog. Nice, though. I'm going back to bed."

"Ho-o-old it!" Sara's lips folded together to form a tight, firm line. She inhaled to a slow count of three and exhaled noisily, a sign that she was trying to control herself, which usually meant the big explosion was right around the corner. "What are you trying to hide?"

"Hide? Sara—" Nettie sighed. "Okay, I might as well tell you. You're bound to find out, anyway."

"That's right."

"I am hiding something from you."

"I knew it."

"But only because I don't want you to get upset."

Immediately Sara became upset. "I'm not going to get upset. Why would I even care? Why does everybody think—"

"Sara, you don't even know what it is yet."

Shoving at the heavy red waves that were slipping out of her braid, Sara crossed her arms. "Fine. Let's have it."

Nettie pulled her robe more closely around her and tightened the sash. "Well. I've been kind of lonely lately, you know. You've been working extra-long hours since your deputy moved to Minot, and I'm here a lot by myself, and…I adopted a dog."

Sara stared. "Dog."

"Yes. Well, not adopted, officially. It probably belongs to someone up the road. But it comes around, and I…pet it. Talk to it. Feed it leftovers. He loves salmon patties. Isn't that funny?"

"You expect me to believe you were feeding a dog at midnight?"

"I know. He likes to eat at the oddest times. I didn't tell you, because…this dog looks just like poor old Skipper, and I know how upset you were when Skipper died."

"I was ten when Skipper died. I'm over it."

"Good for you!" Nettie yawned again. A great, noisy, stretched-arm yawn. "Oh, boy, I'm pooped. I'm going to bed." She walked past Sara and up the porch steps. "'Night."

Sara stood with her arms crossed. She didn't say a word, just let Nettie walk past her and into the house. As the screen door clanked shut, Nettie expelled a pent-up breath. Lying was not something that came easily to her. On the other hand…

She giggled. She was doing lots of things tonight that didn't usually come easily to her. A delicious jittery excitement tingled through her. She'd almost been caught kissing Chase Reynolds by the side of her house at midnight. Sounded like a country-and-western song.

Heading up the stairs to her bedroom, she realized that sleep was the last thing on her mind. Why go unconscious when there was so much to think about, so many wonderful sensations to relive while they were still fresh?

Two weeks. She had two weeks to make new wonderful sensations that she would remember long after he was gone and this lovely interlude had ended. A tiny dullness threatened to encroach upon her mood. Resolutely she shook her head. She had made a decision, struck a bargain, in a sense. Whatever happened over the next two weeks, she would accept the inevitable finality of her parting from Chase. Two weeks and no regrets.

Call me tomorrow...

Nettie returned to her bedroom, closed the door softly and climbed under the covers once more. The sheets were cold and she had to mush the quilt around her to retain some warmth. She would have fourteen exhilarating days to look back on when nights got cold in the future.

And, she had tonight to wonder what "temporary girlfriend" would mean for an experienced man like Chase and a daredevil woman like herself.

Chapter Six

Sara moved around the house like an angry bear the next morning. Plagued by a spate of post-fib guilt, Nettie cut into her own work schedule to prepare waffles for breakfast, but Sara declined, grumbling that she was watching her weight. Standing over the sink, she crunched her way through a bowl of shredded wheat, which she detested, then left the house without saying good-bye.

Wishing she really did have a dog to stuff full of leftovers, Nettie dumped the waffles and wrapped the sausage up for later. Darn it! Sara never watched her weight, and she never turned down pecan waffles. She never turned down food, period. Her gusto for life was all-encompassing.

That's all I'm doing now, Nettie thought, feeling gusto. She simply wanted to do it without an audience.

Heading upstairs to her studio, where work on her sixth There I Go Again! book awaited her, Nettie decided to put everything—Sara and the future and even Chase—out of her mind until later.

"Later" came midmorning.

Working on a particularly fun section of a watercolor painting that depicted her little-boy hero, Barnaby, wandering through a Moroccan bazaar, Nettie was vaguely aware of noise downstairs. Thinking it must be Sara coming home for lunch and perhaps a truce, Nettie continued to work as she waited for her sister to let herself in. A series of firm thuds on the front door convinced her to put down her brush. She wiped her hands on the rag she kept looped through her jeans. Tugging at the blue, paint-smeared man's shirt she wore over her T-shirt and jeans, she headed downstairs, but even as she reached the front door, she was thinking "Sara" or "delivery person," not—

"Chase!"

Dressed in pale blue jeans and a blue shirt—as she was, but minus the paint—Chase stood on the front porch, facing out toward the road, apparently thinking about leaving. He turned when he heard his name.

A smile so naturally sexy it should have been outlawed lit his face. "I saw your wagon, but thought you might be out on another run." That intriguing almost-dimple on his left cheek deepened. "I know I said I'd call first, but I realized I didn't have your number."

"Actually, I was supposed to call you."

"That's right." Chase snapped his fingers. "I forgot."

Nettie leaned against the edge of the front door, but left the screen closed. "That is a big fat lie."

Affecting deep dismay, he placed a hand over his heart. "Journalists do not lie. We interpret facts."

"The fact is you're lying."

Chase moved in so close, his nose almost touched the screen that separated them. "The fact is I didn't want to wait. And I'm usually very good at waiting." The glibness, the teasing was gone. "Were you going to call?"

Thudding happily, Nettie's heart responded before she did. A fall breeze streamed gently through the screen door, the sun shone and a beautiful man stood on her porch. All in all, not a bad morning.

She took a moment to appreciate "the facts": His hair looked like a sea of coffee-hued waves. His even white teeth were perfect. Ditto the muscular shoulders that tapered to a lean waist and truly excellent hips. Shallow physical attributes aside, however, Chase Reynolds also had an exciting life and a wonderful future.

And all that perfection wants me!

She grinned. To deny the pleasure of this moment would be to look a cosmic gift horse in the mouth.

"Well, I thought about calling, but then—" shoulder and hip against the door, she swayed with it slightly "—I remembered what my sister Lilah said about making men wait."

Chase grimaced. "I'm not sure I want to hear this," he murmured. "What did Lilah say?"

"She said, 'Men who wait seldom hesitate.'"

"What does that mean?"

"I have no idea. But Lilah's always had a healthy social life."

"Mmm." Chase turned away to walk toward the porch steps.

Amazed by the disappointment that socked her square in the chest, Nettie opened her mouth to call out to him, to tell him she'd only been teasing and that Lilah had said that back in high school and who took high-school dating advice seriously, anyway? but then Chase plunked himself down on the top step of the porch.

She opened the screen. "What are you doing?"

Picking up a small twig lying next to him, he tossed it lazily into the yard. He checked his watch, stretched his legs out and leaned back on his elbows. "I'm waiting." Arching his neck, he looked up at her. "Any idea how long this will take?"

Nettie ran over and swatted him with her rag. "Brat!"

Smiling broadly, Chase raised an arm to fend her off. "Hey, I'm not complaining. It's just that it's almost lunch time and I may get hungry." Grabbing one end of the cloth, he held on and tugged, pulling so that her only choice was to let go or bend down.

Nettie bent.

Inches away, he said quietly, "I'm sorry for coming over without calling. Have lunch with me anyway."

She usually worked right through lunch. She usually ate a sandwich that wound up having watercolor fingerprints on the bread. She usually adhered to a firm work schedule, and she'd already deviated from it this week when she drove out to Nick's. She was under deadline....

"There's nowhere to go in Kalamoose where we wouldn't be

seen.'' Whispering just seemed right when you were literally face-to-face.

"We'll have to come out of the closet or go someplace farther away.'' The tension remained taut on the towel they both held.

"Farther away," Nettie chose.

"Done." He tugged the rag, levering up at the same time to plant a swift, firm kiss on her lips. Jumping smoothly to his feet, Chase raised the towel between them. "This is wet." Water-based paint stained his palm lightly.

"I was working when you knocked." She examined his hand and giggled. "It looks like a henna tattoo."

"Mmm. Very exotic. You a painter?"

"An illustrator. Come in the house. I'll show you where the bathroom is so you can wash off while I change."

"Okay. What do you illustrate?"

Chase followed her into the old farmhouse. Nettie had grown up here. It had been her home on and off for most of her life, and it offered a simple comfort she loved. The house provided a good indication of the kind of life she led: simple, perhaps even provincial when viewed through the eyes of a man who'd traveled in style all over the world.

In the living room, Nettie turned to gauge Chase's reaction to braided rugs, rough-hewn floors and an overabundance of checks.

He appeared to be holding up pretty well under the "Country Living" assault. His gaze roamed from the fireplace mantel, wreathed in dried flowers and branches and topped by family photos, to the old sofa covered with throw pillows, including the needlepoint cushion Nettie's mother had made which read God Bless Our Happy Home.

Returning his smiling gaze to Nettie, he took a stab at his own question. "You illustrate the *Saturday Evening Post*."

She thwacked him again with the towel. "I suppose you're a chrome and leather man."

"Depends on whether we're talking about furniture or ladies' lingerie." Laughing when Nettie went speechless, Chase addressed her with utter sincerity. "I like your house. I like the way it's decorated. It looks like you."

"Oh." She mock-winced. "Comfortable?"

"Welcoming." He indulged himself by delving his fingers

into the black-as-night waves she'd clipped up in some kind of loose twist behind her head. "A sight to come home to," he said, having had no idea until that moment that he'd been thinking any such thing. "Like open arms."

Once the words were out of his mouth, Chase realized that he absolutely meant them. Still, it was the wrong thing to say, truthful or not.

"That's nice," she responded simply, smiling but obviously not reading anything deeply personal into the comment. Chase should have been happy for small favors. Instead, he wanted to kick his sorry butt. This was exactly what Nick had been talking about. Chase's future resembled a jigsaw puzzle with too many pieces. He and Nettie had already agreed—wisely, maturely—that their relationship would be…non-permanent. The line between "for now" and "forever" should not be blurred—not in her mind. Not in his own.

He dropped his hand, but didn't have to recover verbally, because Nettie had apparently moved on already in her own mind. "There's a downstairs bathroom in the hall by the staircase." She walked him over to it. "It used to be a closet. These old farms typically had lots of bedroom additions, all built around one poor, overworked bathroom. My father put this one in after I was born. I think he anticipated a loss of good humor if he had to share one bathroom with a bunch of women."

"A man with vision. I like him."

Nettie inclined her head. "You would have, I think. Politics and current events fascinated him."

"Nick mentioned your parents passed away when you were very young."

Nettie nodded. "Uncle Harm, my father's brother, pretty much raised Sara and Lilah and me."

"Uncle Harm was a bachelor?"

"Yep." Nettie moved up a few stairs and leaned on the banister. "Except for us. He blessed my father's foresight on the bathroom facilities every time Lilah had a date." She grinned. "Actually, we all did."

Chase, too, leaned an arm on the banister. "And you? What were you like on date nights?"

"Like any other girl, I guess."

Chase shook his head. "No, I don't think so. Teenagers are notoriously narcissistic."

"Were you?"

"Of course." He grinned shamelessly. "Still am. Not you, though."

Nettie inclined her head. "You sound awfully sure."

"I am. I'm a reporter, remember? Good at interpreting the facts."

"You don't have all the facts."

"No. So tell me more."

For some reason Chase couldn't fathom at the moment, the mood had changed. Pushing away from the banister, Nettie tried to maintain her smile. She tried too hard. "I think that's enough family history before lunch."

She was too eager to stop talking. Chase wasn't sure whether the reporter in him demanded to know more or whether the man did. In any case, he persisted. "You were raised by a bachelor uncle. You had one sister who was obviously a tomboy and another who grew up, I'm guessing, a little more interested in boys than homemaking. But the jail windows are all curtained and this place is a paean to family life." He nodded to the photographs, contemporary and old, that decorated the wall behind her. "Somebody worked hard to make that happen. My bet is on you."

"The curtains in the jail only mean I'm no Martha Stewart. I'm sure she'd recommend something more appropriate. Maybe a *Shawshank Redemption* theme."

Chase laughed. "Or *Papillon*." He reached over the banister to tug on the lapel of her shirt. "I like the blue curtains. Nice little ruffle on the bottom. Very cheery."

"Sara's regulars seem to like it."

"Her regulars?"

"Lefty Bruener, Otto Callendar and Violet Jenks."

Chase shook his head. "This I have to hear."

"Lefty shoplifts from Otto's market every Tuesday like clockwork. Otto gets furious and chases Lefty down the block, throwing old produce at him, which causes a public nuisance. Otto insists on pressing charges against Lefty, and the other shopkeepers want to press charges against Otto because he has terrible aim and usually winds up lobbing moldy cantaloupes at the hair salon. Sara finally figured out that arresting both of them right away keeps everyone happy.''

"This goes on every Tuesday?''

"Haven't missed one in years.''

"And Violet?''

Nettie leaned her forearms on the banister again. Her smile softened, becoming once more the winsome curve of lips Chase found so irresistible. "Violet is seventy-eight, almost ten years older than Otto, but she's been in love with him for as long as anyone can remember.''

Chase held up a hand. "Don't tell me. I want to guess. Miss Violet attacks Lefty in defense of her true love.''

Nettie grinned. "Don't be silly. Violet wouldn't hurt a fly.''

"What does she do?''

"Spits in front of the jail.''

Chase took a beat to process this information. "And Sara arrests her for that?''

"Violet spits repeatedly.''

"Because…''

"Because she thinks it's a crime. She wants to get arrested. That way she can stay up all night in the next cell, reading love poems out loud.''

"Otto likes to be serenaded with love poems?''

"Hates it. But Otto is German and Violet makes the best *mandelbreidt* cookies in town. Otto says they taste just like his mother's. Lefty likes them, too. So for Christmas a few years back, Lefty bought a pair of very discreet earplugs for Otto and another pair for himself. Now they can sit in their cell eating cookies all night while Violet reads next door.''

Chase rested his forehead against the banister. His shoulders shook with laughter.

"Hey, don't laugh at us,'' Nettie protested. "We small-town folk take our romance seriously.''

That sobered Chase up right away. Strolling around the banister he took the first stair. She was standing on the third. Paint stains streaked her shirt, reminding him that she was an artist and that he didn't know nearly enough about her yet.

Burning with curiosity now, he moved up to the second stair. "Do you have an Otto?'' he asked quietly.

Nettie's hand trailed farther up the banister as he advanced. "What—" she cleared her throat "—what do you mean?"

Standing on the adjoining steps, they were almost eye-to-eye. "You're a beautiful woman. Is there somebody out there who would be willing to get arrested just to be close to Nettie Owens?" His hunger to know amazed him. Was there a man out there somewhere who wanted this woman completely, who would fight to win her and sacrifice anything to keep her? Chase had always believed that degree of emotion was reserved for books and movies. God knew he'd never noted any evidence of it in the real world. As far as he could tell, people fought for land, for power; they fought to stay alive.

But to risk everything for the privilege of loving someone who may or may not always love you in return?

At another time he would have written Violet off as a silly old woman. Yet at the moment, all Chase could dredge up was a kind of grudging admiration for the old gal.

He looked at Nettie closely. She hadn't answered him. Perhaps he hadn't asked the right question.

Moving forward on the deep step, Chase said, "Would you risk everything for love?"

Even as the words left his mouth, his heart began to pound and he decided to tape his tongue to the roof of his mouth till he got sane again. Nobody—nobody—risked everything for love. People looked out for themselves first whether they thought so or not. And there was nothing wrong with that.

What a damn dumb question he'd just asked.

But the really, really damn dumb thing was how much he wanted to hear her answer "yes."

Nettie felt so immobile suddenly, she couldn't even swallow. How could she answer Chase honestly? If she said, "Yes," she would only invite more questions: Who? When? What happened?

She didn't want to talk about the two great loves of her life, her late husband and her son. Time with Chase hung suspended—no past to mourn or regret, no future to fear.

A person always risked everything for love, whether they knew it or not, because the chance always existed that you might outlive or out-love the person who held your heart and hopes. Nettie stiffened against the feelings that rose like a reflex. She would never love like that again. Not ever.

"No," she said hoarsely, with Chase's mouth hovering mere inches from hers. She could see every fleck of bright gold in his eyes. Stubbornly she infused her tone with strength and finality. "No, I wouldn't risk everything for love."

She saw his eyes blink in what appeared to be surprise. A sudden pang of sadness for the trusting girl she'd been filled her, but only briefly; she shoved the feeling right down again. That girl was gone, and the woman who'd taken her place meant what she'd said.

It wasn't the answer Chase expected.

He'd intended to kiss her, had been aching to kiss her from the moment she'd answered the door. Her response should make everything easier. She wanted what he did—an absence of strings. And he, who had mastered the art of transient attraction, ought to feel mighty pleased.

He leaned forward, about an inch. He *was* mighty pleased. It would take only an inch or two more to show her *how* pleased.

Open and watchful, her eyes remained steady as she awaited his kiss. Chase gave her a small, sexy smile. The moment his lips curved, he realized with a jolt that the pre-kiss smile was a standard part of his repertoire. His brows swooped into a frown.

Until this moment he hadn't consciously recognized that he had a repertoire.

Swallowing a weird lump in his throat, he pulled back. His throat was dry. In fact, he felt like he was coming down with something.

"We ought to get going." He sounded hoarse. "I mean, if we're going to have lunch someplace else. It'll take time to drive." The frown turned into a scowl. He sounded like a damned kid.

Nettie nodded, appearing no happier than Chase felt, but she recovered, quickly and deliberately. "Good idea. I'm starving. I'll get cleaned up and meet you back down here in ten minutes."

Mutely, Chase nodded.

Nettie backed up the stairs. "Help yourself to a drink in the kitchen, and there's candy in the jar on the coffee table if you can't wait for lunch." She tossed him a smile, then turned to continue up the stairs and out of sight.

For some reason, Chase began to perspire. He shook his head, wishing he could shake out the cobwebs that had collected there recently. He'd been under too much stress. He was starting to question himself, to lose his intrinsic confidence. He was a knife with a dull edge, that's what he was.

Words began to flash in his mind. Unwelcome words.

Two weeks and no strings. *No strings...no strings...*

A dull throb started in his temples. He shook his head again. Oh, yeah, he was definitely coming down with something.

No, I wouldn't risk everything for love....

The dull throb intensified.

"What difference does it make?" he growled to the empty room, "I wouldn't risk everything, either."

Chapter Seven

Glory Bea's Café was located ten-point-eight miles due east from Nettie's house. Not too far, but Nettie was a sweaty, shaky, dizzy mess before they'd gone halfway.

For some reason, Chase had turned silent and glowering—at least that's how it looked from the passenger seat.

Clutching her purse with one hand, the door handle with the other so she'd have something solid to hang onto, Nettie tried to relax by focusing on the road ahead. Unfortunately, it seemed to be spinning.

Wondering what *Cosmopolitan* magazine would say about projectile vomiting in her date's Porsche, Nettie gave up on the idea of relaxing and attempted simply to *endure* the drive to Glory Bea's. Shutting her eyes against the traitorously undulating highway, she tried to recapture that ain't-life-grand delight she'd experienced while flirting with Chase on her front porch.

No dice.

In the time it had taken her to run upstairs and change clothes, Chase had changed, too—into a different man. The Chase who had welcomed her return with a low whistle was smooth and polished, with the demeanor of a man who dated often. Too often. Nettie felt awkward, uncertain and, well, cheated, as if suddenly she were going to lunch with Chase's plastic soap-opera twin.

Risking vertigo, she opened her left eye and glanced at him. Ray Ban sunglasses hid his eyes, and the remaining three-quarters of his face wasn't giving away any secrets, either. She was seated just a little over a foot away from him and yet she felt as if she were in the car alone.

Alone. She hated feeling alone.

Her nausea increased. She wanted to be breezy, sophisticated. She wanted to laugh and flirt and pretend she didn't have a care in the world.

Chase hit a pothole. Nettie slammed her one open eye shut. Oh, lordy! What if she became really and truly ill, right here, right now? What if she had the panic attack to top all panic attacks and couldn't hide it from Chase? That would be entirely too much reality to interject into a relationship that had a shelf life of two weeks, tops. A relationship like theirs was meant to be fun, casual and distinctly un-serious. She squeezed the door handle harder.

"Are you all right?"

The question pierced her fog of distress. Wanting desperately to appear calm and poised, Nettie turned toward him and forced a wide smile. "Just fine." Unfortunately, she forgot to open her eyes, which somewhat marred the effect she was after.

Gradually, she became aware of the car slowing as Chase pulled to the shoulder of the road and shifted to Park. She felt him turn in the bucket seat.

"Are your eyes closed for a reason?"

"Yes. I'm resting."

"Ah. Would you mind not resting for a moment?"

"No." She shook her head. "I don't mind." Gingerly, she let her lids flutter open, testing for spinning scenery. Thankfully, the world beyond the automobile appeared to be fairly stable for the moment, so she turned to look at Chase. He'd pushed his sunglasses on top of his head and was studying her with one of the expressions she had come to know and appreciate: intent, curious and sincere. It was a sexier look than any hey-baby grin he could have manufactured.

"What's wrong, Nettie?"

"Wrong?" *Remember, think fun. Think casual. Think "fling."*

"Nothing's wrong." She attempted a laugh that unfortunately made her sound like a demented canary.

The mouth that had so fascinated her the night before lifted slightly. He nodded toward the passenger-side door. "Can you let go of that handle?"

Nettie looked down, surprised to see that she was still squeezing the door handle to within an inch of its life. When she tried to let go, her frozen fingers refused to unfurl.

"They're stuck," she murmured.

"Mmm. So it seems." Gently, Chase reached for her other hand, the one grasping her purse, and eased first one finger, then another from around the leather straps. Transferring the purse from Nettie's lap to the floorboards, he palmed her hand with both of his, massaging slowly. "What's going on?"

Oh, dear. She glanced away, searching empty space for a reasonable answer.

With a crooked finger, Chase nudged her chin, insisting that she look at him again. He leaned across the center console, his gaze dark and penetrating. "I've been told I'm a pretty exciting guy. But I can't recall making a woman hyperventilate in the first ten minutes of a date before. Tell me what's happening here."

When her shoulders stiffened around her ears, Nettie tried consciously—and futilely—to relax. *Oh, what's the use,* she conceded silently. *Tell him.* Bluffing wasn't working, and if she became any more tense from the effort it would start to look as if rigor mortis had set in.

Frustration and resistance mingled with surrender. She had wanted the next two weeks to be her Camelot, with Chase starring as Sir Lancelot, the one passionate, wild indiscretion in her otherwise painfully cautious existence. But there were no panic attacks in Camelot, no pasts to overcome or wounds to heal. That didn't happen until after the wild indiscretion.

Defeated, Nettie sighed. This would be, she was sure, her only date with Chase. He had signed up for a two-week fling, not a double dose of reality.

Even if *he* wanted to try again, she wasn't sure *she* could live through it.

"I'm having an anxiety attack," she confessed as her gaze drifted away from his. "I get them from time to time."

A little understatement. When she'd first started having the attacks after Brian and Tucker died, "from time to time" had sometimes meant around the clock. She couldn't count the nights she'd awakened with the dreaded symptoms already in full swing, her heart pounding, her body sweating and her mind so convinced something awful was about to happen that she had wanted to run screaming from the house.

She felt Chase studying her before he responded. "It embarrasses you?"

Her gaze snapped back to his. "Yes, it embarrasses me. Of course it does." Letting go of the door handle, she gestured expansively. "I'm in an air-conditioned Porsche having a hot flash. And I'm only twenty-five."

"What do you usually do when you have an anxiety attack?"

"Usually?" Her lips quirked. "I panic more." Chase smiled and brushed her cheek with his finger. The touch felt infinitely soothing. "Lately I've been listening to self-help tapes."

"And what do they suggest?"

Nettie rolled her eyes. "You don't want to talk about this."

Chase raised a brow. "How do you know? Maybe *I* need the help. I'm a little anxious myself."

"You are." Nettie scoffed. "You don't strike me as someone who panics over nothing."

"Nothing?" His knuckle ran lightly down her cheek, following the curve to her full lower lip. "Why wouldn't I be anxious? I'm on a date with a beautiful woman." He spoke softly, hypnotically. "My mind is racing. Does she like me? Will I say something I shouldn't? What if I move too fast?" He smiled. "Or not fast enough? What if I don't want this date to end, and she can't wait to go home?"

He shook his head slightly, his voice dropping to a murmur. "It's like being sixteen again."

Mesmerized by this man who had spoken her thoughts, Nettie nodded. "Yes."

His thumb grazed her lower lip. "What would your program suggest in a nerve-wracking moment like this?"

She swallowed as the pad of his thumb circled around to her upper lip, tracing its shape. There were no other moments like this. "It suggests accepting the feelings, the, uh, body sensations and then, um… What are you doing?" Her lips were moving beneath his fingers. It was the most incredibly sensual sensation.

"You have a beautiful mouth," he said. "Like an angel's. After you accept the feelings what does your program tell you to do?"

Bemused by his effortless hop from personal to prosaic, Nettie smiled. *And they say men can't multitask.* "Then you float."

"Hmm. Float?" He arched a brow. Leaving her lips, his fingers trailed lightly down the side of her neck.

"Float." Nettie tried to concentrate. "Distract yourself, get involved in something else." When his knuckles dipped into the curve of her collarbone, she thought she might do something embarrassing, like moan in broad daylight. Before lunch, even.

"Then?"

"Then you, um, let time pass." How curious. Until now she'd had no idea her collarbone was an erogenous zone.

"Let time pass," Chase repeated, adding, "Surrender."

Nettie's eyelids drifted all the way closed. "Surrender?"

"Be willing to lose control." He drew closer, and she wondered how he did that with his fingers—touched so lightly, yet left a trail of sensation that said, *I was here.* "Are you willing to lose control, Nettie?"

With her eyes still closed, she felt him brush so close that his mouth almost, but not quite, met hers. She smelled his skin, warm and clean and spicy, as he passed by her neck to rest his ear against the uppermost part of her chest. Nettie's heart pounded against her breastbone. She shivered.

"Strong," he said, staying where he was for another moment. "Your heartbeat is quick and strong." Lifting his head, he followed the same path up her neck, past her chin to her lips. This time he stayed right there, a hair's breadth away, as he reached for her right hand to place it over his heart. "Mine is the same. Quick, strong—because of you. There's nothing wrong with that, Nettie. Is there?"

Lord, no. Willing herself to open her eyes, she looked directly into his. He was going to kiss her, and, no, there didn't seem to be a thing wrong with that.

* * *

Chase closed the passenger-side door to his Porsche and watched Nettie skip lightly up the porch steps to her front door.

"Thanks for lunch. I've never—" She turned as she spoke, laughing when she saw him still standing by the car. "What are you doing down there?"

"Admiring the view."

Her gaze flicked over his head to the green fields beyond her property. "You're facing the wrong way."

Slowly, he shook his head, his mouth curving into a grin. "Nope." Pushing away from the car, he made quick work of the porch steps and stood in front of her, looking down.

He simply didn't tire of looking at her, he thought, not even when he tried.

After he'd kissed her in the car, he'd asked her if she felt distracted enough to forget about the anxiety. "What anxiety?" she'd murmured on a sigh so breathy and sexy he'd kissed her again. In a cherry-red, scoop-necked T-shirt and blue jeans, she was sexier, more feminine and classier than any woman with whom he'd ever been involved.

Smiling at him smiling at her, Nettie said, "I was going to say thank-you for lunch. I've never eaten french fries dunked in a chocolate shake before."

"No?" Seeing that she had her house keys in her hand and aware that in her effort to keep their relationship under wraps she might not want him to linger, Chase placed a palm on the screen door high above Nettie's head. Classic male-takes-control pose. He hadn't tried it since high school; he hadn't needed to since high school. "So, what's your verdict?"

Nettie glanced at his hand, back at his face, appeared to know exactly what he was doing and didn't seem to mind. "Not bad. A little messy, but somehow they tasted…right…like that."

"I told you. Once you try them that way, you never go back." He'd fed them to her himself. Picking out the longest, skinniest fries on his plate, he'd dipped them leisurely into the frosty drink, held them up and dared her to taste. He had absolutely loved watching the ice cream drip onto her chin, watching her giggle and lick it off and then watching her eyes widen with surprise when she realized he hadn't been kidding, that the odd combo really did taste good. Most of all, though, he had loved the way her crystal-blue gaze had held his while he'd dropped the fries into her mouth.

Chase shifted on the porch. She engendered the damnedest combination of affection and lust he'd ever felt.

"I had a great time, too," he said quietly. His free hand went to his hip as an idea came to mind and he considered whether to pursue it. Before he progressed to a conscious decision, the words poured out. "Listen, Nick offered to let me use a little cabin or, I don't know, a hut or something on his property while I'm here."

Nettie giggled. "It's not a 'hut.' It's the Enchanted Cottage."

"Come again?"

"Haven't you seen that movie?" Still sheltered by his raised arm, she leaned against the screen door and chatted as if she didn't have a care in the world or a single thought of shooing him away before they were seen. "*The Enchanted Cottage* is a lovely romance. Lilah and I must have watched it twenty times when we were teenagers. There's a little house on Nick's place that's only been used off and on for years, so we'd sneak in and camp out there sometimes with our girlfriends. We'd tell ourselves we were in the enchanted cottage from the movie."

She looked impish and winsome as she spoke. Chase felt her carving a permanent smile on his memory. "You'd sneak in, huh? Breaking and entering."

"Don't tell Sara."

He raised his free hand in a Boy Scout salute. "Your shady past is safe with me. For now. So what would you do there?"

"Ooh, fun things. Talk about boys and eat graham crackers with canned frosting."

Chase laughed. "Pretty wild." He lowered his head toward hers. "Let's get down to the nitty gritty. Did you ever take a boy there?"

Nettie squinted an eye as if she couldn't quite remember and was trying to see back into the past. "I think Lilah may have. Trespassing with girlfriends was about as daring as I was willing to get. At the time."

"I can't give you the thrill of trespassing, but I could use your input."

"About?"

"Nick offered me the use of your cottage, because he thought

I might want a little privacy while I'm here. I think he might want me out of his hair, too.''

A dimple appeared in Nettie's cheek. ''The farmhouse is too small for two big strapping individualists like you?''

Actually, what Nick had said was, *If the boy turns out to be yours, and you want to get to know him without anyone else in the way, I've got a little place…*

Chase shook his head. He still wasn't ready to talk about this. Several times during lunch, he'd tried to direct the conversation to a more personal level. Each time, she'd turned the tables on him, deflecting his questions. He'd discovered that she wrote and illustrated kids' storybooks for a living and that her favorite Christmas gift had been a set of forty colored pencils when she was eight, but that was it. She hadn't allowed the conversation to get any more personal, except to make it clear that she was a career girl.

A career girl who accepted the fact that he was a career man. The rules had already been set. A few weeks. No strings.

''I thought a little privacy might not be a half-bad idea,'' he said and then scowled. That had sounded better in his head than it did out loud. Aloud it sounded like he was making a play for her. Like he'd been thinking about it, planning for it. *Which,* he reminded himself, *you are.*

''What I meant was—''

''I think privacy is a good idea.''

Chase sucked in a breath. At another time, with another woman, he would have anticipated that response. He'd feel pleased. He'd begin to envision the rendezvous, but in a relaxed, even lazy way. He might not think about it again at all until the moment was at hand, except perhaps to pick up a bottle of champagne.

So why, now, was his heart hammering and his brow starting to perspire?

When he realized he was starting to sweat all over, Chase dropped his hand and shook his head. This was the damnedest thing.

''What?'' Nettie asked, tilting her head.

''What…what?'' *Ah, you are an articulate son-of-a-gun,* Chase applauded himself. *You've been a journalist for how long?*

"You were shaking your head," Nettie answered him.

"Right." He wiped his palm on his jeans as discreetly as he could, then swiped the perspiration from his upper lip.

Where was his will? He was a fighter by nature. He possessed a strong mind. If he wanted to be casual, then, dammit, he ought to be able to *make* himself be casual.

"I know you've got a work schedule," he began.

She nodded. "But I'm due for a vacation."

Chase swallowed. That's it. He was a goner. "I'm picking you up tomorrow at nine. Nick's driving into Minot. He'll be gone until early afternoon. I make great French toast, so be hungry."

Nettie groaned. "You dare say that while I'm still digesting a Giant Dakota Burger, fries and a chocolate shake? After those calories, we women tend to stick to salad and grapefruit for the next couple of meals."

The confusion and ambivalence Chase had been feeling dried up in a flash. He bent over her. "Not *my* woman."

With a quick, hard kiss, he was back at his car, leaving Nettie open-mouthed, dewy-eyed and slightly off-balance as she stared after him.

"Nine o'clock." He winked. "I hope you like lots of syrup."

Chapter Eight

Nettie awoke at quarter past six the next morning. She had also awakened at three-thirty, four-ten and five-eighteen.

Plunging her feet into the soft, cushioned slippers at her bedside, she moved by feel to the chintz-covered chair where she'd tossed her robe the night before. There was something private and, yes, romantic about the early-morning darkness—lavender sky, pale hint of a moon and birds beginning to arise and sing. She didn't want to lose the mood by turning on a light.

Slipping the robe around her, she tiptoed to the bathroom, trying not to waken Sara, then made her way downstairs to the kitchen. Might as well start the caffeine drip. Not that I'm the least bit tired, she thought. Nope. Not at all. She let her fingers dance lightly along the banister.

Singing a little something from the Dixie Chicks as she scooped Otto's finest French Roast—five twenty-nine a pound; buy one, get one free—into a paper filter, she wondered what Chase was doing right now.

"Probably sleeping." She grinned, knowing she hadn't been this anxious to start a day in longer than she could remember.

Dropping the coffee scoop into the can, Nettie snapped the

filter unit into place and hit the start button on the coffee machine. Searching a cupboard for corn flakes, since breakfast with Chase was still a good three hours away, she marveled at her own appetite. Excitement did that to her, she guessed—woke up all her senses, taste included. She'd felt like this last night, too. Craving music, she'd turned on the radio and blared country and rock. She'd gone back to work and painted with bold strokes and splashes of the most brilliant colors she'd ever used. Later in the evening she'd lit an aromatherapy candle, climbed into a foamy tub and shaved her legs for today, slathering them with moisturizer and then putting on the softest cotton leggings she owned. The feeling of whisper-soft material on smooth skin had been sensuous. And everything she did, every single thing all night long had made her think of Chase.

Grabbing a handful of corn flakes straight from the box, she searched the fridge for bacon.

The coffee had brewed fragrantly and the fry pan was sizzling when Sara ambled into the kitchen around seven.

"Oh, good, you're up!" Nettie sang cheerfully, adding several hot, crisp slices of bacon to the mound already draining on a paper towel. "Now we can up the music." She danced over to a portable radio tucked into a built-in shelf and raised the volume on Billy Ocean. Then she danced her way back to the stove.

Barefoot and squinting from an apparent lack of rest, Sara stomped to the radio and turned it down. "I'm gonna to puke if I have to listen to that this early in the morning."

Shrugging, Nettie hummed "Get Outta My Dreams and into My Car" as she fried bacon.

Sara dragged a mug down from a shelf and slammed the cupboard door. "What's the matter with you? You're acting like Martha Stewart on speed."

Nettie laughed. "I'm happy. It's a beautiful morning. Have you looked outside yet?" Sara grunted, poured herself some coffee and trudged to the table. "Well, it's going to be a glorious day. I hope you're hungry."

"Not really."

Nettie stopped what she was doing and turned toward her sister. "Sara, are you sick?"

"No." The three heaping teaspoons of sugar she dumped into

her coffee more or less proved the point. Slumping over the mug, she stirred.

Nettie brought the first plate of bacon to the table. "Here then. Help me out. I can't possibly eat all this myself. I'm having breakfast at nine."

Sara's head whipped up. "Why are you cooking now if you're having breakfast— Who are you having breakfast with?"

Disapproval edged Sara's tone. Nettie turned to pull juice from the fridge, biting her tongue before she let her own irritation show. Like Nettie, Sara was most comfortable when she had a set of immutable rules to follow. Losing their parents so suddenly had made life seem unpredictable and chaotic for the Owens sisters. Lilah had coped by embracing chaos and unpredictability as a way of life. Sara had divided the world into good and bad and literally tried to jail anything that upset her. Nettie had become very, very, very, very, very, very good in the hope that bad things did not happen to *very* good people.

She shook her head, musing. *Maybe we should all be more like Lilah.* Never one to linger over relationships or sorrows, Lilah had once insisted that life was like toothpaste and everyone had a choice: You could give the tube a squish, here a little, there a little, or start at one end and squeeze out every last drop. Either way, the tube was going to get tossed.

Maybe that was the right idea. Enjoy life and, as much as anyone can, keep it simple. Sara, however, would never agree. She considered Lilah wild and unforgivably irresponsible.

"What is happening at nine?" Sara demanded, again with a tone that foreshadowed the litany of cautions to come.

It's my life, Nettie reminded herself and then answered, "I'm having breakfast with a friend." As Sara's lips formed the word *who,* Nettie stated, "I'm not discussing this. My social calendar is not open for examination. Or debate," she added when Sara geared up for exactly that. "Now," Nettie said, tempering her own urge to argue, "do you care for juice?" She raised the carton.

"No, I do not care for juice!" Grabbing her coffee cup and a handful of bacon, Sara marched to the door, but couldn't resist turning around to add, "You know what kind of trouble you could get into? No man who sneaks around is interested in a woman's good name."

Nettie laughed out loud. "I certainly hope not."

Sara stared at her sister in growing dismay, but she said nothing else before pushing through the door and heading back to her bedroom.

Nettie stared at the wood panel, listening to the stomp of Sara's footsteps and determinedly resisting the urge to make peace at whatever cost.

She busied herself awhile, cleaning up and trying not to think, but her mood was less buoyant than before and she had a hard time ignoring the guilt that stabbed at her. All Sara wanted was order in the court.

By eight-thirty, Nettie was more concerned for herself than she was for her sister. Sara wasn't talking, she wasn't eating and she sure wasn't leaving. The door to her bedroom was still closed. She hadn't emerged to shower yet, and Chase was due to arrive in half an hour.

Dressed and ready to go herself, Nettie stared at Sara's door and made a decision: She would head over to the farm on her own, right now, before Chase left.

Running downstairs to use the phone in the kitchen, Nettie remembered how easily Chase had handled her panic yesterday in the car. He'd simply accepted her as she was and effectively distracted her very, very effectively.

Today she would have to distract herself. A twinge of nerves made her legs feel jittery and weak.

Surrender. The word drifted through her mind in a man's voice and with it came a warm, buttery feeling of relief. Surrender. If she chose, she could surrender to the feelings in her body, to the excitement and the nervousness and to the risk inherent in being alive.

With a long, deep breath, Nettie reached for the phone to tell Chase she'd see him in a few minutes. Punching in the number, she felt a genuine smile spread across her face. *This girl's going to squeeze some toothpaste.*

"Where did you learn to cook?" Nettie asked as she and Chase trekked over to the cottage after breakfast.

Wearing a white V-neck T-shirt, denim pedal pushers and lace-up espadrilles, she walked along the grass that bordered

Nick's barley fields. Chase strolled by her side. Breakfast had been wonderful. Thick-sliced French toast dripping with warm maple syrup, sausages that tasted of apple and sage and perfect coffee. Chase had seated her at the kitchen table with a mimosa and hadn't let her lift a finger. She sneaked a glance in his direction. Obviously he hadn't spent all his time chasing stories along the Sudan.

Hoping she sounded casual even as she admitted to herself that she was dying to know, she nudged again, "Fess up. Who taught you to cook? Mother, sister or girlfriend?"

"Who said I could cook? You just tasted a full half of my repertoire."

He'd neatly skirted the answer, but Nettie had no idea how to probe further without being obvious, so she asked instead, "What's the other half?"

"Chocolate chip cookies."

"From scratch?"

"My own recipe."

"Are they really good?"

He twirled a long twig from the fields between his teeth. "People have killed for less."

"You don't say. I make a pretty mean cookie myself. What's your secret?"

A dark brow arched as he glanced her way. "If I told you, it wouldn't be a secret."

Nettie laughed. The day was sunny; the conversation was sunny. If hearts could grin, she figured hers was.

"Come on," she wheedled happily. "I won't blab to *People* magazine, if that's what you're worried about. In fact, if anyone ever asks me what one of the Fifty Most Beautiful Bachelors likes to do in his spare time, I give you my word never to mention how natural you looked in your sweet little apron, holding a fry pan."

Clamping his teeth around the twig, Chase scowled. "I wasn't wearing an apron."

"Makes a better story, though, doesn't it?" Laughing, she skipped ahead of him, then turned to walk backwards a few paces while he stood still, glowering. Until now, Nettie had had no idea that teasing someone could be this much fun. "Ah, I know what's bothering you," she sang out. "You're afraid *Peo-*

ple's female audience will find out that you're beautiful *and* you bake chocolate chip cookies and you'll be hounded by single women. Hungry single women. You know, I think you're actually very shy."

Disposing of the twig, Chase gave her a wide, unarguably sexy grin. "Why, Nettie," he said, his voice a silky smooth purr, "I had no idea you think I'm beautiful."

This time Nettie stopped walking as he strolled on. "I didn't say that," she claimed while he strutted like a peacock with its tail feathers spread.

Chase wriggled the twig with his tongue. "Did too."

"I was referring to the article."

He shook his head. "I don't think so."

Catching up with him, Nettie fell into step without glancing his way. "Well, think again." Under her breath, but loudly enough for him to hear, she muttered, "Egomaniac."

Chase didn't even blink. He simply stretched a leg in front of hers, deliberately tripping her. As she shrieked and started to fall, he pivoted neatly, placing himself in front of her and grasping both her arms. Then in one smooth move, he dropped onto his back, bringing her harmlessly down on top of him.

The sheer surprise left Nettie panting. Chase's hands were warm and firm around her upper arms. "Admit it," he commanded in a low sexy growl. Before she had time to catch her breath, he rolled them over, placing his palms on the ground and hovering over her. "Admit you want me badly."

Bracketed by his arms, Nettie shook her head. He was teasing, but the energy that sizzled between them was no joke. "I admit I want your cookie recipe," she breathed, refusing to give in. Playing the game.

Chase grinned appreciatively. He lowered his head. "Ve haf vays of making you speak." Closer and closer he moved until he was nuzzling her cheek with his nose and lips.

A strong shiver raced through her body, followed by a dozen tiny, delicious shivers. She tried to mask the intensity of her reaction, but when his tongue came out to tickle the corner of her mouth, Nettie thought she would go berserk if she had to stay silent and still.

"You taste like maple syrup," Chase whispered.

Someone moaned. *Probably me,* Nettie thought, then couldn't have formed a coherent sentence to save her sanity as he used his lips to nibble the spot he'd just licked.

Chase was in control. He was sure of it. Until her fingers delved mindlessly into his hair. Until she arched beneath him with total abandon. Until she moaned.

She was part siren, part playmate. What started out as a game to urge her to say she wanted him had turned into a trap he'd set for himself. He wanted her. Now.

Nettie raised her right knee and his thigh slid between hers. There was no way she could mistake his desire, yet she gave no hint of wanting to pull back.

This is no place to make love, Chase thought even as his mouth covered hers completely. Her lips parted, and he sank into the kiss like a drowning man. On the other hand, it might be the perfect place. Earth below, sunup above. There was another groan, this time issuing from him.

Chase's hand caressed and explored as it roamed from her breast to her waist. Nettie strained against him. He curved a palm around her hip. She began to wriggle, which just about drove him crazy. If she kept moving like that, he'd have them both out of their clothes before their hearts took the next beat.

He clamped a hand on her hip. She strained against him and her hands left his hair, moving to his shoulders, first pulling then pushing until she reached for the hand holding her hip and tried to throw it off.

With a Herculean effort, Chase broke the kiss and raised his head. "Sweetheart," he groaned, his voice hoarse. "I want to give us what we both want, believe me, but I—"

"Off," she gasped.

Chase frowned. *Off?*

"Get. Off." This time she pushed the words through gritted teeth. There was no mistaking her intention as she brought the heels of her hands to his shoulders and shoved as hard as she could. *"Now!"*

Chase leaped up. Nettie followed. Before Chase's ever-widening eyes, she grabbed her T-shirt and all but ripped it from the waistband of her pants.

"Fire ants!" she cried.

"What?"

"Fire ants." Wriggling like a trapped lizard, Nettie indicated, "In my shirt."

She began a mad dance, hopping up and down and flapping the hem of the shirt as she tried desperately to rid herself of the biting insects.

Chase watched with a kind of fascination and some notion that he ought to help, but damned if he knew how. He was a guy. A guy would just—

"Take off your shirt," he shouted above her yelps. She didn't hear him. Chase strode over and grasped her wrists. When he had her attention, he directed again, "Take your shirt off."

If he was afraid she wouldn't comply, he was in for a surprise. Nettie flung the shirt over her head and onto the ground faster than lightening. Unmindful, at least initially, of the fact that she stood in her bra, she rubbed her skin with her hands, reaching around to her upper back.

"Are they all gone?" she asked, twisting and turning.

Chase was not unmindful of the fact that she stood in her bra. Not for a second. He clasped her shoulders, turned her around and held her steady while he brushed the last little clingers off her skin. Perfect silken skin. His touch should have been purely clinical under the circumstances, but to claim that it was would have been pure fiction.

The back she presented to him was a work of art, the shoulders broad for a woman, but the bone structure refined and graceful. Her ribcage tapered to a waist he wanted to span with his hands. Gently, almost tentatively, he splayed his fingers across her back. Like a kid, he thought. Like a kid who's breaking the rule "look, but don't touch."

"Are they gone?" Nettie repeated the question over her shoulder.

Attempting language, Chase managed only a grunt at first. He cleared his throat. "Yes." His hand, he noticed, stayed right where it was.

Slowly, Nettie faced him. His palm skimmed her waist as she turned, and goose bumps rose on her flesh. He felt them. So did she.

Every sense Chase possessed sang at this new sight of her. She wore a gossamer bra of pale blue lace and satin that cupped her round breasts, emphasizing their fullness. He made no attempt to mask the direction of his gaze, deliberately touching her with it, feeling unabashed pleasure when she visibly responded, her nipples growing and tightening beneath his eyes. She was all gentle female flesh, shapely but lush, no evidence of a personal trainer who'd carved curves into angles. Most of the women he knew were aggressively lean. Nettie's definitely female body was, Chase realized, the perfect expression of her personality.

Two-weeks-and-no-strings could go to Hades. It wasn't going to work. *It wasn't,* and he wanted to hear her admit it more than he wanted to deny the truth to himself.

Conveniently disregarding the fact that his hand was still on her waist, Chase swore to himself that he wouldn't touch her again until they'd had a chance to talk. Because…

…he watched her eyes darken to an impossible shade of blue as she raised her hands to his chest.…

…because they needed to talk before…before…

His thoughts scattered as he noted the quickening of her breath. Unerringly, her fingers found the third button of his shirt and unfastened it.

Okay. All right. He needed to stop her because they had to talk. The rules of the game had changed and she needed to know that before she went one step further.

She undid the next button.

Nettie. Her name made it into his mind, but not out of his mouth.

As the buttons popped free, she explored his chest with interest and tenderness, the likes of which he'd never before experienced. When she brushed his nipple with her fingertips— whether intentionally or inadvertently he couldn't quite tell— Chase actually growled.

The effort to maintain control under the circumstances was inhumane. And, anyway, he didn't want to. New plan: Touch now; talk later.

Good plan.

The instant Chase cupped her breast with his palm, a host of new feelings and thoughts rushed through him, including a sense of triumph. *Mine. This woman is mine.* The whole two-week thing was a stupid safety net. In the midst of a flight this high, a safety net was only extra baggage.

Nettie's eyes closed, and she swayed toward him, palms pressed flat against his chest. Chase slid his hands around her back, pulling her close. Abandoning any notion of holding back, he kissed her so there would be no mistake: He was asking to have her, body and soul.

Like whispers of smoke, Nettie's arms wound around his neck. She raised onto her toes, straining closer, returning his kiss with a gusto and sweetness that made him ache.

Just as Chase decided it was time to get off this field and into a house, the relative privacy they had was shattered by the sound of hooves pounding the earth as a horse and rider bore down on them.

Thankfully this time they heard Nick before they saw him, which gave Chase time to yank off his own shirt and toss it around Nettie. Acting almost reflexively, she managed to shove her arms through the sleeves, but was still fumbling with the buttons when Nick reined in.

The three of them stood awkwardly, Chase naked now from the waist up and Nettie clothed in his shirt.

Chase eyed the buttons she'd stuck in the wrong holes and felt a rush of pure affection. *Mine,* he thought again and this time a smile of happiness started in his chest and rose to his lips. It died when he looked at Nick's sober face.

"What?" Chase glared, communicating via expression that he would welcome another big-daddy lecture about as much as he welcomed a case of head lice. He reached for Nettie's elbow in a show of protectiveness and support that was altogether deliberate.

Nick, who had mastered the art of the inscrutable expression, merely nodded a greeting. "Sorry to interrupt. I saw Nettie's car when I got home and thought you might have headed this way."

Nettie said nothing, but Chase noted the tiny frown between her brows and the distracted look in her eyes. He couldn't tell if she was beginning to regret what had taken place, if she was embarrassed, or if it was simply the interruption that bothered her. In any case, he wanted to get rid of Nick and talk to her alone ASAP.

He turned his attention back to Nick, but before he could speak, Nick held out a large flat envelope. "I picked this up while I was in town. Thought you should have it right away."

Chase easily identified the envelope. Express Mail. Without dismounting or riding closer, Nick forced Chase to step away from Nettie in order to accept the envelope, a symbolic move if ever Chase had seen one. Nick, too, understood what was in the envelope.

Intending to snap the flat package out of Nick's grasp, Chase was startled to witness his own hand shake. Inside that thick envelope was the answer to the question *Am I a father?* His lawyer had offered to intercept the results of the DNA tests and then phone, which now seemed like an excellent idea. Unfortunately Chase, being Chase, had wanted full control. He'd insisted the results be mailed directly.

Cursing his shaking hand, he looked at Nettie, who was paying more attention now. His trembling increased.

He grabbed the envelope with a tersely muttered, ''Thanks.'' Feeling like a jackass, standing there with his shirt off, holding an Express Mail envelope he had no intention of opening while Nick leaned on the pommel of his saddle and Nettie stared at him, waiting.

As far as Chase could see, there were no really good options available. He did not want to open that envelope in front of Nettie. With his forehead and palms starting to sweat, he turned to her. ''Maybe we'd...''

He paused as she tilted her head in question. Wearing his shirt, her kissed lips full and red as summer cherries, she looked at him with absolute trust and interest in whatever he had to tell her.

Chase felt sick to his stomach.

All along he'd known what he wanted to find in that envelope: Proof that someone else had fathered Julia's child.

''We'd better get back to the house,'' he said, his voice a pathetic croak.

Nettie simply looked at him, beautiful and surprised and confused.

Accurately estimating Chase's predicament and the discomfort both his friends were feeling, Nick dismounted. ''King's been nursing a fetlock.'' He gave the big horse a solid pat. ''Think I'll give him a break. Mind if I walk along with you?'' He addressed Nettie, whose questioning eyes fastened on Chase. Cursing himself, wanting to kick his sorry butt for the first conscious act of cowardice he could remember, Chase shrugged and immediately looked away.

With Nettie by his side, Nick headed toward the farmhouse. Carrying the envelope and a million colliding thoughts, Chase brought up the rear by himself.

Chapter Nine

"So what kind of kiss was it?"

Nettie dug a paint scraper into the side of the house with both hands while she clamped a cordless phone between her shoulder and chin. Phoning her sister Lilah for a little commiseration and some solid dating advice had seemed like a good idea twenty minutes ago. Did people actually describe kisses out loud? Help. Dating was going to be the end of her.

Evidently hesitant, she asked, "What do you mean, 'what kind'?"

Lilah shifted the receiver of her own phone as she slapped a bottle of nail polish several times against her palm. "Soft?" she prompted. "Wet, dry? Long or short? I need details."

A yellow paint chip went flying. "Lilah, I don't know! I wasn't taking notes."

"You don't want to kiss and tell, you mean." Nettie heard the grin in the other woman's voice. "I still can't believe my little sister got up close and personal with a bona fide celebrity."

"I'm not your little sister. I'm a grown woman."

"You'll always be my little sister, silly," Lilah agreed easily.

"Besides, when it comes to flirtation, darling, you really are a youngster. If I'm Methuselah, you're practically neonatal."

"Thanks a lot."

"We have to embrace our strengths. So, let me get this straight," she said. "You kiss like there's no tomorrow, then Nick rides up with the mystery mail. End of date?"

"End of date, end of story unless you help me. When we got back to the farmhouse, Chase was so ruffled he couldn't get away fast enough."

Lilah hmmed on the other end of the line. "How did he excuse himself?"

"He said he had business to take care of."

"Maybe he's a workaholic. Although the pictures I've seen of him suggest he plays as hard as he works."

Already Nettie was experiencing that swallowed-a-cannon-ball sensation in the pit of her stomach. "What kind of pictures?"

"He was splashed all over the pages of *Premiere* magazine during the Cannes Film Festival last year. Charlize Theron couldn't keep her hands off him."

"Charlize Theron. The actress who looks like a twenty-year-old blond Elizabeth Taylor?"

"Only better. Yep."

Nettie glanced down. She'd changed into jeans, a thin red sweater that was starting to pill and red Keds. The epitome of Kalamoose haute couture. "Was Charlize wearing deck shoes?"

"Beg your pardon?"

"Nothing. Cannes is in France, right?"

"Yes." Lilah sounded wistful. "On the beach. Wall-to-wall superstars. Parties all night long. Fabulous entertainment. Heaven." In the backround a refrigerator door opened and closed. "How long can you keep egg salad?"

"A few days, max."

"Rats."

Nettie rested her forehead on a paint-scraped shingle. "Do you have to cross bodies of water by air or ship to get to Cannes?" she muttered sickly.

"Of course." Lilah laughed, then sobered. "Oh, Net, are you worried about having to travel with him? Are those anxiety tapes helping at all? They say they can help you overcome any phobia, even flying.''

"I'm not worried about having to travel with him," Nettie sighed. "Our relationship isn't going to last that long."

"Yes, it will. Any man would be crazy not to hang on to you."

"Your sisterly devotion is duly noted, but I mean we've already agreed on a two-week fling. And before you rake him over the verbal coals," Nettie said as Lilah inhaled loudly, preparing to do exactly that, "I'm not interested in anything permanent. Or even remotely stable." There was silence and then another inhalation, which Nettie again cut off at the pass. "I mean it. I know what I want."

"Okay. What?"

This time Nettie paused, but briefly. "More. More of the feeling I get when he kisses me."

"That good?"

"Yes." Relief wooshed through her, relief and glorious freedom. Oh, it felt wonderful to say it out loud. "I want this for myself, Lilah. For two weeks I want to live without a past or a future. I want to forget everything but how good I feel when I'm with him. You know what I mean?"

"Yeah," Lilah responded quietly. "Yes, I do. Is that what he wants, too?"

"I think so." With a fingernail, Nettie picked at the chipping paint.

"Or, I thought so. He turned off so quickly today, now I'm not sure. Maybe I'm a terrible kisser." The prospect was so depressing, she lowered her head and groaned.

"Don't be silly," Lilah rebuked. "You are not."

"How do you know? Have you ever met anyone my age with less experience, sexually speaking?"

"That's part of your charm."

"Part of the novelty, you mean. Novelty wears off. Suppose I kiss like a fish?"

"Will you stop it! And if Chase Reynolds is interested in you because you're a novelty to him, then he can go to—"

"He's a novelty to me, too, Lilah," Nettie interrupted with rigorous honesty.

"If you think you're in this for sex and nothing else, you're lying to yourself, Net. I know you better than that."

"Not this time. I told you."

"Yeah, 'Seize the day,' *Carpe Diem.* I understand the principle. I live in Hollywood. We seize the second out here. But that's not who you are. And I don't care what you say," she insisted when Nettie tried to rebut. "Your heart is in everything you do. I don't want you to get hurt."

Concern traversed the miles. Nettie walked the tightrope between gratitude and frustration. "Think about who you are talking to for a minute. 'Try not to get hurt' is my mantra. I feel like a turtle with its head hermetically sealed in the shell." The strength and confidence of a decision firmly made infused her body. She stood straight, spoke straight. "I'm going to do this, Lilah, so don't go all 'Sara' on me. I need advice! What would you do if you were in the middle of a great date with your fantasy man and he suddenly decided he had some pressing e-mail he had to take care of?"

"I'd put on my highest heels, my shortest dress and a lot of very red lipstick. Then I'd find him and make him forget he even had a computer."

"Wow." Nettie took a moment to admire the spirit of her sister's approach. "But my highest shoes are a pair of Dr. Scholls and my shortest dress ends an inch above my knees."

"That's bad. In your case, I'd try to find out what was in that envelope or at least where it came from. See if that's what dimmed the man's lights. Then I'd do some serious shopping. I mean, really—Dr. Scholls?"

If she'd had a pen, Nettie would have taken notes. "How can I investigate the envelope? The postal service gets so prickly about dispensing that kind of information."

"Pry it out of Nick. He must know or he wouldn't have made a special trip to give it to Chase."

"Right!" Nettie frowned. "How do I do that?"

"Are you kidding?" Lilah sounded more like Lilah now— blithe, carefree. "You can wrap Nick around your little finger if you give it half a shot. There's always a way to get what you want, baby doll, remember that. Sara drives him nuts and he thinks I'm decadent, but he's always had loads of respect for you."

Nettie smiled. "Now I'm going to ruin it by asking him to snitch on his friend?"

"You're in the market for a new image."

"True. Thanks." Nettie heard Lilah open and close a cupboard door.

"Can peanut butter go bad?" she asked.

"Does it smell like old axle grease?"

There was the sound of a lid being unscrewed. "Rats!" The peanut butter jar rebounded against the inside of a trash can. "I'm starving. All I've had today was ginger tea and a stale tortilla."

"Lilah, don't you ever have any food in the house that won't cause botulism?"

"I'm an actress. I'm not supposed to have food in my apartment, only Slim Fast. I'm gonna go now. Are you okay?"

"Yes, fine. Thanks for the advice. And for listening."

"No problem, but Net…?"

"Yeah?"

Lilah hesitated. "Don't throw the baby out with the bathwater, right? Who you are is damned fine. I admire you. Everyone admires you."

"Okay. Thanks. I won't. Go eat." Lilah hung up and Nettie let the phone and the paint scraper drop to her side.

Admired. She was admired. A Pyrrhic victory if there was no fun or relaxation or lust in her life. Lust *for* her life.

Checking her watch, Nettie realized it was only a quarter past one. Plenty of time to mix a batch of brownies—Nick's favorite—and a pitcher of frosty lemonade. Then she'd phone him and ask if he could please take a look at the kitchen faucet, which was going to start leaking as soon as she loosened the elbow joint. It was sneaky, it was manipulative—not one bit admirable—and it might work. If she could weasel enough information about Chase from Nick, it was possible that she could make sense of why her fling had begun to flop. Then, if she knew Chase's withdrawal was nothing personal, she could embark on an exhaustive application of all her seductive skills. Which, given what she knew, wouldn't take long.

Acting before she could talk herself out of the vague plan she had only barely talked herself into, Nettie raised the phone, punched the Talk button and phoned Nick.

* * *

"How are the brownies?"

"Just the way I like them." Nettie hovered near the kitchen sink she had deliberately sabotaged so Nick would come over to fix it. He leaned against the counter, a fat fudge brownie in one hand, tall, cold drink in the other.

"And the lemonade?"

He winked his approval. "Icy cold."

"Good." Baring her teeth she offered a facsimile of a smile. Why wouldn't Nick sit down? He was making her nervous, standing there as if his sole intention was to eat his brownie quickly and then go. Nettie felt pressed to acquire her information *now,* before he left. How did investigative reporters stand the pressure?

She'd thought of and discarded a dozen different ways to ask Nick about Chase. She wanted to appear casual, sure of herself. Nick, she sensed, was being deliberately obtuse. He hadn't even mentioned finding her in his field wearing Chase's mis-buttoned shirt. She'd known Nick long enough to know he was thinking a lot more than he was saying.

Draining his glass, Nick set it on the yellow-tiled counter. "Thanks. Let me know if you have any more trouble with that sink. I'm around if you need me."

He started toward the door and Nettie watched her chance to pry walking right out of the kitchen with him.

"Wait! I do need you! I need to, uh…"

Nick turned. Nettie wondered what she could run off and break in the bathroom while he waited here, then quickly snapped herself back to sanity. *Be direct.*

Nick's brow rose. "Something you want?"

"Yes." She stiffened her spine and met Nick's gaze full-on. "What was in that envelope you brought Chase?"

Whoa! Nettie felt as surprised as Nick looked. He recovered fairly quickly to plaster a bland smile on his face. "How would I know?"

"You knew it was important." In for a penny, in for a pound. She waved a hand. "Oh, look, Nick, I know it's none of my business, but I don't care. We were getting along very well before you rode up. Then you handed him that envelope and he couldn't leave fast enough. I want to be sure it was the contents of the envelope and not me that turned him off.''

Nettie took a deep breath. *Whoa with a bullet!* Folding her arms, she dared Nick to deny her the information she sought.

His poker face faltered as he wrestled with and finally reached a decision. Re-entering the kitchen, he set the covered pan of brownies on the table and pulled out a chair. ''Let's sit down.''

Finally! Releasing the breath she'd been holding, Nettie moved eagerly to the table. Nick took the chair opposite her. His obvious discomfort as he searched for a way to begin aroused her guilt, but not enough to call a halt.

''I can't tell you what was in the envelope. Not definitely. In part that's because Chase hasn't told me and partly because it's his information to keep or to share. I can tell you a few things, though. Things I think you should know.''

Nick's gravity gave Nettie the impression they were both going to need something stiffer than lemonade.

''Do you know who Chase's parents are?'' he asked.

Surprised, Nettie shrugged. ''His father is a newscaster, isn't he?''

Nick shook his head. ''Not 'a newscaster.' Lloyd Williams is the Walter Cronkite of cable. He owns most of his station.''

''Chase's last name is Reynolds.''

''It's his mother's maiden name. Lana Reynolds, the heiress to Reynolds Worldwide Shipping and the Sojourners Cruise Line.''

Nettie had never heard of Lana Reynolds, but she'd seen zillions of ads for the cruise line. ''Oh, Good Lord.'' She gulped. ''I can't date him. It was bad enough when I thought he was just your everyday average celebrity.''

That elicited a brief smile from Nick. ''Not quite. Chase was raised with the proverbial silver spoon. Lloyd groomed him from the cradle to take over the anchor desk. And Chase made it easy to believe it would happen. He has the looks, the voice, and the intelligence. Everything he needs to make Lloyd's dream come true.''

''Isn't that what Chase wants, too?''

Nick emitted a gruff snort that passed for a laugh. ''Not by a long shot.'' He shifted in his seat as if he found it uncomfortable. This was, Nettie realized, the segment of the conversation about which Nick felt guilty. "You can't understand Chase without understanding his background. His mother and father divorced when he was young, still in grammar school, I think. His mother hit the society trail, which left Chase to be raised by a series of housekeepers."

Nettie couldn't conceal her shock or disapproval. "She walked out on a little boy?"

Nick's lips twisted sourly. "She managed a visit every other Christmas or so."

"And his father?"

"Lloyd wasn't well endowed with parenting skills, either. He believes in three things: hard work, power and power. He expected a lot from Chase."

The tug on Nettie's heart was swift and strong. Lilah's words came back to her and Nettie struggled to remember that she'd made a deal with herself: Keep your heart out of this. As far as her heart was concerned, it was winter and she was hibernating.

Focus, she told herself. Find out about the envelope. That's all you need to know.

"Chase is very successful," she said. "His father has to be pleased with all he's accomplished." Her nose wrinkled. How pat did that sound?

Nick didn't seem to notice that she'd turned into the mother on "Leave It To Beaver." He shook his head. "I don't think Lloyd has ever given Chase the thumbs-up. In college, Chase said he wanted to be an 'in-the-mud, get-the-story journalist,' that he wanted to report the news, not become it."

Nettie gritted her teeth. She was caught, like a fish who'd seen the hook, but couldn't resist the bait. "What happened?"

"The more Chase pulled, the harder Lloyd pushed. Chase was offered jobs no struggling young journalist could possibly refuse. He thought he was getting them solely on his own merit—that's why he took his mother's name—and he didn't find out until later that Lloyd was pulling strings. Lloyd directed the spotlight on Chase every way he could and when an anchor position came up, he expected Chase to sit right down and say, 'Thank you.'"

"Chase didn't?"

Nick shook his head. "And Lloyd barely spoke to him for the next two years. Nothing Chase did was good enough."

Two years. Holidays flashed immediately to mind. Nettie

couldn't imagine being without one's family by choice, or because you were trying to punish someone. She'd never, ever been alone for the holidays, and a part of her didn't even want to ask, "What about the rest of his family?"

Nick's shrug was eloquent. "He has a half sister who travels—he rarely sees her. His mother he sees once every couple of years when he arranges to be in the same city she's in. Chase tells it all with a lot of humor, but it's part of who he's become, Nettie."

"Why are you telling me this?"

Nick clasped his hands atop the kitchen table. "Chase gets a lot of attention, but he's a private man. I don't enjoy betraying his confidence, but if you're dead set on a relationship with him..." The low slash of Nick's brow told her how he still felt about that. "You need to know that he doesn't stay in one place because he doesn't *want* attachments. If he ever did decide to settle down—" after a brief struggle with guilt, Nick spoke with firm conviction "—I don't think he'd be good at it."

This was the point, Nettie knew, at which she was supposed to remind the world once again that she was *not* in the market for settling down. But that's not what came to mind. What came to mind was how blasted unfair it was for other people to take what they knew about you—a bunch of cheap facts—and then pigeonhole you for the rest of your life. What came to mind was that, despite everything she'd told herself, Nick was wrong about Chase.

"Chase is honest and caring, and he's kind." The words spilled out with equal measures of confidence and indignation. "If he decides that putting down roots is what he wants, then I say he'll be great at it!"

Pushing away from the table, she stood. She realized she hadn't achieved her objective this afternoon, but at the moment, she couldn't quite recover the reason she'd thought the envelope and its contents were so bloody important. She would see Chase again, regardless.

She had to.

Nettie's legs wobbled as she excused herself to use the bathroom. She wanted to splash some cold water on her face and collect her thoughts. Attempting to appear far more poised than she felt, she straightened her spine and moved toward the swinging door between the kitchen and living rooms. She walked swiftly and pushed firmly, startled by a loud thud and sharp cry on the other side of the door.

Nettie poked her head through the door. "Sara!"

Behind her, Nick scraped his chair across the linoleum and repeated her exclamation.

Sara walked sheepishly through the door, a hand over her eye. "What were you doing?"

Sara looked at her sister through her good eye and shrugged.

"She was listening at the door. Weren't you?" Nick growled. "When did you sneak in here? With that kind of stealth, you'd make a better criminal than sheriff."

Sara rallied under Nick's censure. "I didn't have to sneak. This is my house."

"No, you didn't have to sneak," Nick agreed, "but you did." He stalked forward. "What are you up to?"

Sara's expression spoke volumes as she glanced between Nettie and Nick. "Seems to me there's been a lot of sneaking going on around here." She stabbed a finger between the two of them. "You've been seeing that reporter guy and everybody—" she glared at Nick "—knew about it but me. How do you think that makes me feel? I thought…" She faltered.

Nettie put her hands on her hips. The skin around Sara's injured eye was starting to bruise, but she refused to let herself feel guilty or try to fix it. For once, she was putting her own life first. "You thought what?" she demanded.

Sara's cheeks turned red. She had trouble, suddenly, meeting Nettie's gaze and couldn't look at Nick at all. Her hands went to the back of her uniform, where she fiddled with her belt. "I thought…uh…" Unable to defend her eavesdropping, she returned to the offensive, where she was clearly more comfortable. "You've been so secretive lately, I didn't know what to think. And now that I know you've got yourself stuck on the pretty boy, I see I was right to be concerned." Her freckled nose lifted an inch. "For once I agree with Nick."

"How reassuring," Nick murmured. "I may rescind my warning."

"I don't want warnings," Nettie interjected before Sara could strike back. "And I'm not interested in an opinion—from either of you." Splitting her gaze between the people she'd known all her life, Nettie said, "I know you think you're trying to help. But people change. Their desires change, their beliefs change. All you know about me is what you *think* you know about me. You have no idea what I really want."

A car pulled up in front of the house. Nick and Sara were too busy staring at Nettie to react to the sound or to the open and slam of the car door, but she crossed immediately to the window above the kitchen sink. Already, she recognized the sound of that engine, and her body reacted before her mind. Chase. Through the open window, she saw him head toward the front door. "Stay there! I'll be right out," Nettie called through the kitchen window.

Momentarily startled, Chase stopped, located her and then nodded. He looked different. Slightly uncertain. Less perfect, more human. Her heart responded instantly. She sent him a reassuring smile because she thought he needed it, and almost immediately his features relaxed. She didn't even bother with her purse or to offer a word to the two people who watched her in silence.

I'm choosing, she thought, facing them once, briefly. I'm choosing me. I'm choosing Chase. Over you, over your opinions of what's good for me. Damn the torpedoes, and if you don't like it, lump it!

As tremulous, as thrilled as if she were sitting at the top peak of a roller coaster, Nettie flew out the back door and around the front of the house, where Chase stood waiting.

"Let's go for a drive," she said, as breathless as a teenage girl about to sneak off with a forbidden love.

Bemused but agreeable, Chase moved without a word to open the passenger-side door.

Nettie glanced at the kitchen window. Sara and Nick stood side by side, peering through the glass like two old biddies. Following an impulse stronger than reason, Nettie reared back, gave Chase a swift, solid kiss somewhere between his mouth and his cheek and got into the car.

Now there were three people staring at her in varying degrees of surprise.

Chapter Ten

Clover fields waved before Chase like a verdant carpet, more brilliantly green than he would have supposed before arriving in North Dakota. Studded with wild mustard, the landscape looked like a impressionist painting, composed of an infinitude of tiny green and yellow strokes.

Chase inhaled deeply, having to remind himself that mere days ago he had envisioned the area as dry, if not barren then certainly brown and unappealing.

Days ago. He shook his head. How had so many things changed in such a brief span of time?

A few yards behind him, Nettie stood beneath a squat tree. They had spoken little on the drive here. He had something to tell her—two things—and his reluctance to begin amazed him.

Swiping at the perspiration that popped out along his upper lip, Chase endeavored to convince himself it was the heat and not his thoughts that elicited the moisture. The erratic pumping of his heart, however, told a different story.

Through experience, he had come to believe he could usually get what he wanted. He believed in the bulldogged pursuit of a goal, but also in matching a goal to one's capabilities. Now he had the unfamiliar feeling he was in over his head.

Moving toward Nettie, he watched the corners of her mouth turn up. With her back against the tree, she stared at the vista behind him.

"Lovely, isn't it?" she said. "Chicago was so big and fascinating. I was never bored there, but it's the kind of place that happens to you. Know what I mean? All you have to do is stand still and there are a million things to see or do. North Dakota is much, much subtler. You have to look with a more patient eye, interact with her, seek her beauty. Then she can be a wonderful place."

Chase nodded, swallowed and tried to breathe through the tension gathering in his chest. "You lived in Chicago?"

"For a few years. I went to college there."

"College," he murmured. "Not so long ago for you."

She rolled her eyes. "Seems like forever."

Chase smiled. He'd never asked her age, but guessed her to be in her mid-twenties. "Yeah, you're ancient. What did you get your degree in?"

"I don't have one." She shrugged, smiled as if to say *no big deal,* but she seemed awkward suddenly, her cheeks turning pink. "I didn't graduate. You know how kids are."

"Mm." *Not really,* he thought, but because he saw her discomfort, he didn't pursue it. Career had always meant everything to him and college had been a stepping-stone. It had never occurred to him to let anything get in his way. At least, not for long. Personal goals were another matter, however, largely because he'd never had any. Until now.

More perspiration beaded along his upper back and chest. He gestured toward the shaded spot where she stood. "Let's sit down. Do you mind?"

Nettie shook her head and settled herself on a carpet of grass a short distance from the gnarled roots of the tree. Chase hesitated a moment, trying to decide if he wanted to sit beside her or face her head-on.

Irritated by the immediate surge of sick tension that threatened to destroy his stomach lining before the day was through, he sat opposite her. *Head-on. Head-on and get to the point.*

Nettie toyed with the grass. Her long hair was loose, spilling casually over her shoulders as she plucked a green blade and looked up at him. The light breeze and the shade from the tree cooled some of the heat inside Chase, eliciting a brief gratitude as he forced himself to begin.

His reputed silver tongue felt more like brass.

"I have no idea how to start," he admitted, trying candor on for size.

Nettie exhaled. "Sounds ominous already."

"I hope not. I hope…" Dragging a hand over his cheeks and jaw, Chase shook his head. *Oh, man.* He looked at her, telling himself he would replace the trepidation he saw with something better. *He hoped.*

"About this morning… I acted like an idiot, and I'm sorry."

She frowned. "When?"

"When?"

"Yes. Do you mean when we kissed or when you left?" Clearly embarrassed by her own question, she nonetheless held her ground. "Because if you're talking about the kiss," she shook her head, lips thinning to a firm line while her eyes filled with fire, "don't you dare. I thought it was wonderful!" Her mouth rounded to a surprised *O* as a thought struck. "You didn't think it was wonderful?" Pressing fingertips to her forehead, she cringed. "I knew it! I kiss like a fish!"

"What?"

She tossed the blade of grass and flapped her hand in a gesture of surrender. "I know. I'm just…not that… Ohhh! I wanted to appear sophisticated, so I haven't said anything, but the truth is I'm not very experienced. Sexually speaking."

Chase endeavored to appear far more surprised than he felt, and a whole lot less pleased. "I never would have guessed."

She started to say something else, but stopped, shifting gears. "Really?"

He nodded. "Where does the fish come in?"

"Well." She raised both hands this time, letting them slap against her jeans-clad thighs. "I've never kissed me, so I'm only guessing, but if you're sorry—"

"Hold on, I'm not sorry we kissed. I'm not sorry about anything we did. It was great. I'm only sorry I ran out on you."

"You're not? You are? It was?"

"Hell, no! And, yes. Of course. Nettie," he reached for her

hand, but told himself he'd never get through this if he was actually touching her, so he pulled back to rake his fingers through his hair. "Kissing you was one of the sweetest experiences of my life. Don't make a face," he laughed when her smile fell on the word *sweet*. Matter-of-factly he told her, "I've been pretty short on sweet experiences. Nobody," he leaned forward to caress her with his eyes, which felt far safer than any other manner of touch, "but *nobody* would ever accuse you of kissing like a fish."

She leaned forward, too, her smile nearly killing him with its innocence and its pleasure. "I'm glad."

"Nettie." He cleared his throat, determined to stay on course. "I'm usually a man of my word, but this time I'm going to break it. When we agreed to a fling..." Feeling his jaw tighten even as he said the word, Chase slowly shook his head. "That was a bad idea."

Nettie's brows dipped. He could see her swallow. "Was it?"

Chase began to smile. "Oh, yeah. Very bad. I think we should renegotiate."

He loved the way surprise entered her expression, the way it evolved slowly but surely to expectation. "Will I need a lawyer?" she asked.

"Nah." Grinning now, so entranced by her reaction that the cannonball of tension in his chest began to melt, Chase said, "We can work it out ourselves, keep it simple. Keep it," he took a breath, watching her closely, "open-ended. What do you think?"

It was the only time he'd said anything remotely like that to a woman. The words had barely hit the air before his heart began to carom like a pinball against his ribs. Quickly, silently, ferociously he fought every doubt that clawed at him. Not a one of them had to do with her, anyway. They were all about him.

Her expression became a dance of emotion, and the one he sought was the last to come: pleasure. Unfortunately fear followed swiftly behind.

Okay, he could handle that. He was scared, too.

Nettie's insides tingled like a blanket filled with static electricity. She had not anticipated this moment. How could she? He was supposed to be leaving. She hadn't even imagined his wanting to be with her beyond his stay here.

Liar. She'd started imagining it when Nick was telling her who Chase was.

Liar, liar. She'd been imagining it since he'd thrown the first stone at her window. Fantasies had flown in and out of her mind since she'd stood barefoot and blissful with him on her side lawn. Simple fantasies...

Like dancing in the city—she wasn't even sure which city—but somewhere that glittered, somewhere the night was as bright as the day.

And Chase laughing with her as they rode bikes down to Ernie's for the last of the summer's chokecherry pie.

And then she'd imagined the two of them ensconced in the oldest cliché in the book: lying on a rug before a crackling fire, with winter howling outside.... They hadn't even been in Kalamoose in that scenario. She'd pictured a penthouse overlooking sparkling lights.

It was ridiculous. She couldn't do those things, hadn't been to the city in years and never danced anymore.

Then again, before Chase had come to town, she hadn't driven a car in years, either. She hadn't stood up for herself so thoroughly or spent hours laughing, not thinking about anything serious at all.

Before Chase had come to town, she'd been asleep. Now the prince who had kissed her awake didn't want the fairytale to end. Not yet, anyway.

Suddenly Nettie had no desire to deny the sheer gladness that bubbled inside her.

"Are you planning to stay in town, then?" she asked Chase, amazed when she caught herself thinking, *If he says he has to leave and wants me to meet him somewhere, I will. I don't know how, yet, but I'll do it!*

She braced herself, almost exhilarated, as she waited for him to say, *I'm flying to Bora Bora in the morning. The envelope I received held instructions regarding my next assignment. Ever been to Bora Bora?*

Instead he arched a brow. "You haven't answered my question yet."

Shamelessly relishing the power he'd just handed her, Nettie affected a frown. "Hmm. Well, if you need an answer now, let me think..."

Glorious male pride sparked a flash of protest in Chase's eyes. Impulsively, she sprang to her knees and flung out her arms, catching him round the neck. "Yes. The answer is yes!" She grinned, basking in the surprise and the relief she saw in his answering smile.

Chase clasped her upper arms and pressed her into the grass. "Tease," he growled, letting the rebuke linger as he took the kiss she offered.

He kissed her in a kind of lover's Morse code: long-short-short-very long, each kiss a comment. She could drive him mad with a look, and he loved it. His lips told her so.

With her eyes closed she smiled like a cat full of cream, and Chase knew, he knew in that moment, that he wanted to tell her everything. Here, at last, was a woman he felt he *could* tell. Not just about Colin—his *son*—but about how damn humiliatingly terrified he had been when he'd opened that envelope.

For almost three weeks he hadn't known how he would feel or what he would do if the paternity tests proved he had a seven-year-old son. He'd thought that, quite possibly, he might want to run. Not from the financial responsibility, certainly, but from the emotional commitment. What did he know about emotional commitment? He wasn't sure he could define the term, except to say it was the opposite of everything he knew.

Gently, with a touch he hadn't realized he possessed, he traced an invisible *I* over Nettie's face, across her forehead, down the bridge of her nose and along her lips. Her skin was milky and translucent, but between her brows he saw two small worry lines. She was gentle. She was strong. She was authentic. There didn't seem to be a harsh or critical bone in her body. To her and only to her, could he imagine confessing the truth he hated admitting even to himself: He was thirty-four years old, and he didn't think he'd ever loved anyone.

At the farmhouse he had sat on the edge of his bed in Nick's guest room, the door locked, and he'd stared hard at the sheet of paper stating definitively that there was a child in the world with Chase's blood coursing through his veins. Amazingly, Chase hadn't wanted to run—thank God—but he hadn't felt anything a human being might term love, either. He'd felt clammy and cold and so inadequate it had made him nauseous. Then he'd thought of Nettie and without trying, his muscles had relaxed. Her smile had filled his mind and suddenly his body had warmed.

He'd sat there alone, his thoughts disordered, and finally it had come to him that he was shaking not because he wanted to run away from something, but because he wanted to move toward it.

He had a son. And, for the first time, a woman in his life he would rather spend his time talking to than trying to charm.

Moving so that his shadow fell across Nettie's face, he plucked a blade of tall grass and traced the path his fingers had taken. The feathery touch tickled, and she opened her eyes.

"Keep them closed," he whispered, moving the blade of grass tenderly over her skin. "I have something else to tell you. I should have told you before, but I was…" Sighing, he settled onto his elbow. "I've been pretty confused, Nettie Owens, and I don't like being confused."

To Nettie, the last line sounded more like a growl than a spoken statement. She suspected this conversation ought to be pursued with eyes open, but decided this was one of those Men-Are-from-Mars moments and let him have his way.

Keeping her eyes closed and her tone neutral, she asked, "What's confusing you?"

After a brief pause, through which she remained carefully still, he responded, "The difference between what I want and what I thought I wanted. Ever been there?"

Nettie laughed. "Been there? I own property on that block."

Even with her eyes closed, she could feel his smile and the slow wag of his head. "I'm a new resident. Career hasn't been my top priority, Nettie, it's been my only priority. The whole idea of kids, the white picket fence route—that left me pretty cold." The blade of grass had stopped its patterning. "I have a sister who's been married three times, and she just turned thirty. She's on a world cruise right now with Husband Number Three's money. I never did meet the guy. I think his name is Chuck."

Resting his arm along his side, Chase let his gaze drift to the tree as he continued.

"I haven't done much better in terms of relationships. The only difference is I haven't tried as hard. I figured I'd concentrate on what I was good at and told myself there was a certain honor in sparing the world another screwed-up family. But as it turns out…''

Here, he thought, comes the hard part. Feelings he had no idea how to define poured into his voice when he said, ''As it turns out, I'm going to get a crack at raising a family, after all.''

Nerves suffused his voice, but once the words were out, relief flowed through him, clearing a path for new reactions. Suddenly he felt glad, incomprehensibly, shockingly glad. Blowing out a long-pent-up breath, he flopped onto his back. Maybe the sun and blue sky were harbingers: Everything was going to be all right.

''I have a son,'' he murmured, realizing Nettie would forever be the first person to whom he'd spoken the words. ''I have a son. He's seven. His name is Colin. And I've never met him.'' Placing an arm over his eyes, he decided to let the sun burn away his guilt. From this point on he would begin to make things right. ''I knew his mother years ago in London. We were together a few months and then went our separate ways. Apparently Julia died several months ago. She was in the States, living in Florida. After she died, Colin got shuffled off to some friend of hers, and…it's a long, long story. I didn't know anything about Colin until last month, and I didn't know he was really mine until this morning.''

''The envelope.''

''Yeah. Proof positive. Although, I think I knew when I got the call. It's weird, but I think I sensed the connection the moment I heard his name. That sounds crazy.''

''No. No it doesn't.''

Amazed, Chase found himself laughing. ''My God, Nettie, I have a son! And I want…'' He choked, wondering if every ''new parent'' had to deal with this ocean of undulating emotions. ''I want so damn much to make up for the time we've missed.''

Dropping his arm, he arose, expectant and grateful to be with someone who would understand his burgeoning excitement, someone who had ''family'' stamped all over her. With pride out of the way, he wouldn't mind a few pointers—about what holidays were supposed to look like, for example. Man, he had a lot to learn!

Nettie was already sitting up, looking almost as stunned as he felt.

He shook his head. "I'm sorry I sprang this on you." After another brief struggle with his ego, he admitted, "I thought I could ignore the whole thing until it went away. I don't have much to be proud of in this situation. Not yet."

Raw energy coursed through his system. Feeling he had to move, Chase stood and walked to the tree. "You could put everything I know about being a father in a thimble and it wouldn't be half full. But I'm going to do this." He thumped the rough bark with the heel of his hand. "I'm going to be the best damn—" he actually had to take a breath before he could say the word in reference to himself "—*dad* that kid will ever need!"

His vehemence was utterly male—masking self-doubt, filled with determination and trepidation in near-equal measures. Sitting on her knees, Nettie thought no man had ever looked so beautiful, so powerful or brave or scared. Except…

Tears gathered without warning behind her eyes.

Brian. Yes, except for Brian on the day she gave birth to their son. He'd held the tiny body and though doctors and nurses had bustled around them, Brian had seen only his child. Nettie had thought then it was like watching Columbus discover America. O, brave new world. Where nothing would ever be the same again.

She closed her eyes. Another man. Another child. Another bright, uncertain future. *Ah, Chase. Forgive me, forgive me for what I'm going to do.* Through willpower alone, her eyes were dry when she opened them.

Chase stood beneath the tree, knowing he'd gotten carried away, but his adrenaline was pumping. He'd staked his reputation on maintaining equilibrium in the midst of chaos. Now his legs were so wobbly, he wondered briefly if they could actually buckle.

"You were the first person I wanted to tell, you know." He released a shaky laugh that sounded as though it came from someone else's mouth. "I think that means something. Don't you?" He smiled, waiting for Nettie's sweet smile in return.

Waiting. And then hoping.

She twined her fingers, gripping her hands in a tight ball on

PLAY

7

Lucky

777

and you can get

FREE BOOKS AND A FREE GIFT!

PLAY LUCKY 7 and get FREE Gifts!

Lucky 7

HOW TO PLAY:

1. With a coin, carefully scratch off the gold area at the right. Then check the claim chart to see what we have for you — **2 FREE BOOKS** and a **FREE GIFT** — **ALL YOURS FREE!**

2. Send back the card and you'll receive two brand-new Silhouette Special Edition® novels. These books have a cover price of $4.50 each in the U.S. and $5.25 each in Canada, but they are yours to keep absolutely free.

3. There's no catch. You're under no obligation to buy anything. We charge nothing — **ZERO** — for your first shipment. And you don't have to make any minimum number of purchases — not even one!

4. The fact is, thousands of readers enjoy receiving books by mail from the Silhouette Reader Service®. They enjoy the convenience of home delivery...they like getting the best new novels at discount prices, BEFORE they're available in stores...and they love their *Heart to Heart* subscriber newsletter featuring author news, horoscopes, recipes, book reviews and much more!

5. We hope that after receiving your free books you'll want to remain a subscriber. But the choice is yours — to continue or cancel, any time at all! So why not take us up on our invitation, with no risk of any kind. You'll be glad you did!

We can't tell you what it is...but we're sure you'll like it! A surprise **FREE GIFT** just for playing LUCKY 7!

NO COST! NO OBLIGATION TO BUY!

NO PURCHASE NECESSARY!

**Scratch off the gold area with a coin.
Then check below to
see the gifts you get!**

YES! I have scratched off the gold area. Please send me the 2 Free books and gift for which I qualify. I understand I am under no obligation to purchase any books as explained on the back and on the opposite page.

335 SDL DNKS   235 SDL DNKM

FIRST NAME	LAST NAME

ADDRESS

APT.#	CITY

STATE/PROV.	ZIP/POSTAL CODE

(S-SE-04/02)

Worth **2 FREE BOOKS** plus a **FREE GIFT!**

Worth **2 FREE BOOKS!**

Worth **1 FREE BOOK!**

Try Again!

Offer limited to one per household and not valid to current
Silhouette Special Edition® subscribers. All orders subject to approval.

The Silhouette Reader Service® — Here's how it works:

Accepting your 2 free books and gift places you under no obligation to buy anything. You may keep the books and gift and return the shipping statement marked "cancel." If you do not cancel, about a month later we'll send you 6 additional books and bill you just $3.80 each in the U.S., or $4.21 each in Canada, plus 25¢ shipping & handling per book and applicable taxes if any.* That's the complete price and — compared to cover prices of $4.50 each in the U.S. and $5.25 each in Canada — it's quite a bargain! You may cancel at any time, but if you choose to continue, every month we'll send you 6 more books, which you may either purchase at the discount price or return to us and cancel your subscription.

*Terms and prices subject to change without notice. Sales tax applicable in N.Y. Canadian residents will be charged applicable provincial taxes and GST.

her lap. "I am glad for you, Chase. I am…so glad. Glad you told me, too. And I think you'll be a wonderful father."

Sounding reserved, she offered him…platitudes.

You caught her off-guard, he reminded himself. You're misreading her. You've had time to get used to it. She's probably wondering why you didn't tell her right away. Women like to be told.

Pushing away from the tree, he stepped forward. "I should have brought this up earlier. I wish—"

"No." Nettie shook her head—vehemently, or so it seemed to him. "No, it's not that. I—I could be handling this better."

His muscles tensed. "Handling it?" He shook his head. "Just say it. Whatever it is."

Only by the tiniest flicker of eyelashes did she betray her nerves.

"I've enjoyed every moment we've spent together," she told him, and he sensed immediately that those words were going to be his consolation prize. "But this is all so sudden, and… Under the circumstances, I really can't… I don't think we should…" Annoyed with her hesitation, she paused, cranked her composure up a notch and unloaded the rest of the pistol straight from the hip. "The truth is, I don't want to see you anymore."

Chapter Eleven

Sara sat at her desk in the Kalamoose jail, tapping a pen rapidly against a stained blotter while Nettie balanced herself on a cot in one of the cells, measuring for curtains.

New curtains, for crying out dang loud! Just what they needed, more girly stuff to make a perfectly good jail look like a sorority house. As if the old ruffles weren't torture enough.

Tossing the pen, Sara pulled a couple sticks of Juicy Fruit from the desk drawer, blew to remove excess dust, then unwrapped and crammed them both into her mouth. In four days, Nettie had scraped the paint off the entire lower half of their house, slip-covered Sara's favorite TV chair and arranged the contents of the snack cabinet in alphabetical order, which meant Sara had to dig for the Pop Tarts, but the dried apples were right up front. Nothing was safe.

"Come on, let's go," she said, rising from the chair. "It's almost seven, and my stomach's going to cave in if I don't put something in it soon."

Nettie turned from the window. The same cheerful smile she'd worn for days—as if her cheek muscles had frozen solid—wreathed her face. "I didn't realize the time," she chirped, hopping down from the bed. "I've got an Irish stew in the Crock Pot. I made chicken Oscar, too. We can pop that into the oven, if you'd rather. Or I can freeze it for another time. Oh, and there's soda bread, but I could whip up a batch of biscuits if you—"

"No!" Burying a choice swear word beneath her breath, Sara pleaded, "Don't whip anything." Heading for the door, she grabbed her hat, smashing it onto her head. All she wanted for dinner was a triple-decker peanut butter and jelly with a handful of the potato chips that were shelved somewhere between Oreos and Raisinettes. "Let's just go."

Since Nettie had walked to the jail, after Sara locked up, they both got into the squad car, neither of them speaking on the short drive home. Staring out the window with her arms and legs crossed, Nettie knew she had morphed into Heloise and was driving Sara half mad, but she couldn't stop herself. She didn't want to stop herself. Each desperate act of domesticity enabled her to cease thinking and to feel in control, at least for a while.

When they reached the house, she jumped out of the car and ran up the porch steps to busy herself with dinner preparations. With any luck she'd be tired enough to turn in before the last smear of grease was sponged off the last plate.

As soon as she opened the door, she realized something was odd. Lights were on all over the house, yet she didn't remember turning on any lamps before she left. There was also a definite aroma of flowers in the air.

Nettie crossed the threshold, about to comment to Sara, when she noticed several things at once: a shawl tossed over the living-room lounger, chunky-heeled sandals kicked off carelessly at the base of the stairs near a leather carryall, and a huge candle with three wicks, lighted and sitting on the coffee table.

Her gaze rose to the top of the stairs and her mouth opened in astonishment. "Lilah!"

Wearing powder-pink leggings and a soft V-neck sweater that looked as if it had been woven from cotton candy, the second-born of the three Owens girls was the picture of nonchalant glamour. Her golden hair curled halfway down her elegant back. Perfect makeup highlighted a gorgeous smile and brilliant blue eyes that sparkled with life.

"Nettie-Belle!" Skipping down the stairs with the grace of a dancer, the enthusiasm of a puppy, Lilah wrapped her arms around her sister, squeezing until Nettie thought she might see stars from lack of oxygen. "Mmm, you feel good. Let me look at you." Lilah pulled back and sighed. "Beautiful as ever. Come back to Los Angeles with me, baby, I'll make you a star."

"Yeah, that's what we need in this family, more dramatics." Sara's grumble provided a perfect and oh-so-typical foil for Lilah's effusiveness.

"Hello, Eeyore." Turning her attention to her older sib, Lilah put her hands on her hips. "Look who's complaining about dramatics. I haven't seen you for a year and you're still wearing the same costume."

"It's a uniform."

"Mmm." Lilah tilted her head. "Needs a scarf or something." Before Sara could respond, Lilah grabbed her in a bear hug, rocking excessively and planting a smacking, lipstick-staining kiss on Sara's cosmetics-free cheek.

"Oh, for crying out loud." Wriggling free, Sara wiped her face.

Over Lilah's contagious laughter, Nettie realized Sara had shown no surprise at all. "Did you know about this?"

"I'm your birthday present," Lilah answered in her sister's stead. "You know how Sara feels about shopping."

Nettie's eyes widened. Her birthday was still several weeks away. And Lilah's infrequent visits were often rushed. "You don't have to head right back then?"

The blonde shook her head. "I'm taking a long vacation." She tossed an arm around Nettie's shoulders and grabbed Sara in a near chokehold. "Come on. I brought food, Irish Cream and presents."

"Lilah! This is...scandalous!" Laughing delightedly, Nettie held up a scrap of royal purple material that was, she assumed, a thong. "What am I supposed to do with it?"

"Wear it, of course."

Sara grabbed a vanilla wafer and dragged it through a pot of peanut butter melted with the butterscotch morsels Lilah had pulled from her overnight bag. The unusual combination was a classic Owens sleepover snack, something the girls' mother used to make.

"You expect her to wear that thing out of the house?" Sara said with her mouth full.

"Under the proper attire, yes." Lilah swirled her Bailey's Irish Cream over ice.

"Well," Sara picked up a huge strawberry, dunked it in the sweet fondue, tipped back her head and took a bite, "why wear the thing at all then? Looks uncomfortable."

"Sara, if you have to ask what for, you've been alone way too long." Lilah grinned.

They'd been eating, chatting and opening gifts for the past hour. Lilah had brought Sara an autographed copy of the screenplay for *The Quick and the Dead* and a box of designer chocolates from a ritzy store on Rodeo Drive. She'd given Nettie perfume, the thong and a matching bra.

"I know better than to call a shoestring underwear," Sara claimed, flipping through the front pages of the script.

"Men love them."

"Huh," Sara grunted. "They don't have to wear 'em. Try chasing a bank robber in one of those things. You'd hang yourself."

Lilah's bright laughter filled the room. "And speaking of chasing men," she said, mischief darkening her eyes, "How's Nick?"

Sara turned as red as the strawberry she'd just popped into her mouth. "How should I know?" she sputtered, leaping to her feet so quickly, she nearly overturned the coffee table. "I'm going to bed. I have to get up early for work tomorrow. And don't leave that candle burning, when you go upstairs. It wouldn't surprise me if you burned the house down with your candles and your…thongs, and…" Tossing her strawberry stem onto the fruit plate, Sara stalked off.

Lilah took another sip of her drink and murmured, "Still carrying a torch, I see. And not doing a thing about it."

"How did you know?" Nettie asked when Sara was safely up the stairs and out of earshot. She slapped a hand to her forehead. She herself had just started suspecting, but she'd been too immersed on her own life to pursue the thought. "I can't believe I was so blind. How long have you known?"

"She's been ga-ga over Nick since high school, but she makes a second career out of pretending she couldn't care less." Lilah shook her head. "She's so tough about some things, but when it comes to any man who's not on the FBI's Ten-Most-Wanted list, she's a big 'fraidy cat."

"Sara?" Nettie shook her head. "I know she hasn't dated much, but I never think of Sara as being afraid of anything."

Lilah sighed. "Sweetie, when it comes to the opposite sex, we're all afraid of something. Or someone." Curling her long legs beneath her, she settled more cozily into the plaid chair that had always been her personal favorite. "So how about you?" She arched an impeccably groomed brow. "How's your fling coming along?"

Nettie's heart had to squeeze out the next beat, but she managed to shove her cheeks back into smile mode. "Oh, that," she tossed off as lightly as she could. "I'm afraid my fling is *finito*." Rising, she began to gather the used napkins and plates. "You were right. I'm not fling material."

"What happened? Did he say no to a longer commitment?" Sisterly loyalty put palpable anger in Lilah's tone.

Nettie shook her head, mopping smears of peanut butter dip off the oak table.

"Why don't you leave that stuff and sit and talk to me," Lilah suggested. "Sara says you've been doing your Martha Stewart impersonation again."

Nettie stopped wiping and looked up. "Is that why you came?"

"She's concerned. I'm concerned, too. Sara wasn't sure how to help you, so she called."

Lilah shrugged with her customary casual grace. This time it irritated Nettie to no end. "You were both worried when I was planning to have an affair. Now you're worried that I'm not? Seems a little ironic, wouldn't you say?"

"We just want you to be happy, Net."

Nettie gave an uncharacteristically cynical huff of laughter. "Yeah. As long as my happiness doesn't interfere with Sara's feeding schedule or your next audition."

It was a shocking, completely uncharacteristic thing for Nettie to say, and they both knew what she was referring to. Lilah's face went pale beneath her makeup.

''We were scared, Nettie. We thought you wanted…to be alone. We didn't know what to do.''

''Well, that made three of us.''

After Brian and Tucker had died, Nettie had been helpless to take care of anyone's emotions, even her own. It was understandable, but frightening to the two women who had relied on her most of their lives. Even through her own despair, Nettie had seen her sisters' discomfort and though she had felt like a marionette lying limp and disjointed on the ground, she'd somehow managed to scrape herself together and hold her body upright long enough to tell her sisters to go home, get on with their lives…she'd be fine. Like a marionette, she'd been hanging on by a thread.

Guilty but relieved, they had left, and at the time Nettie had felt grateful that she could still ''be there'' for her family. Make everything feel normal and safe for them, just as she always had. Except that by then she'd understood there was no such thing as ''safe.''

Well, this time she was fresh out of illusions. The dream of experiencing a happiness with Chase that couldn't be snatched away was only that—a dream.

Facing Lilah with an uncompromising stare, Nettie said, ''He has a son. Seven years old.'' That was it, all she had to say, really. Tucker would have been six.

Lilah so clearly wanted to respond, wanted to tell her *So what? Go for it,* but she didn't dare.

''Who will be there this time, Lilah, if everything falls apart?'' Nettie drove her point home. ''Sara? You? Will you stick around and pick up the pieces? Because—'' Her voice started to break. Relentlessly, she pressed on. ''I wouldn't survive it another time. I don't think I'd want to.''

''But maybe it won't fall apart this time, Net. You've had your share—''

''You think that's how the world works? You still think it's *fair?* Tragedy isn't dealt out like a deck of cards—everyone gets five and then you go around in a circle and tell the dealer what you want. No one cares what you want! Nobody's checking to make sure you only get what you can handle.'' Nettie slashed a hand through the air. ''That is such a crock! Mother and Daddy were thirty-four when they died and they had three children. And everyone else on that plane had people who loved them and needed them. You want to talk about fair? Brian was twenty-three. *Twenty-three.''* She didn't even say Tucker's name; she couldn't. ''Maybe the truth is some people get more than their share because they're jinxed. Maybe I'm doing Chase a big favor—''

Nettie began to shake. As if she were standing with her feet in ice, the shivering started from the legs up, until her entire body quivered without control.

All she'd wanted was a little bit of joy to remind her she was still alive. What she'd got instead were reminders she didn't want of a life she'd never have again.

Leaving everything—plates, napkins, Lilah—right where they were, Nettie turned to run up the stairs. If a life lived in avoidance meant she was only half alive, fine. It was also half the pain.

It had taken seven years for Chase to discover he was a father, mere hours to travel to Florida to meet his son for the first time, a couple of minutes to note all the physical resemblances between them and about two seconds to realize he was in over his head. Way over.

Twisting the top off a bottle of cold beer, he slumped into a chair at the kitchen table. Given an aisle seat on the plane ride back to North Dakota, Colin had preferred to gaze silently out the window, rather than converse with his father. Chase wondered if they should have spent a few days at Disneyworld, or if he should have brought a gift, something to break the ice. Hell, he hadn't thought to take along a single thing a kid might want to eat or play with or wear.

On the ride from the airport to Nick's, Chase told his son about Nick's horse, received an encouraging but brief flicker of interest and then…zilch.

Now Colin was upstairs, preferring to unpack on his own while Chase remained downstairs, nursing a cold beer and a gutful of self-doubt rather than the walloping sock in the chest of fatherly love he'd expected to feel.

Chase took a long pull from the bottle of Budweiser. Yeah, this father gig was a real piece of cake.

Elbows on the table, he dropped his forehead onto his palms. He wanted to talk to someone. But not just any someone.

Nettie.

She was the first person who came to mind. And the second. Furious with himself, Chase shook his head. She'd bailed. Only moments after those robin's egg eyes had said, yes, her mouth had uttered no to any possibility of a relationship. Because he had a kid.

Chase put a hand on his breast pocket, remembered he'd foolishly given up smoking and rose to pace to the window.

He knew firsthand what it was like to be an unwanted kid. Nothing…no one…would make his son feel that way.

Forget her, Chase ordered himself. Forget her, it's done. He must have had too much adrenaline in his system, anyway, to imagine that he was ready for a relationship with a woman *and* a child. One at a time would be more than enough.

Returning to the table, he grabbed the beer and opened the refrigerator. Nick was out of town for a few days, which meant he and Colin were on their own for meals. Unfortunately, Chase didn't cook. He had no reason to; he was never at home. Peering at the shelves, he searched for something that looked like kid food.

Catsup, bratwurst, more beer, butter. There was a loaf of bread and a box of cereal on top of the fridge. Bratwurst on bread with catsup? Slamming the refrigerator door, he hung his head. He was in serious trouble.

Leaving his beer on the sink, he headed upstairs, heart thumping as if *he* were the kid. When he reached the guest room, he halted at the door. Colin stood at the window, staring out. His small sloping shoulders appeared to hold the weight of the world. Chase felt his anger rise at anyone—everyone, himself included—who had contributed to that sadness.

The simple act of drawing his own child's attention filled Chase once again with an aggravating self-doubt. He didn't know how to address his own kid—how pathetic was that? It was on the tip of his tongue to say, *son,* but that seemed wrong, as if he hadn't earned the right.

Resigning himself to indecision, high blood pressure and ulcers for the remainder of his natural life, Chase cleared his throat and smiled when Colin turned. "Listen I'm getting hungry, and

I thought, uh…'' *Come on, this is easy. It's only food.* ''My
favorite dinner is a cheeseburger, french fries and a vanilla
shake. How about you?''

Huge brown eyes gazed warily beneath a mop of straight
coffee-hued hair. ''I like chocolate.'' No smile and only a halting
enthusiasm, but Chase was encouraged.

''Ever been to a real old-fashioned diner?'' Confused, Colin
shrugged. Okay, no frame of reference for a diner. ''Come on.''
Chase gestured to the door. ''Have you ever had a milkshake
served in a tall silver cup? No?'' Feigning disbelief, Chase followed his son down the hall. ''Aw, man, are you in for a surprise.…''

Given its status as ''the only restaurant for twenty miles,''
Ernie's did a fairly brisk business in the early evenings, particularly when the weather was good. Chase ushered his son into
a dining room that was crowded, relatively speaking, and filled
with the aromas of grilled meat, homemade gravy and pie that
smelled freshly baked.

Obeying a sign that read Take a Menu, Take a Seat and Wait
Yer Turn, Chase chose a booth near a window, watched his son
crawl across the vinyl seat and then slid in opposite him.

Ernie arrived almost immediately with a pot of coffee, pouring
before Chase could accept or decline.

''Welcome back!'' Ernie displayed overly large dentures in a
sincere greeting as he sloshed hot liquid into a brown ceramic
mug. ''Thought you might carry a few hard feelings after you
got yourself arrested the first time you was here, but I can see
you're a man with a sense of humor.'' He slapped Chase heartily
on the back.

Chase lurched forward, amazed by the wizened old codger's
strength. ''Yeah.'' He reached for the creamer. ''I love a joke.''

''Glad to hear it. And who's this good-lookin' fella?''

Colin stared at Ernie with more interest than he'd shown in
anything so far. It was understandable. Ernie resembled an elf
come to life. Smiling, Chase made the introduction exactly as it
first came into his head. ''This is Colin, my son. He just got
into town.''

''Happy to meet you, Colin.'' Ernie stuck out a knobby hand
which Colin accepted and manfully shook. ''This your first visit
to North Dakota?''

Colin nodded.

"Well, that's fine. There may not be much to do, but we got plenty to see. Say, did your dad tell you he spent the night in the same jail that once housed the great Toothless Shoeless Pistol Pete and Dead Eye Dunnigan the night before they was both hanged for bank robbery? Same thing your dad was arrested for."

Colin's eyes bugged wide. He stared at his father with new interest. Chase winced. Turning to Colin, he said firmly, so there would be no misunderstanding, "I didn't rob anything. It was a mistake. The sheriff mistook me for somebody else."

Colin's interest didn't dim a bit. "You were in jail?"

Chase shifted uncomfortably, earning another whack from the old man. "Now, don't be embarrassed, son. Plenty a folks has been falsely accused. Important thing is no one was shot." Ernie went into another fit of cackling. Obviously at least some of the story had made the rounds in town. Interestingly, Ernie didn't seem to be distressed by the part he'd played.

"I was never really 'in jail,'" Chase insisted. "The sheriff took me to jail, but I was never officially booked for any crime."

"I want to be a policeman." Colin announced.

"You oughtta meet our sheriff, then," Ernie said. "She knew she wanted to be sheriff from the time she was your age."

"The sheriff is a girl?" Colin seemed doubtful.

"Yep." Ernie looked proud. "She's our very own Calamity Jane. I bet she'd give you a tour of our jail."

"Really?" Powered by enthusiasm, Colin's feet smacked the legs of the table. "When can I go? When are the tours?" He hopped out of the booth.

"Okay, Colin, sit down. We're going to have dinner—"

"Sheriff's right over there." Ernie pointed to a booth across the dining room. "Why don't you ask her?"

"Oh, boy!" The seven-year-old took off like a shot.

Ernie chuckled. "Kids." He shook his head. "They got so much dang energy."

Chase twisted around, sliding to the edge of the bench-style seat.

"Don't worry." Ernie hastened to reassure him. "He's not bothering anyone. We're all friends here."

But Chase was worried. His body stiffened as his gaze settled

on the three women in a booth across the restaurant. Digging
into a huge slice of pie à la mode that was placed on the table
between them, the women were laughing, wielding their forks
like swords as they battled for control of the dessert.

When Colin skidded to a halt at their table, they glanced up.
Chase spared only a glance for the redheaded sheriff, who was,
as usual, dressed in uniform, and for the unfamiliar blonde who
smiled at his son.

Now that he was at their table, Colin seemed to suffer another
attack of reserve, twisting his small hands behind his back as he
addressed himself to the local law. Chase had no idea what was
spoken between Sara and his son, but he realized Colin must
have identified him as "father," when, almost as a unit, the
women turned to look in his direction.

Nettie's gaze locked with his and she looked, he thought,
exactly the way he felt—as if he'd suffered a punch to his sternum.

Briefly, he considered staying right where he was and waiting
for Colin to return to the table. In fact, he might have—thereby
letting both himself and Nettie off the hook—except for one
thing: Before she'd noticed him, Nettie had been having a perfectly good time. The relationship she'd killed wasn't even cold
in the grave, and she'd managed to put it behind her. And that
irked him. Big time.

Sliding out of the booth, Chase begged a cursory pardon as
he brushed past Ernie.

From her place in the corner of the booth, Nettie watched his
approach. Shifting her gaze between father and child, she felt
the few bites of pie she had taken turn to cannonballs inside her
churning stomach.

This was Chase's son, the boy she hadn't wanted to meet. He
stood, nervous yet fascinated, gazing at Sara. Tall for his age,
sturdy and obviously hale beneath a too-sober countenance,
Colin bore a striking resemblance to his father, though his hair
was a shade darker and impossibly thick, sitting atop his head
like a thatched roof. His mother must have had a devil of a time
running a comb through it.

Feeling herself smile, Nettie abruptly reined in her thoughts.
That was exactly the kind of thing she didn't want to think.

When Chase reached their table, he put a protective hand on

Colin's shoulder. His expression stony, he looked at Nettie but remained silent, almost daring her to speak first.

Nettie had no idea what to say. From her peripheral vision, she noted Lilah turning her head, assessing the situation. When no one ventured a word, Lilah took the bull by the horns, thrusting out a hand.

Chase reacted in slow motion, pulling his attention off Nettie and putting it on the vivacious blonde.

"You must be this charming young man's father." Taking the hand Chase proffered, she flashed him a dazzling grin. "I'm Lilah Owens. And your name is?" To Nettie's amazement, Lilah tilted her head, actually batting her long, mascara-laden lashes.

Flirting? She was flirting with him? In disbelief, Nettie watched Chase respond with a smile that said he was duly charmed. "My name is Chase, Ms. Owens."

"Lilah," she corrected.

"Lilah," Chase agreed, keeping her hand. "I'd know you anywhere. From the photo on the mantel in your family's home," he clarified when she arched a brow in question.

"Such an old, old photo," she laughed.

"But so clearly indicative of the great beauty to come."

"I may hurl." Sara could have been referring to the quantity of pie she continued to consume, but Nettie knew better and for once she shared the sentiment.

Lilah continued as if Sara hadn't spoken. "Ah, you've been to our house?" Gracefully withdrawing her hand, she glanced around the table and then back at Chase. "You must know my sisters then." Her surprise was a shade too enthusiastic to be genuine.

Chase's eyes met Nettie's. She longed to kick Lilah beneath the table. What kind of game was her sister playing? Sitting in the corner of the booth, Nettie felt her anger rise. Now Chase was going to think she hadn't cared enough about their relationship to tell her own sister about it! On the other hand, she corrected herself sternly, it made no difference. She certainly didn't want him to think she was carrying a torch for him. Did she? No! Of course not.

Afraid she looked as fidgety and uncomfortable as she felt, Nettie tried to use the pie as a focal point to gather her racing thoughts, but Sara kept hacking away at it with her fork. And

Lilah kept staring at Chase in that *irritating* way. And Chase…
Already he'd removed his gaze from Nettie and returned it to
her blonder, sexier sibling. Irrationally she felt more piqued.
What kind of inconstant jilted would-be lover was he, anyway?

With a lazy smile, he confirmed for Lilah, "I've had the pleasure of getting to know both your sisters. My stay in North
Dakota will always be highlighted by the memory of your family's…unusually warm welcome."

Nettie's eyes narrowed. Unusually warm? Either he was referring to being handcuffed and nearly shot or…to being prop-
ositioned by a country widow within a week of his rolling into
town. Either way, it didn't sound like a compliment.

"Excuse me," she said, finding her voice at last and determined to nullify his insinuation that they had somehow embarrassed themselves, "but the fact is, we greet everyone like that."

His brow rose. "That must be a boon to North Dakota tour-
ism."

Nettie lifted her chin and tightened her jaw to keep from grimacing. *Damn. Damn!*

Chase squeezed his son's shoulder. "Come on, Colin. I'm
sure these ladies want to get back to their dessert, and we've
got some great burgers waiting for us."

Colin craned his neck to look up. "But we haven't ordered
yet."

"Right." Chase laughed. "That's right. So let's do that.
Ladies." Studiously avoiding Nettie, he nodded.

"But I want to see the jail," Colin resisted his father's tug.
"Will you show me your jail?" he asked Sara. "I want to be a
policeman."

Judging by the expressions on their faces, Sara and Chase
were in a dead heat for Least Enthusiastic About the Idea. On
the other hand, Nettie watched the eager face of the child and
wanted to kick both adults for allowing their personal grievances
to stand in the way of a simple request. The child had lost his
mother. He'd been shuttled to a new place with a father he barely
knew. A tour of local points of interest wasn't much to ask.

"We can see about that later, Colin," Chase said, trying to
move the boy along.

"Come by anytime and take a look around." Stated with
resolve, Nettie's offer surprised everyone. Beneath their stares,

she addressed herself to Colin. "If Sara's not too busy, I bet she'll even let you stand inside a cell." She smiled and received a tentative smile in return.

Sara looked as disgruntled as a mule and Chase regarded Nettie with a wary mix of curiosity and reproach. Nettie stared back at them both. True, she'd taken into her own hand matters that weren't hers, but in this isolated instance she wasn't sorry. It was simply meant to quench a child's thirst for adventure.

After an abrupt nod, Chase led his son back to their booth. Pretending a renewed interest in dessert, Nettie picked up her fork and stuck it into the sliver of pie still remaining. She felt her sisters' stares like lasers blazing through her skin.

"I thought you were through with that guy," Sara said, her disapproval blatant. "Now he's going to show up at the jail— him and his kid—and that'll be nothing but trouble. If you ask me— Ow!" She jerked in her seat. Reaching below the table to rub her shin, Sara glared at Lilah, who had obviously kicked her. "You nearly broke my leg."

Lilah smiled unapologetically. "Oops. Sorry," she said, utterly insincere. "My foot slipped. Ow!" Lilah's gorgeous features scrunched into a furious scowl as her own leg took a blow. "Revenge is childish," she growled at Sara. "Or hadn't you heard?"

"That one was from me." Nettie forked a bite of sweet dark berries and flaky crust into her mouth and chewed calmly. She swallowed, nudged Lilah with her elbow this time and said, "Scoot out."

"I'd love to, but my shin bone has been fractured. What was that for, anyway?"

Moving with enviable calm, Nettie gathered her sweater and purse. "Lilah Owens, you are still the most outrageous flirt in Kalamoose County."

At first Lilah appeared ready to launch into an automatic protest. Then she changed her mind and shrugged. "So? He's good looking, he's single—he's a celebrity, so he's probably rich—if you don't want him, why should we let him go to waste?"

"Listen to you!" Sara leaned far over the table before Nettie could respond and sneered at Lilah. "Not let him go to waste. As if he's got an expiration date! Men are just so much hamburger to you. Like that time you kissed Nick at your sweet sixteen party.''

Lilah rolled her eyes. ''You're still harping on that?''

'''Sweet sixteen and never been missed,''' Sara taunted, '''Every guy she saw, she kissed!'''

''All right, kiddies,'' Nettie said equably. ''Time to go home and clean up your rooms now.'' Again she nudged Lilah. ''Slide out.''

Lilah remained stubbornly right where she was. ''Not until you tell me whether Chase Reynolds—'' she lowered her voice ''—is up for grabs or off limits. Fish or cut bait, little sister. What's it going to be?''

Nettie saw it then—the challenge and appraisal in her sister's eyes. Lilah was testing her. Pushing her to make a choice. And Nettie, who had believed her choice was already made, understood that in the game of romance minds were made up, changed, and made up again, sometimes over and over. *Choose again,* Lilah was telling her.

''Let's just say I don't want my sister to cast her line.'' Refusing to say more than that, Nettie stared at Lilah levelly until the other woman gave up and slid out of the booth. Keeping her back straight, her eyes focused straight ahead of her—and away from Chase's table—she made her way to the front of the restaurant.

Chapter Twelve

Four days later, Nettie thought that perhaps she'd seen the last of Chase. He hadn't brought Colin to the jail. The only reason she knew they were still in town was that Etta Schlag, who owned the bakery, had rattled on for ten minutes this morning about how handsome Chase was and that he and his son had eaten three of her Bavarian cream donuts yesterday—three, she hoped to tell you, and she made them extra large—plus, they'd each had a cup of hot chocolate, besides. Then Chase—"that sweetheart"—had told her that if she ever decided to move to New York, he'd set her up in a donut shop and they'd be bigger someday than Krispy Kreme. Whatever, Etta said, that was.

Nettie had taken her loaf of German sourdough rye and walked home.

She'd tried hard to concentrate on her work, spending most of the morning illustrating a scene from her latest book, but by early afternoon she'd been too restless to sit still. Lilah had gone into Minot for the day, so Nettie walked back into town. Now she was hanging the curtains she'd made for the jail...and trying not to admit to herself that standing in the cell where she'd first met Chase was far more satisfying than staying home, pretending she wasn't thinking about him.

Sara had gone out on a call fifteen minutes ago, answering a summons from the janitor at the local elementary school. That left Nettie once more alone with her thoughts.

By now she had to confess—to herself only—that she'd been living a four-day-long fantasy about seeing Chase again. The fact that she hadn't seen him left her feeling utterly disappointed.

Yeah, right, she thought, bunching a panel of curtains along their rod. "Flat-out rejected" was more like it. And that was so dumb! She had chosen not to continue their relationship. Reason still told her she'd made the right decision, the one with the least potential for excruciating pain in the long run, but there seemed to be a gap the size of the Grand Canyon between what her reason told her and what desire demanded.

Desire... She desired to see him again. To feel her skin tingle and her heart skip from the look in his eyes. And from trying to judge when, where and how he was going to kiss her. There were certain sensations of danger, she was beginning to realize, that felt mighty good.

Shoving the curtain rod into a bracket, Nettie hopped down from the cot. Emotions were the most illogical things. She was better off without them.

Looking around, she wondered what else she could dust, mop or redecorate to within an inch of its life, but before she could determine her next victim, Sara stormed through the door, grumbling something about "...stray dogs and kittens..."

"Come on," Sara said, holding open the solid wood door. "You're under arrest, so don't give me any resistance or back talk."

Nettie watched with interest as a little boy, his shoulders straight and his eyes huge with curiosity, marched through the door, the most willing prisoner she had ever seen.

Nettie lifted a brow in inquiry.

"He was wandering around Wilbur Elementary," Sara explained. "Hank found him drawing on the chalkboard in a schoolroom that was supposed to be locked. Breaking and entering is a crime, so I arrested him." Colin's thin shoulders were manfully squared. He stared straight ahead, chin up, countenance solemn but oddly dignified, as if he was telling them, *I committed the crime; I'll do the time.*

"The school is almost two miles from Nick's place. Was, uh, your prisoner by himself?" Nettie asked.

"Yep. Rode his bike. Nice shiny new bike. It's in the back of the squad car now. Impounded."

While Kalamoose was by no means the crime capital of North Dakota, Nettie didn't like the idea of a seven-year-old riding his bike two miles in one direction in an area that was unfamiliar to him. "Does your father know where you are?" she asked, receiving a noncommittal shrug in return.

"He says Chase told him he could go wherever he wanted. I called Nick's place. No one's there."

That made no sense to Nettie. She knew she was overly cautious, but to tell a child he could go wherever he desired and then leave so there wasn't an adult at home while he rode off to explore? If that was Chase's idea of parenting, it left a lot to be desired. Every child needed an anchor. She looked at the little boy.

Colin maintained the posture of Repentant Convict until he noticed Sara's police radio. Then he broke into a gallop. "Wow! Does this thing really work?"

"Of course it works!" Following him, Sara grabbed him by the collar of his shirt and hauled him several steps back. Colin didn't seem to mind a bit. "Don't touch it, though. I use it for official police business only. It's not a toy. In fact, nothing in here is a toy." Placing her hands on her hips, just above her gun belt, she added, "I expect you to remember that."

Colin nodded. "I will." He turned around. "Can I look in the cells?"

Sara rolled her eyes, as if the effort to show him around kept her from something hugely important. "Yeah, I guess. You're going to make it quick, though, because I'm putting you under house arrest with my sister in charge."

"What?"

"What's that mean?"

Nettie and Colin spoke at the same time, Colin mildly curious but with most of his attention on the configuration of the cells. Nettie, on the other hand, felt every nerve-ending buzz to life.

"Explain that," she said to Sara while Colin crawled beneath one of the cots, looking for a trap door or other means of escape.

"His father isn't home." Sara tossed her hat like a Frisbee, cleanly hitting a peg of the coat rack. "Nick's not there, either, and I don't have time to baby-sit till they get back. Besides, a jail isn't day care." She lowered her voice, crossing toward her desk. "I've got guns here, too many things I don't want him messing with. I figure you can take him to our place until his wayward parent decides to show up. Anyway, that way if he gets hungry or thirsty, you'll know what to do with him. Little kid rode his bike almost two miles. He's got to be hungry, and I don't know anything about feeding kids."

"Right." Nettie's tone was droll. She refrained from pointing out that Sara fed her inner child several times a day. Looking at Colin as he crawled around on the hardwood floor, she felt her pulse increase. She was about to take responsibility for a little boy again. And sooner rather than later, she was going to see Chase.

"I like these waaayyy better than the ones he got us." Colin sat at the kitchen table, swinging his legs while he ate homemade oatmeal cookies and sipped from a tall glass of milk.

"'He' meaning your father?" Nettie stood with her back against the counter. Colin had seemed shy on the walk home, but a quick tour of Nettie's studio and a handful of cookies had relaxed him considerably.

"He can't cook. He made spaghetti last night and it tasted like barf."

It was stated so matter-of-factly, Nettie burst into laughter. "It wasn't that bad, was it?"

Colin bobbed his head. "Yeah. The noodles were weird."

"Weird?"

Mouth full, he rocked and kicked the rungs of the chair, filled with boyish energy. "Kinda like Goop."

"Goop?" Nettie was familiar with the strangely gelatinous toy, though she'd never had the pleasure of tasting it. "That's not good."

Colin shook his head vigorously. "And he burned the oat-meal. And then he put jam on it 'cause we ran out of sugar!"

Affording his onlooker the courtesy of first swallowing his cookie, Colin mimed throwing up.

"Mmm. This does sound serious." She felt vaguely sorry for Chase. He was probably making a lot of peanut butter and jelly sandwiches to stand in for ruined meals. It certainly explained his gratitude for Etta's Bavarian creams.

"Can I have another cookie?"

Noting his still scissoring feet, Nettie took pity on Chase and vetoed the notion of more sugar. "How about a sandwich?" she suggested. "Have you ever had a roast beef club?"

While she built the sandwich, Colin studied the two books she'd autographed for him. The stories and illustrations were sophisticated enough to hold his attention and he studied them intently, seeming engrossed by the element of magic.

Nettie found herself smiling as she glanced at him, smiling as she sliced cheese and stuck a knife into the mayonnaise jar. All the daily, innocuous acts she seldom gave a second thought to suddenly infused her with a quiet happiness that felt almost…holy. If this had been Tucker, if she'd been making sandwiches for her own son these three mislaid, lonely years, would such commonplace moments have begun to slip by virtually unnoticed?

She'd never know. So for now, each swipe of mayonnaise over wheat bread and each crisp turn of the page as Colin read her book was something that stood out like a little gift.

How, she wondered, trying not to be judgmental and failing miserably, could Chase be so bored with fatherhood already that he'd encourage this child to simply wander off on his own? Besides, a day like this, when the weather hung between summer and fall and the lazy breeze coaxed a person into the sun, a perfect day like this was simply meant to be spent with someone you loved. Chase had told her that commitment and constancy were not his strong suits. Apparently, he'd told the truth.

Nettie sliced the sandwich into triangles, using more force than necessary, but she was angry. Not for her own sake. No, that'd be a waste of cortisol. She and Chase were past history. But for his son's sake—yes. On behalf of that little boy, Chase Reynolds was going to have to learn to commit.

She was hunting through the snack cabinet, in search of Sara's stash of barbecued potato chips, when a car pulled too quickly up to the house. The driver cut the engine and Nettie realized she easily recognized the sound of Chase's car.

Moving as if her heart wasn't racing a mile-a-minute, Nettie set the sandwich and chips in front of Colin, then went to open the door the senior Reynolds was already pounding on. Not just knocking, actually pounding.

He looked as though someone had stuffed him into a washing machine and left him too long on the spin cycle. His hair was disheveled as if he'd plowed his hands through it dozens of times, and in fact he did so now as he entered the house. His eyes were at once tired and sharply alert, like a man standing watch.

"Is he here?" Eschewing preliminaries, Chase marched into the house and looked around. "There was a message on Nick's machine, from Sara."

"He's here," Nettie said. "He's eating lunch in the kitchen. He's fine."

Her last statement was clearly the most important to Chase. Again, his restless fingers raked his hair, but this time he released a long sigh of relief, as well. "Sara said she found him at the elementary school. I've been driving all over! Where the hell is the elementary school?"

"A couple of miles from Nick's."

Chase's reaction was almost identical to Nettie's. "Two miles? He's only seven! He rode his bike two miles?" Obviously intending to relieve some of his agitation in a lecture, Chase started toward the kitchen.

Nettie stopped him with a hand on his forearm. "Let's sit down," she suggested, gesturing to the couch.

Chase sank to the sofa, elbows on his knees and forehead resting against his clasped hands.

"Were you home when he left the house?" she asked quietly, and Chase nodded. "You didn't even know he was leaving, did you?"

"No." He raised his head, pressing his lips against his knuckles. Guilt seemed to emanate from his very pores, and Nettie felt a surge of protectiveness. She was beginning to get a clearer picture of what had transpired this afternoon.

He turned to look at her, his eyes puffy and tired. Several days of hands-on fatherhood had taken a toll. "I blew it. I was working, writing an article." He wagged his head. "I'm trying to figure out how to have a kid and a career at the same time. I can't keep traveling. I mean, he's got to go to school in one place, right?" Frustration and uncertainty coiled his muscles. "I'm no damn good at this! Some people shouldn't be parents. I've always known that. What kind of a father doesn't know where his son is?"

Nettie sighed, immensely sorry for having judged him. Real life so seldom played out like the picture in your head. Chase thought he knew what fatherhood was supposed to look like and figured he was coming up short.

Studying him she felt a surge of compassion—for him and for herself as well. There was such a gap between who we thought we *should* be and who we feared we actually were. And the truth, Nettie was beginning to realize, wasn't either of those false notions. The truth was somewhere in the middle. Like most people, Chase was neither as perfect as he'd hoped nor as puny as he feared. Maybe that's what happiness is, she thought, watching him silently wrestle with his "shoulds." It's making peace with that gap in the middle.

Sensing the coil of energy that was about to make Chase stand up and start pacing, Nettie placed a hand on his. She meant the touch to be a comfort, but a zing that felt like static electricity sizzled beneath her palm.

Unsure of whether Chase felt it, too, she tried to speak calmly. "Tell me what happened."

Searching her face, Chase nodded. "Colin was restless. I was busy, trying to concentrate, and it wasn't going well. So I told him to play in his room while I finished and when he said it was boring in his room, I said then play outside. I bought him a bike a couple of days ago, but I never figured..." Lips thinned, he shook his head, far angrier with himself than his son. "All of a sudden, the article started kicking in for me. I don't think I looked up for the next hour. I wasn't even thinking about him. It was like I completely forgot—" Chase smacked a fist into his palm.

"That is so normal. Yes," Nettie insisted when he shook his head. "Getting frustrated, telling him to play outside, even becoming lost in your work and losing track of the time—and certainly not being able to anticipate a child's next move—it's

all normal, Chase. You are not a bad parent.'' Then more quietly
she said, ''He wasn't running away from you, you know. He
wasn't leaving *you*.''

The hungry expression on Chase's face told her how much
he craved that very affirmation. A faint smile of gratitude curved
his lips, but he shook his head. ''Thanks. I appreciate the
thought. Really. And I hope this doesn't sound rude or conde-
scending, but I think this is one of those things you can't quite
understand until you've been there.'' He gave a brief laugh. ''I
certainly didn't. Being a parent...'' He wiped a hand down his
face. ''I've never felt this responsible for anything or anyone
else in my life. I can't even describe how it feels.''

It was the perfect opportunity to tell him everything. They
had more of a kinship than he had any idea of.

The moment came. The moment went. With another small
smile at her Chase stood.

''I'd better get in there,'' he said. ''I'll be picking him up in
Fargo if we leave him alone too long.''

Raising her brows in appreciation of the humor, Nettie stood
and followed him into the kitchen. The ping-pong match between tell and don't tell hadn't lasted long, but residual tension
curled in her stomach.

Still working on the sandwich and chips, Colin was again
immersed in one of Nettie's books. He didn't even glance up
when his father walked in.

''I've been looking for you,'' Chase opened the conversation
with a well-restrained neutral tone, but only by a hair. ''I thought
you were right outside the house, playing. That's where I expected you to be when I told you to play outside.'' He paused.
''When I realized you weren't there and that your bike was gone,
and I wasn't sure how long...''

Trying to be calm and rational was obviously too tall an order.
Colin still hadn't looked up, but Chase knelt by his son's chair.
In one swift movement, he gathered Colin in a hug as fierce as
it was unexpected.

''Don't do that again! Don't ever leave like that without telling me, okay?'' All the emotions Chase said he couldn't describe
filled his voice as he held onto a child who was truly a small
version of him. ''You scared the cra— You scared me,'' Chase
breathed. ''I thought something might have happened to you.''

It was clearly their first hug; the moment seemed awkward and new.

Colin sat stiffly at first, but the break in his father's voice weakened his childish resolve not to care what Chase thought. Held against a man's chest, tears sprang to his eyes and muffled his response. "Okay."

They remained there awhile and then released each other, Chase surreptitiously wiping his eyes before he pointed to the plate with Colin's half-eaten snack. "That's a good-looking sandwich," he commented, trying to normalize the moment. "Are you enjoying it?"

Colin nodded. "She makes good cookies, too." He picked up one half of the sandwich and took an enthusiastic bite.

"Cookies, too," Chase murmured. He turned to Nettie. "Thanks. It seems cooking is not one of my inherent skills. I tried spaghetti last night. Canned sauce—how hard can that be?" He wagged his head. "It tasted like…"

"Goop?" Nettie suggested when he had trouble finding an apt description. She lowered her voice as if slipping him the answer to a pop quiz. "You overcooked the pasta. Also, a little oil in the pot helps keep the noodles from sticking together."

Chase sent Colin a glare that was clearly playful. "Blabbermouth." The little boy grinned. "We wind up eating a lot of baloney. I may be stunting his growth."

"He seems tall for his age. You've probably got a couple of inches to play with." Nettie traded a smile with Chase and time hung, stealing her breath.

It was Chase who broke the moment. "We'd better get out of your hair. Thanks for everything." To his son, he instructed, "I'm sure Nettie has to get back to work. Tell her thank you for keeping you from starvation one more day and let's get going."

"But I still gotta eat." Colin protested, swinging his legs and pointing to the remaining half of his roast beef, turkey and cheese.

"Grab it. You can eat in the car."

"Sure you can." Fighting a wave of disappointment that they were leaving, Nettie wrapped Colin's sandwich in a napkin. "There," she said, handing it back to him, "that ought to keep the guts from leaking all over your father's Porsche. Nothing

sloppier than stacked sandwiches in sleek, shiny vehicles."
Colin giggled while Nettie segued from disappointment to a
buzzing sense of urgency. Would she see them again? When did
Chase plan to leave North Dakota? How inappropriate, stupid
or out-and-out unwelcome would an invitation to dinner be?

Before she had time to find out, Colin used his free hand to
awkwardly scoop up the books he'd been perusing.

"Can I take these to look at some more?" he asked Nettie.

"Sure. Absolutely. I want you to keep them. They're yours."

His eyes grew round with pleasure. "Thanks!" Colin breathed
with the kind of excitement she might have expected him to
reserve for a Harry Potter item. He swung around to look at his
father, awkwardly juggling the large books and his sandwich.
"She wrote these!" he trumpeted, sharing his awe. "And she
drew the pictures. By herself. I can draw by myself. But not as
good as this yet."

Relieving his son of the books, Chase examined them carefully before looking up at Nettie. He wore a somber, largely
unreadable expression. "Not only an artist," he said. "A children's book author." He read from the inside back flap.
"'Gifted author and illustrator Annette Ecklund...'" Arching a
brow, he questioned, "Pen name?"

His eyes narrowed and Nettie saw a hint of censure, heard a
note of betrayal in his otherwise painstakingly even voice.

"Kind of," she answered quietly, holding his gaze, knowing
the time for hiding in the shadows—professionally or personally—was coming to an end. "I use it as a pseudonym now.
Annette Ecklund was my married name."

Chapter Thirteen

Chase lowered the book he'd been reading to his lap and rubbed his eyes. He couldn't remember the last time he'd read a kid's book, or two, in one night. In one sitting. Three times each.

Behind his broad-backed chair, a standing lamp cast an amber glow in Nick's den. A grandfather clock logged the time, its heavy pendulum clicking with slow, even precision. Chase wanted to get up, open the glass door and rip the pendulum from its housing. He didn't need a reminder of the time. This night was crawling by like an arthritic turtle.

Not that the reading material on his lap wasn't entertaining. On the contrary. Annette *Ecklund's* illustrated stories easily held an adult's attention. And she certainly knew how to tickle a child's imagination.

She certainly knew children.

Flipping the top book over, Chase opened the back cover and looked again at the studio portrait above her bio. She was beautiful, as always, but thinner in the photo, with a smile that appeared less spontaneous than it did in person.

Who are you? He demanded of the photo for the umpteenth

time that evening, but it remained stubbornly mum. Like the woman.

He could no longer believe she'd rejected him because she didn't like kids. That excuse had been shot full of holes. And clearly there had been a time when she had wanted commitment in a relationship.

Closing the back cover, Chase laid both books on the table beside his chair and reached for the cognac he'd poured earlier. There was only a little left and he downed it in a gulp, welcoming the fire that burned a path down the back of his throat and into his stomach. Whom had Nettie Owens married? What man had inspired a commitment from her? And what had happened to end that commitment?

Chase's craving to know more—a lot more—about Nettie's marriage had been driving him crazy all evening. After leaving her today, he'd spent the rest of the afternoon trying once again to get acquainted with his son. They had, in fact, had a better time of it, with chatter flowing more easily than it had before. They'd gone marketing at a large grocery two towns over, and Chase had dropped any pretense that he knew what he was doing when it came to the feeding of a seven-year-old boy.

Interestingly, with his defenses lowered, he and Colin had become partners in the search for "bachelor food." Together they had decided that the cooking of chicken was a mystery but that steak was worth a shot. Potatoes were easier than rice, and when Chase saw the vast assortment of frozen spuds, he almost wept, choosing cheese and bacon-stuffed potatoes for himself and letting Colin dump bags of tater tots, french fries and hash browns into their basket. By the time he handed his plastic over to the cashier, he knew he was going to buy the biggest freezer he could find when they moved to his apartment in New York.

That is, if New York was where they wound up. At the moment, he wasn't a hundred percent sure. About anything.

In the past he had taken pains not to base his career choices on anybody's interests but his own. Part of him—sometimes a big part—longed to continue in that vein. It was easy.

But it wasn't the best thing for his son.

Checking the grandfather clock, Chase saw that it was almost 11:00 p.m. Colin had been in bed for two hours. Already, Chase understood that enforcing bedtime was as much an opportunity to exert a little parental power as it was a way to make sure that Colin got his rest. Unfortunately for Chase, the hours between 9:00 p.m. and 1:00 a.m., when he typically retired, stretched like miles of inhospitable desert.

Half sighing, half growling, he rose with his empty glass, deciding not to pour another. Prowling to the kitchen, working on the premise that a light snack might make him sleepy, he grabbed a box of the frozen toaster pastries Colin had suggested as a breakfast option—and which Chase had forgotten to freeze…oops. Well, they'd heat faster this way, he comforted himself, pulling two from the box.

Nick's ancient toaster took forever to spit anything out. Reaching into a bag of cream-filled wafer cookies that tasted like two pieces of cardboard stuck together with vanilla grout, Chase munched while he waited for his pastries, and then realized what he was doing. He was going to wind up in a diet group, learning how to make cottage cheese dip if he didn't work out what to do with his nights—soon.

Figuring at least one of the pastries had to be warm enough to eat, he reached into the toaster. He plucked gingerly, expecting the toaster to be reasonably warm, but apparently it worked faster and better than he'd originally assumed, and he burned his fingers.

"Ow!" Pulling back and shaking his stinging hand, Chase stuck the two fingers in his mouth to cool them off. Anger made him more determined. He reached in again.

"Ha, gotcha!" he crowed, extracting the rectangular Danish just as the doorbell rang. Startled, he whirled around, dropped his snack on the floor and swore.

Who would be ringing Nick's doorbell at this time of night? Taking an automatic step toward the living room before the late-night caller could awaken Colin, Chase brought his foot down directly on top of the fallen Danish. His bare foot. Hot raspberry filling squooshed out.

"Ow! Sonova—"

Hopping around, he swiped at the burning goo. A soft but insistent knock sounded at the door, and a split second later the toaster spit out the other pastry. Chase swore all the way around.

Walking as much as he could on the side of his abused foot, he limped to the door and yanked it open, eager to vent an anger

that had started long before he burned himself. He would begin
by giving a piece of his mind to the person who dared to ring
a doorbell at 11:00 p.m. out here in the middle of nowhereville,
where decent people had gone to bed by now!

Hand poised to knock, Nettie offered a tentative smile across
the threshold.

She looked as if she was arriving for afternoon tea, dressed
in the same low-necked lavender sundress she'd worn the day
they had first kissed. Fresh as a daisy—that's how she looked,
and it ticked him off royally, considering that she was one of
the big reasons he hadn't slept in several days…the main reason
he was angry…the reason he'd decided to scarf toaster pastries
at 11:00 p.m…the reason he'd stepped on hot raspberry goo.

She widened her smile in greeting.

Chase scowled harder.

He was so damn glad to see her. Too glad. He wanted to grab
her hand, pull her into the house, sit her down and talk to her
about everything. Absolutely everything.

Controlling himself, he leaned—lazily—against the doorjamb.
"It's late."

Undaunted by his rude excuse for a welcome, she nodded.
"It is."

Chase waited, refusing to give an inch, refusing to feel guilty
as her pretty fingers twined together.

"Are you stopping by for eggs?" he baited, sounding like a
snarly, sarcastic old coot. It took her only a moment to pick up
on the reference.

"No." She shook her head and then sighed. "Although I was
about to tell you that I was in the neighborhood, saw your lights
on and thought, 'well, might as well stop by.'" Nettie's straw-
berry-glossed lips inched into a sheepish smile that was bound
to make mincemeat of his self-control.

"But that wouldn't be the truth?"

"Only the part about seeing your lights on. I wouldn't have
knocked otherwise."

"Hm." The truth was he wanted her to knock anyway. He
wanted her to knock if it was 3:00 a.m. and there wasn't another
soul awake or a single light burning for twenty miles. He wanted
to tell her that if this were his home she wouldn't have to knock
at all. "So—"

"Well—"

They spoke at the same time. Chase tipped his head to her. "You first." If she was here for any reason other than to throw herself into his arms and demand passionate lovemaking, he'd save himself a lot of frustration by letting her speak before his hopes or his imagination got the best of him.

Lowering her head, Nettie performed a quick mental recap of why the heck she was here. What had compelled her to put on a dress and makeup and to squirt mousse in her hair when normally she'd be in her jammies by now, preparing to watch "The Late Show"?

This afternoon she'd told herself it simply wasn't right to stand by, doing nothing while a man tried as hard as Chase to be a good father. It was heartless, yes, a veritable sin not to lend a hand. But she could have wandered by tomorrow morning, say sometime after sunup, to drop off a meat loaf or offer advice about children's Tylenol versus Bayer.

Right, so that question again: Why was she here on Nick's doorstep, with Nick out of town, wearing a dress and makeup and a pair of Lilah's high-heeled sandals at 11:00 p.m., staring at a man who was obviously still furious with her because she hadn't had the guts to tell him the truth in the first place?

I'm here because I don't want him to be hurt and furious. I'm here because of the love and protectiveness and fear on his face when he hugged his son. I'm here because if he leaves and I never see him again except on cable news, I want him to know… I want him to know—

Still with her head lowered, Nettie closed her eyes, took a deep breath, opened them again and said, "I want you to know, I…" Something caught her eye. "I want… What's on your foot?"

"You want what's on my foot."

"I…no. What *is* on your foot? Is that blood?" She peered down, squinting in the dimly lit entry. "Oh, my goodness, it is. You're bleeding!"

Pushing him back, she crossed the threshold, half bent to look down.

"I'm not bleeding."

"Yes. Look!" She pointed. "You must have stepped on

something. Did you break a glass? Here, come sit down. We have to take care of it.''

She propelled him backward into the living room, and Chase found her sincere concern so welcome he decided to wait just a minute before telling her the "blood" was raspberry jam.

He plopped backward onto the couch, tracking, he was sure, raspberry goo all over Nick's carpet. But it was worth it. He'd call a carpet cleaner tomorrow, but right now it was worth any expense or extra effort to feel the first gentle touch of her fingers on his bare skin. Even if it was only his foot.

As she probed softly, Chase let his eyes drift closed for a moment. Just a moment. Did she have any idea how good it felt to be touched like this…ministered to…cared about? Did she know the simplest touch from her could make him feel weaker than a newborn colt…and more powerful than a tiger on the hunt?

He stifled a groan as Nettie lifted his foot, holding the heel and ankle with one hand while she explored in tentative dabs. There was a considerable pause. "This is unusually sticky," she said finally, referring to the red stains.

Reluctantly, Chase opened his eyes. She was a glorious picture, her long hair spilling over her beautiful bosom as she knelt on the floor by the sofa—holding his non-bleeding foot.

"It's not blood," he said.

She sat back. "What is it?"

"Raspberry…stuff. I think. I mean, I think it's raspberry. I haven't tasted it yet."

"You haven't tasted it. Yet. I see," she murmured, pondering his foot a moment. "Is this anything like drinking champagne out of a woman's slipper?"

Chase grinned. He couldn't help it. He couldn't stay angry and he couldn't remain aloof, not when every cell in his body was trying to convince him he was sixteen again.

Leaning forward, he said, "This is nothing like drinking champagne from a woman's slipper." Rearing back a bit, he regretfully eased his ankle out of her hand to rest it on his opposite knee. "What a mess. I'd better get cleaned up."

He started to rise, but Nettie touched his knee. "Why don't you sit tight for a minute? I'll get something so you can wipe this off before you walk on it."

On behalf of Nick's carpet, Chase accepted her offer. She disappeared briefly, returning quickly with a damp kitchen towel.

"Here we go," she said. He expected her to hand him the towel, but instead she knelt again and began to wipe off the stains as if the action were the most natural thing in the world, almost nonphysical.

It certainly didn't feel nonphysical, though, not to Chase. After her first automatic swipe, Nettie, too, seemed aware that no physical contact between them could be classified as platonic. Her swabs slowed to a crawl, which only made them more potent and torturous for Chase. He clamped a hand on her wrist.

She gazed up at him, eyes wide and unfocused. They were both breathing harder than a little cleanup could account for.

Chase swore he could feel her pulse beat beneath his fingers. He felt his own pulse throbbing in his temple and the side of his neck and wondered if she could see it. Playing it cool no longer seemed an option.

"Why are you here?" His tone sounded as ragged as the question was blunt.

This time Nettie didn't even think to prevaricate. "I was afraid I might never see you again." She wagged her head slowly, gaze linked with his. "I don't want that."

Chase firmed his grip on her wrist. With his other hand, he reached for her upper arm and pulled her onto the couch beside him. A hairbreadth of time passed while they looked at each other, but even that hairbreadth seemed like an eternity.

Chase let go of her wrist and they came together like spark and fuel.

Nettie felt the heat inside her, deep inside. Where there hadn't been an ember for years, now a conflagration roared to life. In the past, lovemaking, or merely the anticipation of it, had made her tremble, left her giddy and pleasantly weak. Not now. Chase kissed her, opening her mouth with his, no preliminaries, no tentative probe to inquire if she was willing. He knew. She knew. And the certainty of it filled her with strength.

As his arms curved around her and one of his hands cupped the back of her head, she wound her own arms around his neck, plowing fingers into the thick hair at his crown. Molten lava flowed through the center of her body, a long lusty river of it, when his tongue entered her mouth. She met it with her own and they dueled. Nettie surprised herself and Chase: In the sweet, cunning dance of desire, she didn't want to follow; she wanted to lead. Just like he did.

Her fingers tightened in his hair, holding him as she pulled back, deliberately depriving him of the mouth he wanted to control. She took his lower lip between her teeth and bit, tugging as she held his head still.

Chase groaned, and Nettie felt a surge of delight in her own power. Her control, though, however sweet, was short-lived. Chase wanted it back, and when he took it his groan turned into a growl.

He shook his head like a lion, loosing her grip. Getting off the couch, he reached for her, lifting her in one fluid motion. Nettie circled his neck with her arms, eyes on his face as he carried her into the downstairs guestroom and laid her on the bed.

He'd waited too long for this, waited all his adult life to feel this hunger, to feel a need that was more than just sexual but a damn sight stronger than "sweet."

Bracing himself with one hand beside her head, he smoothed a palm up over her stomach to her breasts. The thin material of her dress moved with his touch. Her eyes glowed as she watched him.

When he reached her breastbone, Chase paused then slid his hand to the right, cupping one full gorgeous globe. She shuddered. Her eyes half closed, she released a sound that started as a sigh and ended in a moan that seemed to rise up from her toes. A desire to possess, to brand and to keep roared through his veins. He searched Nettie's face, gauging her willingness, assessing her hunger, needing to know it if matched his own.

Methodically, wanting her to feel the anticipation as he did, Chase unlooped the small buttons down the front of her dress, pushing the material away until he revealed her bra. Purple. He smiled, but quickly forgot about the hue as he realized the iridescent material was sheer enough to afford him his first access to a bosom he'd only been able to admire until now.

Brushing his thumb across her nipple, he felt it spring eagerly to life. His groin tightened. Urged by her sharp intake of breath and his own need, he bent lower to put his mouth where his hand had just roamed. Biting gently, using his tongue, too, he captured her nipple with his teeth and s-l-o-w-l-y, exquisitely tugged.

Nettie's hands dove into his hair. She arched, writhing beneath him, lifting a leg in a mindless motion that made their thighs brush. The soft bare skin on the inside of her thigh brushed his rough jeans, and she moaned. Chase reached down to hold her leg where it was, halting all motion, because in another second he was going to reach between their bodies to touch her far more personally and that, he felt sure, would be the beginning of the rest of the night.

Rising up, barely able to resist the cry of complaint in the back of her throat, he divested himself of his shirt with quick jagged motions, never taking his eyes from her. If she wanted to stop, this would be the time. The last time. He tossed his shirt to the floor and looked at her in question.

Lips parted, eyes open, Nettie sat up beneath him. She scooted back a bit, giving herself more room to move and Chase felt a flare of crushing disappointment until he saw her hands go to the front of her dress. She unfastened the remaining buttons, watching him all the while, and slipped the dress slowly off her shoulders. Reaching around, she unhooked her bra, and Chase wondered if she could see his heart as it threatened to pound through the wall of his chest.

"Are you—" *Sure,* he started to ask, but she took his face between her hands and answered before he completed the question.

"Does it look like I'm sure?"

Chapter Fourteen

With her palms cupping his face, Nettie leaned back, drawing Chase down with her. She tried to lie still while he kissed her again, to mark and remember every sensation of his hands skimming her torso, eliciting a quiver she knew he could feel.

When his knuckles grazed her belly and his fingers slipped beneath the band of the scanty purple thong, a shudder wracked her. His touch was gentle yet bold and absolutely unabashed. With each stroke, he possessed her, shaking her free of the control she had struggled to maintain for so long. Nettie felt herself open, body and heart, for the first time in forever.

Chase pulled away from her mouth, moving lower to kiss her neck, her breasts, while his fingers explored deeper. He had reached the limit of his own restraint. She could tell by the increased intensity of his touch, by the way his muscles bunched and strained beneath her hands as she moved them along his back.

Moving purposefully, he rolled her flimsy undergarment away then lifted off her to shed his own clothing. When he sank down again, he joined their bodies, and the act was as welcome and gratifying as a summer rain. Tears built behind Nettie's eyes as pressure mounted inside her body. She gripped the arms that bracketed her, clutched Chase's back. Her breath came in pants then gasps that matched and mingled with his. She was standing on the edge of a cliff with a voice urging, "jump."

Her entire body surged upward as Chase's bore down. He growled her name—twice—as he arched over her, burying his face in her neck. The words were almost unintelligible, primal. He stoked the tension in her body, propelling her on until Nettie cried out with the pleasure of release and the incomparable satisfaction of feeling Chase above her, relinquishing his control, too, as he followed her over the edge.

For Nettie, the lingering moments after making love with Chase felt new and exhilarating and awkward and uncertain. She wished she could read his mind. And was grateful that she couldn't.

Reaching for the sheet they'd eventually crawled under, Nettie tucked it around her body and started to rise. Though Chase said Colin was a sound sleeper, she wasn't altogether reassured.

"I'd better go," she said.

Chase looked at her with calm eyes. Grabbing her wrist he pulled her back on to the bed and propped himself on one elbow. "You don't have to go."

"Yes, I—"

"No." Prying her hands from the sheet, he twined his fingers with hers and rested their clasped hands above her head. "I want you to have breakfast with me—with us—tomorrow morning. I want to watch the sun rise over those barley fields with you." There was something almost endearingly serious in his expression. "If you have regrets about tonight, tell me."

Extracting one of her hands from the love knot Chase had created, Nettie smoothed her thumb over the vertical line between his brows. "No regrets," she said, and her voice was strong.

No regrets. She'd made love to only one other man in her life, her husband, and that was after they'd married. She believed unequivocally that she never would marry again, but Lilah had been right when she'd insisted sex could never be casual for Nettie. This night with Chase, even if it never happened again, would be imprinted on her mind and heart the way the feel of his hands would be imprinted on her skin.

"I'll stay." She traced a tiny scar at the corner of his right eye. She hadn't noticed it before. There would be so many things to discover in a relationship that promised tomorrow…and tomorrow…. A pang of sadness tried to encroach on the quiet, sweet moment. Nettie pushed it away. "So what are you making for breakfast?"

Chase grinned. "Toaster pastries."

He gave her a long, lazy kiss. The fact that she was staying filled him with satisfaction. No, more than that—pleasure. The middle of the night was fast approaching, and she would be here. The sun would edge up from the eastern horizon. She'd be here. His son would come downstairs for breakfast, and the three of them would sit at the table together.

It was right. Chase's kiss increased in intensity. If he could transfer his conviction to her via a kiss, he would do it. If by making love to her from now till morning he could convince her they deserved a chance at forever, he wouldn't have let her get dressed in the first place.

Forever. Chase could hardly believe he was thinking about a future with one woman, the same woman, day after day, night after night. Lifting his head, he looked at Nettie while she stood with her eyes happily closed, smiling a little, swaying toward him. A big goofy grin claimed his face. Oh, yeah, he was thinking about it. A few days ago, she'd shut the door on any possibility of a relationship between them. Now it was a whole new ballgame. He had no idea how it would all play out, but that wasn't the point. The point was they deserved this chance.

"Colin won't be up until seven tomorrow. Really," he said when she regarded him doubtfully. "You can set your watch by him. We can sneak out of bed, watch the sun come up and have breakfast on the table before his eyes are all the way open."

"Okay," Nettie agreed, "but try not to make too much noise. I'd hate to have to explain what I'm doing here."

"I don't think I'm the one we have to worry about when it comes to decibels. You are—how should I put it?—surprisingly vocal."

"I—" Nettie frowned, then her eyes grew wide. "What do you mean? You mean during…? I am not!"

Chase laughed. "I'm not complaining." He growled in her ear. "I love it."

Goose bumps raced along her neck and arms. She wriggled in his embrace. "Just the same, I'm not...noisy."

He gave her an Eskimo kiss, the first he could recall ever bestowing. "Noisiest woman I've ever met."

Cheeks flushed beet red, she tried to scowl at him. "Am not."

Chase loved the way she did that—managed to look both virginally innocent and gorgeously wanton at the same time.

"Are too."

"Not."

Bending low, he grinned. "Let's find out."

The next morning Chase felt something so unfamiliar that at first he wasn't one hundred percent certain what it was.

Standing at the stove, wrapped in a ridiculous striped apron Nettie had tied around his waist, he listened to his son chatter about the books she had given him and about a movie called *Shrek* that he'd seen four times. Chase pushed bacon around an iron skillet with the spatula Nettie had placed in his hand and realized that what he felt was happiness. Pure and simple. He felt plainly, cleanly, deliriously happy.

"I hear a lot of talk over there, but I don't hear any offers of, 'hey, I'll set the table,' or 'let me pour the juice.'" He glanced over his shoulder to see Nettie confer with Colin.

"That must be a hint," she said dryly as she scraped back her chair.

"I can set the table. I know how." Colin scrambled down from his seat to gather an excessive number of utensils from the cutlery drawer.

Nettie pulled a carton of juice from the fridge and brought glasses and plates down from a shelf.

Chase grinned to himself. He couldn't care less if anyone helped this morning or if he stumbled through breakfast preparations himself, start to finish. He just wanted to be in on the conversation. Man, what a lovesick bufflehead he had turned out to be!

"What are you grinning about?" Nettie sidled up, peering into the skillet.

"Me? Nothin'." Chase bumped her shoulder discreetly with his. "You get along pretty well with my kid." He lowered his voice, working hard not to turn around and plant a kiss on the tip of her nose.

"Great kid," she said simply, snapping off a bit of bacon from the pile she had shown him how to drain on paper towels. Chase shook his head. Apparently bacon had to "drain." Who knew?

"This is going to be a mighty fine breakfast," he boasted, feeling, he decided, mighty proud of himself, too. The bacon looked good. The juice and waffles were no problem. This was the first meal he hadn't ruined.

Nettie pressed the lever on the toaster and followed Colin around the table, setting down plates. "Toaster waffles, toaster pastries," she said. "I detect a culinary theme."

Chase agreed without apology. "You got that right. And if some enterprising manufacturer comes up with the perfect toaster cheeseburger, I'll be stocking up on those, too."

Nettie laughed. "Remind me to give you a few easy cooking lessons sometime in the near future. Nick's freezer isn't that large."

Chase wanted to cheer at the prospect. More time together fit in perfectly with his plans.

Colin liked the idea, too, but on a different basis. "Can you teach him to make spaghetti," he asked with a child's guileless clarity, "the right way?"

Nettie's eyes sparkled at Chase. "Yeah, I think he could handle that."

"How about garlic bread?" Chase added. "The perfect Caesar dressing and…" He pondered. "Zabaglione for dessert?" The more time he spent with her, the better.

Nettie's eyes widened as she listened to his menu. "You want to learn to make zabaglione? You? The toaster pastry king?"

"Yeah, Miss Smarty." He looked at Colin. "I think a well-rounded menu is important."

"What's zab…ra…" Colin searched for the word.

"Zabaglione," Nettie supplied. "It's sort of an Italian pudding. You won't like it."

"I like pudding!" Colin insisted. He added extra forks to each place setting until he'd used all the utensils. "Can we have zab...zabra...that pudding stuff tonight?"

"It's not the kind of pudding you're used to." Nettie poured three glasses of juice, plus a glass of milk for Colin.

"We have to eat something, though," Chase reasoned, removing the last pieces of bacon from the skillet and bringing the plate to the table. He slid an arm around Nettie's waist as he moved behind her. Lingering there, he drew her gently against him, pleased when she relaxed. Reveling in the clean fresh scent of her and the softness of her hair, he nuzzled the pillow of curls, trying not to be too obvious about it. "I like this home-cooking stuff. How about teaching me to make an Italian dinner tonight? Plus chocolate pudding for Colin?"

While Colin waxed on about his love of chocolate pudding, Chase whispered into Nettie's ear, "I know it's a lot of work—probably the last thing you'd like to do with your afternoon—but I promise to make it worth your while. And tomorrow I'll find a baby-sitter so you and I can go into Minot for dinner. Maybe some dancing?"

Warm and soft, Chase's breath made Nettie tingle. His suggestion made her shiver. He was planning their tomorrow as if they were an average couple. She looked at Colin, at the table they had set, at the food. It all looked so normal; it all felt so right.

When she failed to respond verbally, Chase leaned around to look in her face. "Are you free tomorrow?" he asked, sounding less certain now.

Nettie smiled. She liked that, too.

"No, I'm not free," she murmured, exercising a feminine coyness she'd never really tested before. Turning in Chase's arms, she leaned forward till their noses were almost touching and added, "If I'm spending half the evening in the kitchen teaching you how to cook, it's going to cost you."

They were only halfway through breakfast when the phone rang.

Colin had insisted that he could not eat a waffle unless every "ditch" was filled with syrup, and his father seemed mystified by the universal stickiness that ensued. No part of breakfast, the table itself or Colin, it seemed, was currently maple syrup free.

The phone rang a second time.

"Telephone!" Colin announced loudly, clearly convinced he was the only one in the room who possessed ears. "Someone's gotta get it."

"Yeah, you stay where you are and eat." Chase pointed to his son's plate. "And don't touch anything except the food on your plate and your own fork until I get back."

Nettie grinned. Chase was definitely getting a crash course in parenthood. Breakfast lesson number one: The time it takes a child to make a mess of his meal is only a fraction of the time it will take him to eat it.

Sipping her juice, Nettie kept an eye on Colin while Chase picked up the kitchen extension. Colin asked her if there were lizards in North Dakota, then proceeded to tell her he knew how to make a good "lizard house" and asked if she had any shoe-boxes he could "borrow."

Dividing her attention between answering the seven-year-old's questions and urging him to eat some of his waffle before his father got off the phone, Nettie was vaguely aware that Chase had taken advantage of the long phone cord to pull the receiver through the kitchen door and into the hallway as he spoke.

When he returned to the table some time later, Nettie saw that his mood had changed considerably. She kept up the dialogue with Colin, but Chase seemed unwilling or unable to reenter the conversation. After several long minutes, Nettie rose, ushered Colin into the bathroom to get him started on the process of cleaning up and then rejoined Chase.

"What's wrong?" she asked without preamble, approaching him in concern. Having shuttled Colin's plate to the sink, Chase now leaned heavily on the counter, looking very much as though he was in pain.

He glanced around.

"In the bathroom, cleaning up," Nettie said, responding in unconscious shorthand to the question in Chase's eyes. "There was syrup on his clothes, so I told him to change. It should take awhile." Without giving it any thought, she placed a comforting hand on his back. "What's going on?"

Chase shook his head, keeping his palms braced on the sink

as if he required the support to remain upright. "That was my lawyer on the phone." His voice was low and unsteady. "When I went to Florida to get Colin, there were no other known relatives. Now—" He stopped, turning to scan the kitchen, needing to make sure once again that Colin was not within earshot. "Julia's parents have been located."

"Julia was Colin's mother?"

Chase nodded. "Her parents live in England. Julia was estranged from them. Her choice, apparently, not theirs. They say she wrote them a letter a couple months before she was killed, indicating that she wanted to reconcile and..." Chase shook his head, obviously shell-shocked by the pieces of information he'd been given. "They want Colin. They want custody."

Chase faced her. He looked like a man who'd been sucker punched—disoriented, hurt and angry all at once.

Nettie felt a rush of blood to her head. "But how can they ask such a thing? Don't they know he's with you?"

Chase emitted a harsh laugh. "The news left them unimpressed. Given the fact that I didn't even know about Colin for the first seven years of his life, they have grave doubts their grandson's well-being will be served under my care."

Clearly parroting his lawyer, Chase's words filled Nettie with indignation. How unfair! How...*how dare they?* They hadn't even seen Chase with Colin; they didn't know how much he loved his son already.

A fierce desire to protect this man, this come-lately father who didn't know enough to take the syrup bottle off the table after it had been poured, who'd had no idea how to fry bacon, and who was often clearly uncertain how to talk to his son...but who so desperately wanted to try...rose inside Nettie with the strength of a thousand armed troops.

"Where have *they* been?" she demanded. "How well do they know Colin? Have they ever met him?"

"I don't know."

"Well, then they can't possibly have all the power here. I can't imagine they'd even get to court."

"I don't know," Chase repeated. "My lawyer wants me to call him back as soon as possible."

They heard Colin running from his room upstairs. Nettie saw additional concern cross Chase's face and hastened to reassure him. "I'll take him with me. Lilah's at home. Between the two of us, we'll keep him occupied until you can get there." Moving in close, she rubbed his chest and shoulder.

Capturing her hand, Chase pressed a kiss into the palm. His eyes communicated his gratitude.

When Colin clattered into the kitchen, Nettie gave Chase a moment to compose himself. She forced a bright smile that relaxed into something more genuine when she saw Colin's Don't Sweat the Small Stuff...And I'm Small Stuff T-shirt. "Hey, kiddo. How'd you like to come over to my place and help me draw a picture for my next book?"

Colin proved to be a bit more careful with paint than he was with a syrup bottle, but not much. Nettie hoped his T-shirt was not new, given that yellow ochre, jade and crimson decorated its surface in a variety of blops, smudges and stripes.

Leaving the paint-happy boy ensconced in her studio, Nettie went downstairs, where Lilah waited for her in the living room. Lounging in the wingback chair, bare pedicured feet propped on the coffee table, the inherently glamorous blonde held a tall glass of lemonade in her hand. There was another waiting on the end table for Nettie.

"Thanks." Nettie grabbed the icy tumbler and plopped onto the couch. "I must be out of shape. Keeping up with a seven-year-old has me worn out already and it's barely noon." She pressed the glass against her cheek.

"Is that what wore you out?" Lilah wriggled her toes. "And here I thought lack of sleep was the culprit." Innuendo curled her lips as she sipped her lemonade.

"Yeah, you're funny," Nettie applauded dryly. "Did Sara say anything when I wasn't here this morning?"

"She doesn't know. I closed your bedroom door as soon as I realized you were gone." Lilah wagged a shaming finger. "Then I told her you had a headache and had decided to sleep in."

Expelling a sigh of relief, Nettie toasted her sister in thanks. "I don't feel like dodging the Sara Owens third degree today."

"I don't blame you. She used to grill me if I came home five minutes after curfew when we were in high school. And she's only two years older! Drove me crazy.'' Lilah shook her head. ''So, Nettie-Belle, tell me one thing— What are his intentions?'' Slyly, she grinned. '''Cause I know where you were and who you were with.''

Setting her lemonade on the side table, Nettie covered her face with her hands, pounded her feet on the floor as if she were running in place and squealed. ''Oh, Lilah! It was so, so...not me!'' She lowered her hands and met her sister's affectionate smile. ''I think I seduced him,'' she whispered.

Lilah hooted with laughter. Nettie giggled, too. ''We made breakfast together this morning and it wasn't awkward at all. It was...''

''What?''

Right. It...just...felt....right. But she didn't want to say that. No, didn't even want to think it. It was too much, too soon, too scary. Adages popped into mind.

What goes up must come down....

Every back has a front....

The bigger they are, the harder they fall....

The more right something feels, the more wrong it can go.... Okay, so that last one was hers, but the point remained the same: Keep your expectations simple. Keep plans to a minimum. So, instead of saying this morning had felt ''right'' or ''wonderful'' or, heaven forbid, ''perfect,'' Nettie murmured, ''Nice. Yeah, it was nice.'' An understatement, to be sure.

''And now you have Colin here.'' Lilah watched her sister with loving eyes. ''How does that feel, Nettie-Belle?''

''Not as hard as I thought it would be.'' The truth came as more of a surprise to Nettie than to her sister. ''I thought I'd be sad, that it would be too painful to have a child here. Or that I'd feel guilty, like I was somehow betraying...'' She took a breath. ''Tucker. And Brian.'' Smiling through a pang of sadness that hit her dully in the center of her chest, she shook her head. ''Silly.''

''No,'' Lilah said softly. ''Not at all. So, tell me. Why did you bring Colin here by yourself? Where's Chase?''

Briefly, Nettie explained what she knew about the phone call and Chase's need to converse with his lawyer without Colin around to overhear.

Lilah pursed her lips. "So he might find himself in the middle of a custody battle?"

"I don't know." Frowning, Nettie shook her head. "I can't imagine it going that far. When you watch Chase and Colin together, it's so easy to see they're building a relationship. Who would stand in the way of that?"

"Plenty of people, Nettie-Belle. Plenty of people." Lilah's expression flowed from interest to concern. "Oh, sweetie, you know I want you to get out into the world and live again. But I thought you'd go for the pleasure and shelve the pain for awhile."

"I am." When Lilah looked doubtful, Nettie persisted, "Truly. First of all, Chase is not going to lose that child. I know it. But he does have to deal with this, see his lawyer, rearrange his life to include a little boy." She smoothed her palms over the jeans she'd donned upon arriving home. "Any time now he's going to knock on that door and tell me he's booked their flight home to New York." With an admirably level gaze, she maintained, "I'm ready for that. I was ready for it before he got the phone call this morning. That's why I was able to stay with him last night."

"I don't know if I like the sound of that. I wonder if *he'd* like the sound of that."

Amazingly, Nettie found she was able to laugh and that fact encouraged her. She was going to be okay when Chase said good-bye. She really was. "He's going to like the sound of that just fine. Believe me. He's got more than enough on his plate as it is. He doesn't need a woman clinging to his arm."

"Mm."

Lilah looked like she had more to say, but Colin chose that moment to holler from upstairs. "Nettie!" He clambered down the staircase, skidding to a breathless stop when he saw her in the living room.

There was even more paint on him now.

"What is it?" She rose immediately.

"Um, you know that thing you put the picture on? That folding thing?"

"The easel? Yes."

"Well, um, it sorta fell over, sorta."

"It did?" Relieved there was no real emergency, she asked, "What happened to the canvas?"

"Is that the picture?"

Nettie nodded.

Colin looked worried. "It landed on the ground."

While Lilah covered a smile, Nettie had a moment of gratitude for watercolors.

"Okay. Let's go upstairs and see if we can salvage the picture."

As it turned out, repairing the painting didn't take as much effort as cleaning Colin up for the second time that day. While Nettie tossed his T-shirt into the washing machine, Lilah took a phone call from Chase. He asked her to pass along the message that he had travel arrangements to make but would be over shortly.

Given the message, Nettie found her body responding almost before her mind. With a fluttering heart she realized, *This is it. This is goodbye.*

He's going to tell me they have to leave for New York immediately. Before we make spaghetti. They'll start their life together as a family, and I...

Swallowing heavily, she told herself to buck up. This was simple. She would begin again, too. That's what people did every day, anyway, wasn't it? Especially after losing someone. You woke up, you made the choice to begin again. Every day.

On a deep breath, Nettie looked at Colin as he gobbled more of her homemade cookies and peppered her with questions like, "How come when you put the green in the red it turns brown?"

It had been a fun morning. And that, Nettie told herself, was enough.

Chase arrived while Colin's T-shirt was still tumbling in the dryer. Appearing weary but calm, he greeted Nettie by drawing her into his arms for a long hug. Pulling back, he turned the embrace into a soul-satisfying kiss.

"I needed that," he growled low in her ear. His warm breath sent showers of goose bumps racing down her neck and arms.

He told Lilah he was making travel plans, Nettie reminded herself as soon as she could form a coherent thought.

"Colin's with Lilah," she said. Pull out of his arms now...atta girl...turn away...keep talking... "They're in the backyard, collecting earth in buckets.'' She began edging toward the kitchen. ''Want some coffee? I just a made a pot.''

''Sure.'' He followed her. ''Dare I ask what they're planning to do with this 'earth'?''

''Lilah told him she thought they could make a million dollars by making North Dakota mud packs for rich women in Beverly Hills.''

''I see. So my son shows a precocious entrepreneurial spirit?''

''Mm, mostly I think he liked the idea of digging in dirt.''

''Ah.'' Chase watched her while she poured the coffee, set out milk and sugar and pulled cookies from a ceramic jar in the shape of a merry pig. When she handed him the plate of snacks, he grinned, first at it and then at her.

''What?'' Her forehead creased. ''Is something wrong?''

''No, no. I was just trying to remember the last time a woman handed me a plate of cookies.''

''And?''

''And I can't remember.''

Nettie made a face. ''Wonderful. In an ocean of exotic memories, someday you'll look back and think of me as Betty Crocker.''

''You bet,'' he agreed. Plucking a cookie from the plate, he took a bite, gave her a wink and let his gaze wander slowly down her body. ''Covered in chocolate, frilly little apron, naked underneath…''

Nettie snapped a dishtowel in his direction, but his reply pleased her enormously. ''Shame on you! C'mon, let's go into the living room. I want to know what your lawyer said.'' *Very good!* Her inner coach commended her efforts to remember what was about to transpire here. *Stay on track… simply ignore that nasty woosh of longing to rip his clothes off…or yours….*

Steeling herself to appear poised, sophisticated and serene throughout his account of the call even—no, especially—when he got to the part about heading back to New York, Nettie perched on the edge of the couch and waited for him to begin.

Chase leaned back against the cushions, took a sip of the very strong coffee and sat a moment, simply collecting his thoughts. ''What a day.'' Setting his mug on the table, he opened an arm in Nettie's direction. ''Hey, come here.'' He tilted his head and motioned for her to snuggle against him.

Danger...danger... Do not go there. She stared hungrily at the side of his torso and the warm, perfectly shaped alcove of his underarm.

We-e-e-ll, would it hurt, really, to scoot in for just a moment? There's no harm, she reasoned, *in being comfortable while he says goodbye.*

She scooched over on the sofa, but remained committed—absolutely—to holding her body in a rigid, unyielding line so there would be no mistake about what was going on here: She might be getting physically close, but she was distancing herself emotionally.

Chase folded his arm around her. He brought his other arm up to gather her into what might have been interpreted—by somebody else—as a circle of love and protection.

"There," he murmured, his muscles softening as he sighed manfully. "I've been wanting to do this all day."

"Me—" Catching herself in the nick of time, Nettie mumbled, "Um, so what did your lawyer say?"

Chase released another sigh, this one rough and weary. "He said things I'd like to forget about until Colin is eighteen. Unfortunately burying my head in the sand is not an option if I want to keep my son."

"And you do."

He reared back to look at her. "I like the way you say that. Like it's a given. My lawyer put it somewhat differently. He said, 'Be sure that raising this boy is what you want, because if this goes to court, you're in for the fight of your life.'"

"But why? I still can't fathom how Colin's grandparents can threaten your custody."

"Because of me. Because of things I've done. And said." He settled back against the couch again, and Nettie felt the resonance of his voice as she leaned against his chest. He spoke slowly, carefully. "I've never felt any particular pride in the way I've lived my life up to now. But I can't say I've had any discomfort with it, either. I guess I've lived like your classic bachelor. The only rules I followed were mine."

"Well, you were a bachelor. You are."

Chase gave a wry grunt. "Maybe I should rephrase it more accurately. I lived like a bachelor who's been on the cover of

Star magazine. There are plenty of opportunities for socializing when you're regarded as a celebrity."

"I know." Toying with the hairs on the back of his wrist, Nettie confessed, "I got on the Internet one night and looked you up. You've dated *way* too many models." She gave a couple of hairs a firm tweak. "Weren't you afraid of becoming a cliché?"

She posed the question facetiously, but Chase groaned. "Yes," he said emphatically. "Hell yes, I've dated way too many women, period." He tightened his hold on her. "Are you losing respect for me?"

"Mm, gettin' there." She rubbed the hairs she'd pulled. Then more seriously she added, "If the women were willing, who can fault you?" Nettie was thinking of herself, no question. To a rag magazine like *Star* she supposed she'd be considered just another one of Chase Reynolds's women. The thought poked a finger of jealousy right in her sternum. Jealousy and possessiveness. She didn't even want to explore that and was relieved when Chase claimed her attention.

"A court can fault me," he answered her question and Nettie heard the frown in his voice. "Grandparents can fault me. Social services—"

"Now wait a minute. Aren't you being overly harsh? You didn't even suspect you were a father until a few weeks ago."

There was a pause. "Before you let me off the hook, there's more you need to know. I never wanted kids, Nettie." Rather than shifting to see her better, Chase stayed where he was and Nettie understood it was easier for him to get this out without looking at her. "That's an understatement. Any lawyer with the competence of Daffy Duck will be able to wallpaper the courthouse with evidence of my position on commitment. And for awhile there, I was pretty vocal about being opposed to fatherhood."

"All right, I understand your concern. Maybe I can even understand Colin's grandparents' concern—because they don't know you. But judges are mandated to be impartial. A couple of gossipy articles from your past can't mean that much."

"Maybe not," he agreed. "But one really stupid comment I made a few weeks ago could do us in."

Chase sounded sick with remorse. This time Nettie wriggled

out of his arms to face him. He looked at her, but his eyes held a faraway, unhappy expression. She waited.

Scraping a hand through his hair, he shook his head, then swore beneath his breath, damning himself.

"Julia's boyfriend in Florida was the first person to contact me about Colin. When he told me Julia had a son who was seven and that I was the father, I said—" Chase closed his eyes, wincing at the memory. "I said, 'Bullshit. The kid isn't mine.'"

When he reopened his eyes, he looked like a condemned man so filled with guilt he would refuse his own pardon. Nettie's heart reached out to him. Whatever had made him reject the idea of fatherhood so vehemently, clearly a lot had changed in a few weeks. "Are you afraid Julia's boyfriend will be a witness for her parents?"

"Their lawyer has already spoken to him. I don't think he cares one way or the other who gets custody as long as it's not him. But if he's subpoenaed, it won't be good for us."

"You and Colin have so much to handle right now. Becoming a family is challenging enough without all this hanging over you."

"I just don't want Colin to suffer because his father shot off his stupid mouth." Restless, Chase stood and paced the room. "I came to North Dakota to elude the press as long as I could, but my lawyer tells me the story broke in England today, and it's bound to hit a few papers in the states. That means photographers and pictures of Colin." He swore again, but more mildly. "It's weird, all these feelings I've never had before. I just want to protect him, Nettie. I want to make life...*everything*...better for him, not worse."

The impulse to rush to Chase, to hold and reassure him was so strong Nettie almost gave in. Exerting all her willpower, she stayed where she was. "Lilah said you mentioned something about travel plans. I imagine you'll be leaving..." Traitorously, her voice wobbled. "Leaving soon," she said. To prove she was fine, perfectly fine, with whatever he had to do, she added, "It makes sense. School will be starting in a little while. You'll have to register Colin, and I'm sure you want to be near your lawyer. And your family. We haven't even talked about your family and how they feel about Colin. They must be so excited. When..." Her hands were clutched so tightly on her lap, she feared she might cut off the circulation to her wrists. "When do you leave?"

Standing at the fireplace, Chase looked at her quizzically. "I'm not leaving. I made travel plans for my lawyer, Nelson, to come out. Besides, Colin's grandparents want to meet him, and I'd rather have that happen here than in New York. For the time being, we're staying put. We're staying in North Dakota."

Chapter Fifteen

The relief was dizzying.

Why bother to deny it, Nettie thought as the tension she hadn't even realized she was carrying began to drain from her neck and shoulders. The news that Chase was staying—even temporarily—acted on her like a good antihistamine: all at once she could breathe again.

Outwardly, she strove to present a calm and serene front while she considered the best response. "Gee, that's nice," "Anything I can do to help?" and "North Dakota's glad to have you" all exemplified the poise she wanted to possess.

Shouting "Thank You, God...Thank You, God...Thank You, God!" while throwing her arms around Chase's neck would be more genuine.

In the end, she compromised, walking to him as calmly as she could and circling his waist in a gentle hug while the giddy smile inside her bubbled to the surface. "I'm glad."

Tension drained from him, too, as he hugged her back, resting his cheek on the top of her head.

In the kitchen, the back door opened and closed. Sneakered feet raced noisily across linoleum and over the hardwood, skidding to a stop in the living room. More languidly, feet shod in sandals clicked across the floor.

Lilah halted next to Colin and, like him, stared at the scene in front of the fireplace. "If this were Christmas, I'd turn you into a postcard."

Her wry comment pulled the couple slightly apart. Still with their arms around each other's waists, they glanced over. Nettie was flushed and happy.

"Told you," Colin said in a stage whisper to his new partner in dirt digging. "They kept huggin' like that while I was trying to eat breakfast."

Lilah nodded. "Speaking as a professional actor, I can tell you this doesn't look a bit like 'good-bye.'"

Chase's lawyer, Nelson Dale, was booked on a flight from New York to Minot for the following week. In the meantime Chase accepted Nick's offer to move into the two-bedroom cottage that sat on its own patch of fallow land about a half mile from the barley fields. Nick's father had built the stone-and-stucco bungalow for his second wife—Nick's beloved stepmother, Bea—who had moved to North Dakota from the countryside of England. It was the house Nettie had told him about.

"The enchanted cottage," Chase muttered darkly as he and Nettie stood outside, assessing the work they needed to do. Warned by Nick that the place had been neglected for years, Chase had requested Nettie's expertise in returning it to a state of hominess, but he hadn't expected quite so much disrepair.

"Looks more like the house on haunted hill," he grumbled, hands resting on his hips as he wondered if renting a place in town might be a better option. His lawyer had stressed the importance of presenting a picture of home and hearth.

Chase shook his head. If this place had a hearth, he seriously doubted their ability to locate it. Weeds and a tangled vine that should have been eulogized a long time ago shrouded the exterior of the cottage. A thick crust of dirt covered the windowpanes. Chase could imagine the condition of the interior...but wasn't sure he wanted to.

"If I'd known it looked like this, I never would have asked you to help," he told Nettie, who was already attempting to peer through the grime encasing the window. Some hot date he'd turned out to be.

Swinging around from her preliminary fact-finding mission, she faced him with shining eyes.

Dazed, he surmised. Probably in shock. Wants to tell me to stuff it, but isn't quite certain how. "Nick's description of the place leaves a lot to be desired."

Nettie nodded in agreement. "I don't think he ever appreciated it the way we girls did." She made a sweeping gesture with her hand. "Isn't it wonderful?"

Chase simply stood there, wondering if he heard her correctly. "'Scuse me?"

She stepped off the porch to examine the perimeter. "When Bea was alive she kept an English garden. No one knew how she could nurture so many gorgeous flowers with our harsh weather. The ladies at church suspected she imported dirt from England!" Rubbing her palms with enthusiasm, she urged, "Let's go in."

"You want to see the inside?" he asked incredulously. "After lunch? If the mess is bigger inside than out, I, for one, am in danger of tossing my cookies."

"Don't be silly," Nettie laughed. "This is a great challenge! Wait'll you see the fireplace, you'll love it. This sweet old girl deserves to be returned to her former glory."

Chase withheld comment on her definition of "glory" and produced the key Nick kept on a hook in his kitchen. "I bet he hasn't tried this key in years," he said as he made his first attempt at wriggling it into the lock.

"Probably not. Nick never came here much, anyway. It was Bea's haven. She shared it with the women in town and with us girls. We had the best sleepovers here. I loved it."

"Sleepovers," Chase mused. Good idea. He glanced at the eager woman beside him. If she promised to sleep over he'd work from sunup to sunup making the cottage presentable.

Would he have chosen to remain in North Dakota if not for Nettie? Doubtful. Very doubtful.

His lawyer had advised him to transform his image. A white-carpeted, chrome-and-leather-trimmed apartment in Manhattan with neighbors whose names he doubted he'd ever known, did not seem like a route to that goal. At this point, Chase had no

idea where he and Colin would wind up permanently, though
he knew he could have chosen someplace less rural for their
temporary abode. Connecticut, for instance, or upstate New
York. But then they would have been alone.

He looked again at Nettie and found himself thinking the word
home.

Why fight it? A smile pushed his cheeks into grinning-fool
mode as he opened the rough-hewn door and watched her rush
inside, as thrilled with the dark, dust-laden interior as if he'd
just opened the door to Buckingham Palace.

Chase filled his lungs with the stale, musty air and echoed her
sigh. Yep, he'd toil from sunup to sunup. While visions of sleepovers danced in his head....

Three days later, the "enchanted cottage" was...

"Cute," Chase observed, kicking back on the living-room
sofa, whose overstuffed cushions and garden floral upholstery
managed to seem stylish twenty years after their purchase.

"Cute?" Nettie echoed indignantly. Arranging knickknacks
on the mantel, shifting their positions to satisfy herself, she
grumbled, "Three days of slave labor and the best he can do is
'cute.'"

Chase gladly took the bait, hoisting his tired bones from the
couch to come up behind her, and Nettie squealed when he
grabbed her around the waist, tipping her back into a dramatic
dip.

"Slave labor," Chase chided. "Is that what you call yesterday?"

"Yesterday?"

"Whisking the mattress in the master bedroom?"

Nettie's eyes darkened. He referred, of course, to what had
taken place after the mattress whisking...when they were supposed to have been putting linens on the bed and wound up in
it, instead. Her lips parted unconsciously as she remembered the
moment, and he almost carried her into the bedroom for an
instant replay. Although, he assured himself, feeling his body
respond faithfully, it wouldn't be so "instant."

"How," Nettie asked insouciantly, "does the, um, 'mattress
whisking' negate my allegation of slave labor?"

"You were richly rewarded," Chase growled low in her ear.

Slowly, deliberately she wagged her head. "*You* were richly rewarded."

"Sassy." He grinned, taking advantage of her position to rain kisses down her neck. "Sassy and sooo right...."

Some time later, they resurfaced to begin dinner preparations in the newly cleaned brick and copper kitchen. Chase suggested that dinner out would be a fitting reward for all their hard work, but Nettie insisted on christening the cottage with a simple home-cooked meal around the carved oak dining table. She'd barely won the argument before the doorbell rang.

Lilah, with Colin in tow, stood on the porch, a huge picnic basket in her hands. "There's more in the car," she tossed over her shoulder at Chase as she breezed by. "Place looks spiffy," she added on her way to the kitchen.

"Yeah. Spiffy." Colin trotted happily after his babysitter, lugging a small Igloo ice chest. He wore, Chase noticed, a brand-new pair of sunglasses—like Lilah—and had mousse in his hair.

Lilah had been a great help the past few days, sometimes pitching in to set the house aright, sometimes baby-sitting Colin when it was clear the child needed a break from housecleaning. So if she had his son looking like a pint-sized Hollywood producer, oh well. What was the harm?

Agreeably, Chase went to the car, the same huge clunker Nettie drove, and hefted a box filled with covered baking dishes from the open tailgate. "Whoa! What the heck..."

How much food had she brought? He wondered, taking several steps backward under its weight.

"Unless you're psychic," he said to Lilah upon entering the kitchen, "something tells me this is not an impromptu home-cooked meal." He set the box on the small center island, pulled out a large slow cooker and lifted the lid to inhale the savory aroma of barbecued beef. "You can cook," he complimented.

"An Owens trait." She shrugged to suggest it was really no big deal.

"What about Sara? Can she cook, too?" Somehow, he couldn't fathom it.

"No. But I can buy." As if on cue, the sheriff of Kalamoose strolled into the kitchen with a stack of pink boxes.

"Ooh, baby! What kind did you get?" Lilah hurried over to peek inside.

"I dunno. Whatever Ernie had. It's all good."

"Hi, Sara! I've been practicing my quick draw." Colin raced toward the uniformed woman. Miming a holster and pistol, he "drew" three times in quick succession.

Chase glanced at Nettie, who was smiling at his son and her sisters while she unpacked their dinner. "Did you bring the drinks? Oh, good!" From the picnic basket, she withdrew four bottles, two of champagne and two of sparkling cider.

Chase felt a warm glow deep in his chest as realization dawned. Nettie had set up a kind of housewarming. Stowing the drinks in the refrigerator for the time being, she turned with a satisfied look in his direction. The cottage could have fallen down at that point, and he wouldn't have been able to look away.

"Did you do potato and pasta salad?" Sara asked, while she dangled her handcuffs in front of Colin.

"Yes." Lilah answered with her head in a pie box. "Peach! Oh, Ernie, you doll, you!"

"How about baked beans?"

"Of course."

"Hey, Sara, can I handcuff myself to the doorknob?"

"Sure, squirt. I'll come unlock you in a minute."

Conversation eddied around them. Chase and Nettie continued to stare at each other. "Thank you," he mouthed.

"You're welcome." Her smile broadened—just for him—and Chase knew in that moment he could have said much more than "Thank you." And meant it.

Four days later, Nelson Dale arrived to brief Chase on what was now officially his custody case, and Chase began to understand for the first time in his life what "family" felt like.

It wasn't silence, polite or contentious, while silverware clinked on bone china and classical music underscored an abundance of good taste.

It wasn't white carpets, empty apartments, travel that seemed never-ending.

And it wasn't muscling through every challenge in life totally on one's own because to ask for help might be perceived as weak by the people who were supposed to love you.

No.

"Family" was laughter, raucous and tolerant, when your son chose dinnertime to practice his new skill—voluntary belching.

Family was braided rugs that hid dirt, homes with too many people and not enough privacy, and towns where everyone knew your name and too much of your business.

Most of all, he realized that family was, indeed, not asking for help…because by the time you got around to it, help had already arrived.

The news that Colin's grandparents had already decided to pursue custody hit everyone like a thunderbolt. Nelson Dale felt terrible bearing the bad tidings. He closeted himself with Chase for several hours at the cottage while Nettie took Colin for the day.

"You seem…I don't know…content here," Nelson commented, looking comfortable in a leather wingback. "Present circumstances aside."

The two men were holed up in the "library," a small room lined with recessed bookshelves and appointed in rich leather and dark wood. Nelson, a small, wiry fellow with glasses and a hairline more recessed than the bookshelves, eyed his client and friend over the rim of his coffee mug. "If I didn't know better, I could almost believe you planned to stay."

"In Kalamoose?" Distracted, Chase brushed the notion aside without giving it any consideration. "What would I do here?"

"Mmm. That is a point, of course. But still, it's too bad."

"What? Why?" Chase gave Nelson more of his attention. He'd known Nelson since college, had retained him as a lawyer for the past eight years and in all that time, whether they met in a business or social setting, Chase had never seen his friend relax. Not that Chase had ever really noticed before, but clearly the man was wired for city living. Even today, where no one knew him and his only client was wearing jeans, Nelson wore a suit and tie, gold cufflinks and a pocket watch. A pocket watch, for crying out loud. "Since when have you appreciated rural life?"

"Since you became the defendant in a custody suit. When the court assigns a social worker to your case, you could be treated to a drop-in visit.'' He scanned the room behind his glasses. ''This place makes a persuasive presentation. As does your friend.''

''Nettie?'' Nelson nodded and Chase frowned. He didn't like hearing his ''friend'' or his home—even if it was only his borrowed, temporary home—described like something from a movie set. He didn't like feeling compelled to orchestrate his life; he just wanted to live it. Most of all, he detested and resented like hell the hovering sense of fear that he could lose his son.

''I'm not a custody attorney,'' Nelson said, concern puckering his brow.

''You've told me.''

''Yes, but you don't seem to be listening. Soon—very soon— you will have to engage an attorney who specializes. In the meantime,'' he raced on when Chase opened his mouth to swear (he'd been doing a lot of that this morning), ''I'm going to advise you the way I believe a custody attorney would. You have somehow placed yourself in the midst of a lifestyle that bears no resemblance whatsoever to the life you formerly led. In your present situation this is a very good thing. It could, however, also be construed as a ploy to appease the courts. Nothing more than a well-constructed fiction. Needless to say, that would not be good.''

''Yes, it is needless to say,'' Chase growled—rudely, given the fact that Nelson had come here to help. He pinched the bridge of his nose. ''So what's your point?''

''Your past—distant and more recent—does not speak well of your commitment to fatherhood. Your lifestyle does not recommend itself to the nurturing of a small child, nor do these facts compel one to believe that you will be deeply committed to retain your current level of domesticity.''

''What the bloody hell is your point, Nelson?''

Reaching over to a pad of paper on the small table between them, Nelson scribbled ''discuss temper management.'' Chase sighed.

Setting the pencil down, Nelson looked his client calmly in the eye. ''My point is I can think of one thing that might solve all your problems.''

Chase waited a beat while Nelson sipped his coffee, a small

smile playing about his lips and a mischievous glint in his sharp eyes. "Do you want me to guess?" Chase asked, nerves stretching his patience about as thin as it could get.

"Fatherhood is still new to you. I imagine the sheen hasn't worn off yet. We haven't discussed it, but you could agree to share custody with Julia's parents. For that matter, you've always spent a good portion of the year overseas. With sufficient visitation—"

That did it! Chase bolted from his chair.

Calmly setting his cup on the table, Nelson showed his palms in a gesture of surrender. Sadly, he shook his head. "Everyone blames the messenger. All right." Getting serious, he leaned forward. "How badly do you want full custody? To what lengths are you willing to go?"

"Any lengths." The answer was swift, adamant, and Chase's tone stated clearly that this was not a topic up for debate.

Nelson nodded. "There is a very effective cure for the problems plaguing this case." Again he paused, as if his client was supposed to supply the answer himself.

Chase hissed through gritted teeth. "I'm waiting."

"Yes, you are. And you know what they say about he who hesitates? Always a bridesmaid, never... No, that's not it." Nelson tapped a thin finger against his lips. "What is that...? What is it they say...?" He shrugged in defeat. "Ah, well." Folding his thin, lawyerly hands neatly over his flat stomach, his myopic eyes never blinked. "Get married."

Nettie drank flavored iced tea from a bottle, taking a brief pause from the amusing domestic anecdote she'd been sharing. Chase was hovering around the kitchen, listening to her, but obviously distracted and tense, a product, no doubt, of his current circumstance and of spending the past two days in a small enclosed area with a lawyer.

Hoping to relax him, she continued her account of the past two days at her house, where she and her sisters had babysat Colin while Chase tried to figure out how not to lose him.

The irony of Chase's situation in relation to her own was not lost on Nettie. It was an uneasy balancing act she played. On the one hand, nothing seemed more important than helping

Chase keep Colin. She wanted to devote herself to the cause, do anything she could to help him through the desert of uncertainty, share with him that she understood, as well as anyone and better than most.

On the other hand, the closer she got to father and son and the more she imagined the unthinkable—that Colin could be whisked away to England—the more nervous and frightened she became, for Chase and for herself. She doubted she would see Colin again, ever, if he went to live with his grandparents. England, after all, might as well be on another planet as far as she was concerned.

She hadn't thought much about anxiety for the past few weeks. She was still using the program Lilah had gotten for her and was able to drive all over Kalamoose and even into the two cities flanking her hometown. After three years of being afraid of life—and even more afraid of the fear—getting back in a car, driving and actually enjoying herself felt like an accomplishment of heroic proportions. "Excitement" was replacing "fear." But flying across a continent and an ocean? That was another matter entirely. Imagining Colin on a plane ride that long made her as jittery as a jumping bean. Picturing him in another country with people she didn't know and had no reason to trust, wondering if he was happy and well and never truly knowing…

That was something she couldn't think about at all. So the balancing act was to accept her desire to help, while reminding herself that caring about Colin and Chase was a temporary occupation. A goodbye was coming; it was just a matter of time. The only uncertainty lay in the details.

Reaching into a grocery bag, she continued her story, finding solace and distraction in the chatter. "So this afternoon Colin told Lilah he wants to be an actor, like her, when he grows up. But before you panic, a half hour later he told Sara he wants to be a police officer. Now here's the absolutely adorable part. He looks at me and obviously doesn't want to hurt my feelings, either, so he says—" Nettie laughed at the memory "—he says, 'I'm going to write books and draw the pictures, too. Probably on the weekends.' With that kind of schedule, your son will need a personal secretary by the time he's eight!" Grinning, she set a bag of red peppers on the sink.

"Yeah." Chase stared absently at her growing pile of spaghetti sauce ingredients.

"He has a caring heart, that boy of yours."

"Yeah. He does." Restless, Chase hopped off the tall stool he'd just sat on. "Listen, this all looks great," he indicated the food, "but why don't we go out tonight, just the two of us?" He reached for the tomatoes, intending to store them in the refrigerator.

Nettie slapped his hands. "Drop the veggies, pal. You're not wriggling out of a cooking lesson tonight." Grabbing his cheeks like a respectable Italian mama, she said, "You gonna make-a such a beautiful sauce. The best you ever had." Planting a quick hard kiss on his lips, she patted his cheek and turned back to the ingredients. "All right." She rubbed her palms together. "Let's get started."

Without allowing him time to protest again, Nettie put him to work peeling garlic and onions, explaining the difference between a chop and a mince, a fry and a gentle sauté. Chase tried to concentrate…sort of…but he knew darn well that he was just avoiding the real task tonight.

Task.

He shook his head. Asking a woman to marry you and be your wife and the mother to your child should not be a "task."

Darn it, he ought to go back to covering wars and dodging land mines for cable news; it was a helluva lot less stressful than trying to maneuver in all these relationships.

Tears sprang to Chase's eyes as he macerated an onion with a large rectangular knife. *Terrific.* Nervous as a cat at a rottweiler convention and now crying to boot. Since that seemed like a pretty lame time to ask a woman to marry him, Chase procrastinated awhile longer.

He'd had the most interesting reaction to Nelson's suggestion of marriage as a solution to his present predicament: Immediate dismissal followed swiftly and incongruently by grateful concurrence.

The thought of Nettie and Colin and him together as a family filled Chase with satisfaction, even pride, as if family were some mind-blowing new concept he'd come up with all on his own. *Forever* had always scared the filling out of him. What seemed frightening now was that she might say no.

"The timing couldn't be worse," he grumbled, hacking into the second onion.

"What?" Nettie turned from the sink, where she was peeling the tomatoes.

"Huh? Oh." Surprised that he'd spoken aloud, Chase lifted his arm to wipe his tearing eyes on his sleeve. "Timing on onions and…garlic. Do you sauté the garlic a long time and then add the onions or…not?"

Cleaning her hands on a dishrag, Nettie approached Chase with a smile and a paper towel to wipe his flowing eyes. "I should have sliced a piece of potato for you to hold in your mouth. Keeps you from crying."

"You're kidding." She shook her head, and he asked, "Why aren't you crying?"

Nettie shrugged. "Onions never make me cry. Only movies about old people and animals who have to find their way home."

He smiled. Even a coarse paper towel felt soft with her gentle ministrations.

How could he ask Nettie to marry him? Proposals were supposed to be romantic or lighthearted or tender. Not practical. And the fact was, Chase's need was as great as his desire. A woman like Nettie deserved more than a "practical" proposal.

Nettie started to turn away, back to the cooking, but Chase caught her wrist. When she glanced back in question, he said, "We need to talk." Immediately, his heart rate accelerated. "But not here," he added quickly, cowardly. "Not…"

"Not what?"

"Not…in the kitchen…with all these tomatoes."

Her finely arched brows rose higher. Chase cursed himself. There was an engagement ring burning a hole in his pocket. He'd driven into Minot yesterday and picked it out, barely an hour after he'd told Nelson to mind his own business.

"Let's go out," he tried again. "We'll clean all this stuff up and make the spaghetti tomorrow. I'll spend a few hours with Colin now and you can go home and—" his hand stirred the air "—take a bubble bath or whatever you do, and I'll pick you up for a late dinner. Lobster. And champagne."

"In Kalamoose?" Nettie laughed. "Something tells me Ernie's fresh out of seafood."

"We'll drive to Minot. How about it?"

"We can't. We have to make dinner here because—"

"No. No 'have to's.' Not today." He reached for her hands, realized his were covered in onion and garlic and went to rinse them under the sink. Man, the stench…. "How do you get this smell off?"

"Yeah, garlic does tend to linger. We can rub them with lemon, but the best way, really, is to soak your hands in vanilla."

Chase scowled. "Okay, never mind." He grabbed a dishtowel, dried off and decided not to wait to ask her to marry him.

Colin's grandparents made their first appearance next week; if Chase waited until then to ask her, he would never be able to convince her that his proposal was anything more than an attempt to secure his future with his son.

But if he asked now, if he could somehow find the right words so she understood that this was what he wanted even though it was too soon and they hadn't had enough time to themselves and he had no idea how to be a husband, well then perhaps together, over time, they could build a future. One that was rich and worthwhile. One that would last.

Chase began to perspire.

A kitchen seemed like an asinine place to propose, but something prodded him. Now or never.

Taking Nettie's hands in his, he walked her over to the high stool by the center work island. "Here. Sit."

Bemusedly but without argument, Nettie did as he asked and Chase felt some minor encouragement.

Now, if he knelt down as in a proper proposal…

He'd be making his pitch to her kneecap. Chase grimaced. Maybe the stool wasn't a good idea.

"Stand up," he redirected. Nettie tilted her head, looking at him as if he'd lost his mind. "All right, never mind. You sit. I'll stand." Taking a moment to assess their positions before he asked his question, he nodded to himself. "Okay, this is good. This works."

Perspiration gathered with ever-increasing momentum along his brow and above his upper lip.

Letting go of one of her hands, he touched the ring in his pocket for reassurance. His throat felt dry as dust. Attempting to clear it once, he tried to swallow, then hacked again more forcefully.

"Do you want something to drink?"

"Do you have champagne?"

"No." She looked confused. "I thought maybe water for your—" she touched the base of her neck "—congestion or whatever...."

Congestion. He sighed. Score one for suave. "No," he said. "I'm fine."

Nettie sat atop the stool, one hand held rather tightly in Chase's and wondered what was going on. She had seen Chase tense, had witnessed his fear and glimpsed his anger. But this was different. This afternoon he was discombobulated.

"Are you especially worried about Colin?" she asked gently. "Did Nelson say something that upset you?"

"You mean something more than usual? No. Well." He nodded. "Yeah, of course. Nelson's mission in life is to say something that upsets me."

"Tell me."

Breathing heavily, Chase swiped the perspiration from his upper lip. Man-o-mighty, his heart was backfiring like a '78 Chevy. He couldn't believe people actually enjoyed this. If Nettie said no, he would just stay single the rest of his life.

"So?" Nettie softly encouraged him.

"Right." Hoarse, he cleared his throat again. "Right. So... Nelson and I were discussing my life, and he pointed out that I've never been the most stable sort when it comes to, well, my life. What he meant was I'm always traveling, can't remember the neighbors' names. In five years I haven't been home long enough to finish a quart of milk."

Great. Good strategy, genius, begin with the low points. "Of course, Nelson knew me in college, so his perspective may be a little—"

"You went to college together? I didn't realize that."

"—warped...what? Yeah. Yeah, and he thinks—"

"Has he been your lawyer since he passed the bar exam?"

"Huh? Yeah."

Nettie beamed. "I'd say that shows stability right there."

Chase thought about it. "Right. That's right! Well, he thinks I should get stable in other areas, too. And I said, 'Which other areas, for example?' And he said, 'For example, women. Most of your relationships haven't outlived the average housefly.' So after I punched him—'' Chase laughed heartily ''—I said, 'What do you suggest, Nelson?' And he said, 'Turn over a new leaf. Get married.''' Chase paused, lips peeled in an unnatural smile.

What an idiot! He expected her to say yes to *that?* Mentally Chase kicked himself. How could a man who had been all over the world, who had previously been hailed as the king of self-assurance, turn into such an incontrovertible doofus?

Nettie Owens was either the best thing that had ever happened to him or she'd be the end of him before he hit forty.

He needed to begin again. Dropping the smile, he asked, ''Can you forget everything I just said?''

''No.'' Nettie studied Chase with an unblinking frown. ''No, I don't think so.'' Perhaps, she mused, she felt as calm as she did because he was so obviously keyed up. She didn't feel any of the emotions she might have expected to feel under the circumstances. Or under what she thought were the circumstances. ''Are you proposing to me?''

''No!'' Chase grimaced. ''I mean, yes, but not like that.'' He blew out a long, forceful stream of air. ''You ever feel like you were trying to order filet mignon and you wound up with hash?''

Nettie smiled. He *was* proposing. Her heart thumped strongly but steadily in her chest. ''Hmm. I suppose I have.'' There was something both sweet and endearing about his utter lack of confidence.

He let go of her hand finally, and Nettie flattened it on her jeans. Her nails were clipped short, serviceable for work and for sticking her hands in a bowlful of bread dough. She wasn't a decorative person.

''I'm not the filet mignon type,'' she admitted aloud. ''I like hash.''

Chapter Sixteen

Chase looked up from his scowling contemplation of the linoleum, and the hope that suffused his face was a sight to behold. Nettie felt her first flutter of nerves.

"Lilah and I were talking last night about you and Colin. She said pretty much the same thing Nelson did."

Chase winced, but some humor returned to his countenance. "What? That I'm a relationship-shy workaholic?"

"No." Nettie tilted her head. "I think she said 'commitment phobic.'" Chase gawped. "Just kidding."

Inching a hand out to fiddle with a bunch of parsley, Nettie said, "Lilah watches reruns of 'The Practice' and 'LA Law' in case she ever has to play an attorney, so she gets most of her ideas from TV, but she thinks that if Colin's grandparents thought you were getting married, they'd have to back off."

The parsley leaves began to wilt as she toyed with them. She couldn't believe she was saying this to him. She couldn't believe she was this relatively calm.

Last night, her conversation with Lilah had seemed like nothing more than the result of an overactive imagination and too much cable TV. But with Chase bringing up the topic of marriage and clearly feeling so clumsy and awkward it seemed merciful to admit that she and Lilah had talked about it, too.

"Lilah thinks you and I ought to pretend to be engaged for a while until they can see for themselves that Colin belongs with you. Once they're reassured and they go back to England, the engagement could just naturally break up." Letting go of the greens, she laughed a little. "See? You and Lilah had the same idea. Not that Lilah's ideas are exactly *mainstream.*"

Nettie released a breath that felt a bit shaky. Was she accepting his proposal? Defining terms of the agreement? Or simply reassuring him? She braved a look at Chase's face. He was frowning.

"Let me get this straight," he said. "We pretend to be engaged for an indefinite period of time."

"Yes—*if* we decide to actually do it...if it seems like getting engaged is really a good idea, then yes. I imagine the time period will be indefinite. But closed-ended. No one will be able to fault you if the breakup is timed properly. Lilah says timing is everything."

"It sure is," Chase muttered. He looked decidedly less than pleased as he muttered, "A fake engagement."

"Temporary engagement," Nettie corrected. "Lilah says that when you're playing a role, you want to believe in it as much as possible. So anytime you discuss it, even if you're only rehearsing, you should talk about it as if you believe it's true."

There was a long, heavy pause. "You'd agree to something like this?"

Nettie breathed in. *Now* she was nervous. Very. Her mind began to race. What would she be agreeing to? A temporary engagement for the sole purpose of preserving the relationship between a father and son. Put like that, it sounded rather altruistic. Of course, for a few weeks...or what, a month at the most?...she'd be pretending that she had a commitment to the man and child who made her days hum with life and purpose again. Put like that, it sounded altogether dangerous.

Feeling her arms and legs quiver, Nettie reminded herself there was a built-in safety net in the knowledge that the relationship was not meant to last. The stated end gave her a sense of control. Her main intention was to keep Chase and Colin together; stealing a few more moments of joy would be her reward for a job well done.

A woosh of adrenaline sent her heart skittering, but she told herself to embrace the sensation; after all, she was about to do something that would make anyone's heart palpitate.

Surprised by the strength in her tone, Nettie said, "Yes. Yes, I'd agree to a temporary engagement."

Slowly, Chase nodded.

It was a strange way to accept a proposal, he thought. But then, it had been a strange way to extend one.

She'd misunderstood him entirely. Heat filled his chest. Dammit, he hadn't been talking about temporary. Now he felt like an ass. A frustrated and angry ass.

But he could get this right. If he could report the news with bullets whizzing a hundred feet behind him, he could propose in a way that made his intentions clear: No one could predict the future, but when it came to marriage and family, he intended to give "open-ended" a run for the money.

"Listen, about tonight—"

The doorbell rang. Bullet number one. *Whizzzzz.*

"One of us should answer that," Nettie said when he stood like an animal caught in a mud hole.

Reluctantly Chase stomped to the door, prepared to quickly dispatch whoever it was. A moment later, however, he was stalking back into the kitchen, carrying yet another grocery bag, this one from a specialty store in Minot. Trailing behind him was a happily chirping Lilah.

"...so I bought two pitiful-looking avocados that cost an arm and a leg—this is why I moved to California—and the parmesan cheese, but I couldn't find the exact red wine she asked for. Oh, Nettie-Belle, you're already cooking!" Lilah strolled to the sink, where Nettie had resumed peeling and seeding tomatoes, hoping the activity would calm her down. "Anything I can do?"

Nettie hesitated, shooting a glance in Chase's direction. "Actually, I think we're going to handle this on our own."

"Oh, right, it's a cooking lesson." She winked at Chase. "Real men make pasta?" Grabbing a jar of cured black olives, she unscrewed the lid, plucked out an olive and popped it into her mouth. "Mmm, salt."

"I need those for the sauce," Nettie said.

"Okay, I'll go home and eat potato chips. What time do you want us here, by the way?"

"Umm...." Guiltily, Nettie cast another glance at Chase.

"We're cooking for company?" he grumbled without a shred of hospitality.

"I thought it would be more fun." She shrugged, half apologetic, half persuasive. Chase could have sworn he heard another bullet whiz by. "It's Nick's homecoming."

"Nick's coming?"

"And Sara, of course." Lilah reached into the jar for a few more olives. "And that cute little lawyer of yours. Nelson."

Whiz.

Nettie confiscated the olive jar. "Colin is with Sara right now, I assume."

"Yep. I told Chase when I came in. Colin didn't want to go shopping, so he's hanging out with *la sheriffe*. Probably learning how to spit and shoot. You don't mind, do you?" she asked Chase.

"Mind? I'm beyond minding," he said, "about anything."

He and Nettie shared a long look.

"Am I interrupting something?" Lilah eyed them both speculatively. "I suddenly feel like the fifth wheel on a bobsled."

Nettie made a face. "Bobsleds don't have wheels."

"Exactly."

"You're not interrupting anything."

Chase crossed his arms. "Yes, she is."

Someone knocked on the door to the mud porch. Chase closed his eyes. *Whiz.*

"Come in!" he shouted, crossing to the women, grabbing the olive jar and carrying it back to the other side of the kitchen to dig into it. Nick opened the door.

"Hey," he smiled, newly returned from Chicago, where he had participated in a panel lecture about twenty-first-century agricultural techniques and the environment. "This place looks great. I ought to feel ashamed for letting it sit so long."

Chewing an olive, Chase nodded an acknowledgement, the best he felt like doing at the moment. No one else seemed inclined to speak, either.

Nick glanced around. "Something wrong?"

Nettie shook her head and smiled. "No."

Lilah overlapped her, shrugging. "Seems like it."

Chase overrode them both. "Yes! Dammit, I was in the middle of proposing."

"Proposing?" This time Lilah and Nick spoke in surround-sound.

They glanced back and forth between Nettie and Chase.

The protracted silence while Nettie wondered how much to say proved to be too hard for Lilah to handle. "Well, what did you say?" she demanded, bouncing up and down like a kid.

"I said yes," Nettie answered and was rewarded immediately with a squeal and a huge bear hug from her sister.

On the other side of the work island, Nick approached Chase with an outstretched hand. "Congratulations." He sounded almost as pleased as Lilah. "Good choice."

Trying to settle her bouncing sister, Nettie whispered, "It's temporary, remember. It's what we talked about last night."

Lilah pulled away. She glanced at Chase. "Right. I know. But it's still a cause for celebration."

Nick stepped forward. "What did you say? Temporary?"

Chase felt a ferocious scowl cover his brow. He was a split second away from kicking the two interlopers out of the house, barring the door to dinner guests and then kissing the word *temporary* right out of Nettie's vocabulary. In fact...

He opened his mouth, intending to do just that, when Lilah began explaining to Nick, "They're doing it for Colin. The grandparents are showing up next week."

"I know. Chase told me." Nick looked at his friend. "So you're going to put on a show for these people?"

"And for the court, if it comes to that," Lilah answered.

"I'm afraid you're going to be sucked into this, too, Nick," Nettie warned him. "I think it's really important that we all act as natural as possible."

"That's right. We have to act as if this engagement is the real thing. So that means absolute commitment to the situation." Lilah purloined the wedge of Parmesan cheese, withdrew a sharp knife from a wooden block on the counter and began cutting. "You know, I don't think we should tell Sara that your engagement is only temporary. She has a lousy poker face. No acting technique whatsoever." She bit into the cheese. "Yuck. Too dry." She swallowed, then clutched her throat.

Nettie poured a glass of the blush wine she intended to serve with the hors d'oeuvres and handed it to her gagging sister. "I hate to make Sara feel like she's been duped, but I agree with you. One stray comment and this whole thing could backfire. You know what I really hate, though?" She poured another glass and handed it to Nick.

Chase saw his private afternoon turning into a damned cocktail party. He had to intervene now and get this train back on the right track. "Listen, everyone—"

"I hate lying to Colin. I don't want to hurt him."

"Yeah." Lilah sipped her wine and nodded. "But maybe now is not the time to think about the end of your engagement."

Damn straight. Chase nodded.

"Right." Nick frowned in Chase's direction. "That's putting the cart before the horse. Seems to me you ought to concentrate on what you're starting before you try to figure out how to end it."

Well, you don't have to tell me! Chase felt a very male need to hit something. "All right, look, everybody—"

"Hey, open up! We're carrying stuff!" The call came from the back door.

"Sara!" Nettie said, appearing rattled.

"It's okay, stay calm. No one's doing anything wrong here." Nick reassured in an even tone that absolutely infuriated Chase. *Duh*, they weren't doing anything wrong!

He gritted his teeth until his jaw hurt. This was a miserable situation, but it was *his* miserable situation, and he had totally lost control of it.

"Don't tell her to stay calm," he growled, stalking over to stand nose-to-nose with Nick.

"Why not?"

Chase put his hands on his hips. "Be...cause."

A thoroughly obnoxious grin curled up Nick's face. "I just meant she shouldn't worry. We'll handle Sara." He indicated himself and Lilah.

"Wrong." Chase stabbed a finger at Nick's chest. "There is nothing to handle. My *fiancée* and I have everything under control." He glared around the room. "This is an engagement, not espionage. Got it?" This time he let his gaze linger on Nettie.

"Got it," she murmured.

Lilah leaned over to her sister. "He must be a Method actor."

Ignoring that, Chase strode to the door, giving instructions over his shoulder. "Colin is obviously with her, so I want to keep this as low-key as possible for the time being. We don't even have to mention it tonight. Not until we have the details worked out."

He'd shout news of their engagement from the rooftops if he thought Nettie was committed to a permanent union, or a decent stab at one, anyway. How the heck had a simple marriage proposal turned into a bad scene from a B movie?

Chase felt a rise in blood pressure and knew this was not the time to settle anything. He'd talk to Nettie later when the peanut gallery had disbanded. She'd realize she had misunderstood him, he'd show her the ring, and the whole situation would be straightened out. In the meantime...

With a hand on the doorknob, he turned to the expectant group. "We're all in agreement here, right? Low-key. Underplay."

Nods all around. Nettie spoke up. "Absolutely."

"Hey, c'mon! Hurry up, already! I've got two half-gallons of ice cream you'll be able to drink through a straw if you don't—"

Chase opened the door to his son and, he hoped, future sister-in-law. She wrinkled her face in disgust. "'Bout damn time." She glanced at Colin, who stood beside her, weighed down by a smaller grocery bag. "Oh, sorry, kid. Remember what I told you about bad language."

Colin nodded as he walked past Chase into the kitchen. "Toilet mouths wind up with their sorry butts in a sling."

"Right."

"Sara!" Nettie shook her head.

"What?" Sara dumped her bag on the counter with the rest of the food and then reached down for Colin's.

"You spent too much time with Uncle Harm, that's what," Lilah said in disgust.

Bemused by the comment, Sara shrugged. She pulled a container of mocha-almond-fudge ice cream out of the sack, followed by a carton of a flavor called fresh summer peach. "So what's the big celebration tonight? We already had a housewarming."

Nettie took the ice cream to the freezer. "Nick wasn't here, though."

Looking up, Sara noticed her old nemesis across the room and curled a lip ungraciously. "Thought I saw your truck. Back from the big city, huh?"

"That's right. And looking forward to heading out again as soon as I find a good excuse."

"Is that what we're celebrating?"

Lilah poured a couple more glasses of blush wine. "Of course not. We're celebrating Nettie and Chase."

"Li…" Nettie cautioned, nodding pointedly at Colin.

Chase cleared his throat.

Sara glanced between the two of them. "What about Nettie and Chase?"

Unable, apparently, to contain her enthusiasm—or to recall a conversation that took place only two minutes ago—Lilah faced her sister and bounced up and down on her high-heeled sandals. "Chase proposed to Nettie. They're getting married!" She squealed like a debutante with a new Nordstrom's card.

Nettie opened her mouth in a disbelieving *O*.

Sara's eyes bugged wide at the news. Lilah grabbed her arm and shook it. "Isn't that great?"

Sara nodded. "Yeah." Slowly a wide smile spread across her face. "Yeah, it is." She didn't bounce like Lilah, but when the other woman embraced her, Sara hugged back. "So when did this happen?"

"Just before you got here." Nick strolled over to pick up a glass of wine. "I think it calls for a toast."

"Nick!" Nettie gave him a pleading look. He and Lilah had promised to help, not dig a hole for Nettie and Chase to jump into!

"Oh, right," Nick said, remembering Colin, who was all eyes and ears. "We'd better get juice for you."

Distressed, Nettie turned to Chase. He shrugged, but his eyes narrowed in assessment. No two people could be this lame. Lilah and Nick were clearly working their own agenda. With little effort, they had just turned a "phony" engagement into the real thing.

He smiled.

Colin wore a huge grin as Nick poured him a tumbler of

cranapple and then clinked glasses with him before raising his goblet in a toast.

"To Nettie and Chase." Then, including Colin, Nick added, "And family."

"To family," Lilah and Sara repeated.

Moving forward, slipping a hand around his fiancée's waist, Chase accepted the wine Lilah poured for him. Nettie appeared absolutely stupefied. He looked around at the others as they beamed, truly happy and blithely ignoring his orders to keep the "temporary" engagement under wraps. And Colin was in the middle of it all, a bit dazed, but clearly enjoying the hoopla.

Nothing today had gone according to Chase's plan. On the other hand, what was that saying? All roads lead to Rome.

Yes, indeed, he thought, raising his glass. "To family."

"So where are you planning to have the wedding?" Sara asked. "Because, you might not have thought about it, but the jail's available."

Lilah choked on her wine. "The jail! Are you joking?"

"No. Hey, it happens to be a good idea. It's where they met. They could have a theme wedding."

"Ohhh." Lilah snapped her fingers. "Of course. I read about theme weddings all the time in *Martha Stewart Living*. Nettie can wear something from the Vera Wang penitentiary collection."

Sara scowled. "Sarcasm is a sign of weakness."

Swirling the wine in her glass, Lilah rolled her eyes. "Whatever."

"Well, I still say—"

When the phone rang, Chase kissed Nettie's temple. "Good luck," he murmured, hating to let go of her. At the first opportunity, he would take her aside, just the two of them, to talk.

"Hello." Grabbing the phone in the kitchen, he had to stick a finger in his ear to hear above the noisy argument behind him. "Nelson! What's up, man? Are you coming to dinner tonight, too? What? I can't hear you? Who's coming over? Who— Wait a minute." Covering the mouthpiece of the phone, Chase called out, "I'm not dressing like Wild Bill Hickok, Sara. Can you guys keep it down for a minute? Nelson's on the line, and I can't hear."

Lilah and Sara continued the theme-wedding debate, but at lower decibels.

"Okay, Nelson, shoot." Chase listened as his attorney filled him in on the status of the custody case. His stomach began to churn and sweat tickled his upper lip. "I thought you were going to make sure we had some advance notice." He paused. "Yeah, well, I'm not talking about two weeks. Anything over two hours would be fine." His sarcasm was unmistakable. "Yes, I understand spontaneity is the point, but you're *my* lawyer. Aren't you supposed to fight for my rights? I know you're not that kind of lawyer, will you stop saying that!"

The talking in the kitchen ceased. All heads turned toward Chase. Breaking away from the others, Nettie came to stand by his side. Without knowing what had him so riled, she put a hand on his shoulder. Her touch was surprisingly strong, affirming; it communicated support not suppression, but Chase found himself relaxing almost against his own will.

"Sorry," he said, to the people watching him and into the phone. "I think I need a blood-pressure pill."

"You have high blood pressure?" Nettie murmured, sounding concerned.

"Only when I'm talking to Nelson." He offered a quick reassuring smile to Colin and shot a pleading look at Nick.

Taking his hint, the three adults started talking to Colin at the same time.

Chase pulled Nettie into his arms, amazed by the immediate comfort of having her so near. "All right," he said into the phone. "Tell her we'll expect her around seven."

With his arms resting casually on the small of her back and his chin settled on the top of her head, he murmured for Nettie's ears only, "We're having company for dessert."

Dinner was not quite as festive as Nettie had planned. The mood in the little cottage changed considerably when Chase announced that a social worker would be arriving later in the evening to "evaluate" him. Everyone but Colin understood the significance of the meeting. Chase and now Nettie, too, would be scrutinized. All the adults at the table seemed to share their nerves and apprehension. Only Colin, in fact, ate with gusto, somehow managing to maintain a running monologue about dead outlaws between noisy slurps of spaghetti.

Nelson arrived late, between the salad and pasta courses, and he, too, appeared distracted by concern, so as soon as the last noodle had been twirled, Sara took Colin outside to ride the tractor lawnmower, leaving the others to speak freely.

"We all need to be on the same page," Nelson said, eyeing them over his steepled fingers. "Being engaged is a good thing, a very good thing. But the timing is suspect. I think it's important to point out tonight that you two—" he nodded to Nettie and Chase "—began to have strong feelings for each other prior to finding out about Colin."

"I can vouch for that," Nick said. "I've known Chase for fifteen years, and I saw him falling for Nettie the first night they met."

Chase looked surprised. And sheepish. He literally squirmed in his chair.

"And Nettie called me a couple of weeks ago absolutely besotted." Lilah grinned. "I haven't heard her like that since…" she faltered. "In a long time."

"I—" Nettie started to protest, but Lilah had, after all, only spoken the truth. Still, she shot her sister a quelling glare.

Chase cocked a brow. "Come on. I'll confess if you confess."

Nettie felt four sets of eyes upon her. Her blood heated. Without a chance to speak with Chase alone since his proposal, she felt like a ship being tossed at sea. Nelson wanted them to be "on the same page?" She wasn't sure they were reading the same book!

Addressing herself to Chase only, she said, "I take the fifth. For now."

Nick and Lilah grinned. Chase gave her a look that promised he'd weasel a confession from her later.

Nelson shook his head. "No good. The social worker's name is Georgiana Rees, and Ms. Rees is going to want to hear that this love affair, of which she has not been apprised, was rock solid before there was even the hint of a custody battle. In fact it will send your attorney into paroxysms of joy to learn that you two have been meeting on the sly for a considerable time, say months or even years. Not that I'm advising you to lie, but if Chase visited Nick over the years…"

Chase shook his head.

"…or perhaps Nettie has traveled to New York…" Nettie gestured in the negative. "Or overseas…"

"No. Sorry."

Nelson tapped an index finger against his lips and looked at his client. "When did you propose?"

"This afternoon. You know that."

"What I am aware of is that you *announced* your engagement today. I imagine you proposed…" he waved a hand "…a week ago?"

Chase glanced at Nettie. She took a breath and nodded. After all, if the purpose of the engagement was to protect Colin, what difference did it make *when* they got engaged?

Though his distaste for lying couldn't have been more clear, Chase agreed. He rubbed his eyes, clasped his hands on top of the dining-room table and looked at Nelson. "Why don't you tell us about our engagement."

"How come I hafta wear a tie?"

Standing in front of his father, Colin tugged on his too-tight collar and made faces into the mirror. Chase attempted to put a part in his son's impossibly thick hair, but the comb barely made an impression.

"Because we're having a guest. It's a gesture of politeness."

"We already had guests. We didn't hafta wear ties for them."

Chase smiled. Tempting logic. His own tie felt like a noose. "This guest is different," he said, smoothing a hand over Colin's hair. He'd had hair like this, too, at Colin's age, hair that stuck out all over even with the shortest cut. It had driven his ultra-conservative parents crazy.

"Why's this guest different?"

Chase hadn't told Colin about the custody dispute. He hoped he never had to tell him. The last thing he wanted to give his son was more instability.

Speaking quietly, while Colin continued to experiment with the myriad shapes a mouth could make, Chase explained, "Nettie and her family are our friends, so we don't have to be formal with them. But Ms. Rees is sort of a…business acquaintance. She's coming over to help us."

"How?" Colin stuck out his tongue and tried to see if he could curl it up at the edges.

"She's going to make sure I'm taking good care of you. She'll probably ask you some questions. You okay with that?"

Colin's tongue retracted quickly, like a lizard's. He stared solemnly at Chase's reflection in the mirror. "You take good care of me."

Simple words, but Chase had to consciously remind himself to speak. "Think so?"

Colin nodded. "How come you keep holding my head?"

Chase looked down. His palm still capped Colin's thick hair. Hmm.

Because it feels good. Chase thought to himself. It feels right to be your parent, to touch and protect you. And because I don't ever want to stop holding and protecting you...my son. Suddenly Chase remembered all the ways in which he'd tried to measure up when he was a kid—the parent-approved clothes, tamed hair, impeccable manners, the achievements. His achievements had been his defining characteristic.

"What do you want to wear to meet Ms. Rees?" he asked.

Colin mulled it over. "My 'N Sync T-shirt...no, maybe my purple sweater?" The purple V-neck pullover was a new purchase, not a bad choice at all.

"Go put it on."

"No tie?"

"No tie." Chase felt like he'd actually scored a major parental success when Colin whooped and began digging through a dresser drawer. "One more thing," he said. Colin looked over, and Chase put his hand once more on Colin's head. This time he mussed up his son's hair. "That's better."

Colin looked in the mirror and grinned up at his dad.

With hugs for good luck, Sara, Lilah, Nick and finally Nelson left the cottage, intending to wait at Nick's place till the coast was clear. Nettie knew she should talk to Chase alone before the social worker arrived. Trying to calm herself had been an uphill battle all afternoon. The knot in her stomach felt like the boulder in *Raiders of the Lost Ark*.

Prepping for their interview, Nettie slicked on lipstick, although "slick" was a misnomer. She dabbed her lips with the tube whenever her quaking hand got close enough to make contact.

Lowering the lipstick, she rested her palms on the bathroom sink and took a deep breath. She'd been extra jittery for days, which seemed pretty normal under the circumstances, but she knew there was something more tweaking her emotions. It was hard to concentrate on anything lately. She felt sad and clingy, and several times this week she'd wanted to cry for no obvious reason.

Nettie examined her eyes in the mirror. Red and puffy. Maybe she was coming down with something or it was time for her period or...

Oh.

"It's August fourteenth." The awareness hit her like a moving freight train. Tucker's birthday was on the sixteenth.

"How could I have forgotten?" She thumped the heel of her hand on the porcelain sink. What kind of mother simply forgot? What kind of mother didn't even think about her child's birthday until she was practically right up on it?

Each year Nettie picked out a gift, something small, something Tuck would have liked at the age he would have been. Should have been. All at once the memory of putting the photo of herself and Brian into the desk drawer came rushing back.

"It's our baby's birthday," she whispered, wishing that somehow, somewhere Brian could hear her. Closing her eyes, she tried to picture a heaven in which her husband and son would be together on Tuck's birthday, eating Tuck's favorite cake and remembering how birthdays used to be. And maybe thinking of her for a few minutes and feeling how much she loved them.

Opening her eyes again, she wondered what Brian would think of her current situation. Pretending to be engaged for the sake of a child. Infatuated with the father. Living a temporary fantasy.

"You always said I overcomplicated things." She smiled, but an uncomfortable heaviness grew in the pit of her stomach.

She tried to put a name to the feeling. It wasn't guilt. Brian would never begrudge her the chance to be happy. He'd been an uncomplicated man, incapable of severe judgment or blame. She might think the dance of hello and goodbye had the most intricate steps, but he would have said the pattern was simple: just listen to the music and don't fight the beat.

The doorbell rang. Nettie jumped, sending the tube of lipstick clattering into the sink. She checked her watch. Seven on the dot. The boulder in her tummy transformed into a hundred fluttering butterflies. Ms. Georgiana Rees, MSW, had arrived.

Plump and no-nonsense, with a striking resemblance to Julia Child, Georgiana Rees shook hands with Chase, nodded brusquely to Nettie and boomed down at Colin, "Hello, young man. Show me your room."

Perfectly amenable to the request, Colin displayed his books and several toys while Nettie and Chase watched anxiously from the doorway. Bored with a Buzz Lightyear doll that had seen better days, Colin announced, "I got better stuff at our other place. We didn't bring it all over here, yet."

"Your other place?"

"Yep." Colin tossed Buzz onto the bed. "We used to live at Nick's."

"Ah. Do you like your room?" Ms. Rees queried, looking at a framed print of a very British foxhunt. Not exactly Disney memorabilia.

But Colin nodded. "My dad's getting me a bed shaped like a car."

Dad. The three adults in the room all noted the name. Only Chase, though, feared his legs would no longer support him.

Dad.

Feeling her fiancé's body tremble beside her, Nettie looked up. She saw the tears in his eyes and remembered the first time Tuck had called her Mommy. Shakespeare, bless him, was dead wrong on that "rose by any other name" issue.

With one word, a seven-year-old boy had just given a grown man his place in the world. Forevermore.

Chapter Seventeen

"My what a yummy, yummy fudge sauce." Ms. Rees—Georgiana—licked the back of her spoon, wiped a drip of chocolate from the rim of her dessert glass and sucked her finger. She made a loud smacking sound. "Is it purchased?"

"Ah, no. I made it." Try as she might, Nettie could not reconcile the stolid Ms. Rees with a word like *yummy*. Georgiana had spent an hour with them and had done little more than chat thus far. Nettie's nerves were tight as piano wire, and Chase appeared to be ready to jump out of his skin. Lilah had called to ask how things were going and even she sounded nervous and tense. Only Colin and Georgiana were able to concentrate on their ice-cream sundaes.

Ensconced on the couch, the formidable woman made one more swipe around her dessert glass while Colin, seated on the floor with his sundae in front of him on the coffee table, found a more interesting pursuit in lifting his spoon to create a mini waterfall of melted peach ice cream.

Nettie and Chase sat on side-by-side chairs facing the social worker.

"Well," Georgiana said, dropping her spoon into the glass

with a clatter and clapping her knees. "Let's get down to business." From her large handbag, she dug out a yellow legal pad and a pen. Balancing a pair of old-fashioned bifocals low on the bridge of her nose, she scribbled with strong stokes and made a bold slash beneath whatever she had written. She glanced up at them, smiling.

"I was surprised to hear you two were engaged. Rather sudden, was it?" Her voice was energetic, her gaze uncompromising.

Chase felt his hackles rise. *Calm and cooperative,* he reminded himself, realizing he'd gain little by suggesting she mind her own damn business. First, though...

"Colin, would you take your dish and Ms. Rees's into the kitchen, please?"

"I'm not done."

With a pointed glance at the melted sundae, Chase nodded. "Yeah, you are. Put the dishes on the sink and then run out back and rewind the hose for me. You can water Nettie's flowers first, if you want."

Because there was nothing Colin liked better than to spray the world with a garden hose, he was on his feet in an instant. "I know how to water them. Nettie showed me." As carefully as he could given his haste to go outside, he transported the dishes to the kitchen.

Georgiana scribbled furiously.

Chase waited until the back door opened and closed. Then he said, "I've known Nettie three weeks. I've never been married or engaged before and never wanted to be. Whatever you've heard about my reputation where relationships are concerned is probably true, and I don't know if I would have been smart enough to notice the diamond in my path if we'd met even a few months ago." He looked at Nettie and his harsh gaze softened considerably. "I like to think I would have." Turning back to the attentive social worker, he said, "I do know this— Whether or not Colin had turned out to be mine, I would have pursued my relationship with Nettie. With or without a custody hearing, I would have proposed."

Georgiana raised a brow dyed I-Love-Lucy red. "What about you?" she questioned Nettie. "Would you have accepted? With or without a custody hearing?"

Chase knew he couldn't hang on the answer, not in any obvious way.

Nettie appeared startled. Whether by Chase's declaration or Georgiana's question wasn't clear, but it took her a moment to regroup. "Yes. Absolutely. With or without."

Another note went down on the legal pad. Georgiana, however, was not smiling. Chase reached over to take Nettie's hand and give it an encouraging squeeze.

"Your career is quite demanding as I understand it," the social worker said to him. "How do you plan to address the demands of parenthood and a job that requires extended periods of travel to other countries?"

"I haven't had time yet to work out the details, but there will be changes, of course."

"Are you quite confident you can mother a seven-year-old boy?" Abruptly, Georgiana transferred her focus back to Nettie. "It certainly seems possible, given Mr. Reynold's career choice—current career choice," she amended when Chase started to speak, "that you will be called upon to be a so-called single parent at times. Tell me how you feel about that responsibility. In your own words," she added sternly as again Chase attempted to interrupt.

Nettie pulled her hand away from Chase. She had not expected questions to be addressed to her, specifically. And questions about motherhood...

Clearing her throat, she answered, "I take motherhood very seriously. I understand the responsibilities."

"How old are you?"

At least a hundred. "Twenty-five."

"Do you have nieces or nephews?"

"No."

"Would you like children of your own someday?"

Nettie's tongue grew instantly thick. Her head felt fuzzy. "I—That...isn't necessary. Right now I'm concentrating on Colin."

Strategically, it was the wrong answer. She could see that in Georgiana Rees's face. Nettie felt Chase's gaze upon her, but refused to meet it.

"What, in your opinion," the other woman pursued, "are the qualities that make a good mother?"

A horrid, prickling heat bubbled in Nettie's veins. She couldn't think. Dumbly, she stared.

"Have you given it much consideration yet?"

An awful urge to scream filled her throat. *Every day. All day.* And whatever else she came up with, Nettie always returned to the conviction that whatever the qualities were, she didn't possess them. If she did, her three-year-old child would not have died without his mother there to help or to hold him. But those were the nighttime thoughts. The two-in-the-morning-when-you're-all-alone-and-can't-push-them-away-anymore thoughts. Useless, useless thoughts that yielded neither to reason nor to compassion.

Was that what Georgiana Rees wanted to know? If Chase suspected how dark Nettie's musings were when it came to motherhood or marriage, if he had any inkling of the fears that robbed her of her usefulness, he wouldn't have asked her to be his fiancée, even as a ruse.

"Are you all right?" The man she had optimistically offered to help sat forward in his chair.

She had to speak. If she continued to sit dumbly like this, she might cost him the custody of his son singlehandedly.

"I— Yes. No," Nettie confessed, "I'm not feeling very well."

Chase left his chair in an instant. "I'll help you to the bedroom. You can lie down."

"No." Unsteadily, Nettie rose. "Actually, I'd like to go home." Belatedly, she realized she had no car here. She'd have to walk to Nick's, where Sara and Lilah were waiting, and surely it would appear odd to Georgiana to see Nettie walk away from a cottage in the middle of a lonely field while her fiancé stayed behind.

Alternatively, she could call Nick's and have one of her sisters come get her, but that option required more explanation. She began to feel trapped, which often led quickly to feelings of claustrophobia, which led to panic and the horrid, indefinable dread that accompanied an attack. She wanted to run. She wanted to run now and she wanted to run far.

Chase frowned at her, but with more concern than anger or disapproval. "I'd like you to stay," he said in a low voice, as if she were the only other person in the room. "But if you definitely need to leave, I'll take you."

He was concerned about her. Let down by the woman he had counted on to help, his first concern was still for her.

Deep breaths, Nettie reminded herself. You are not a coward. It's just anxiety. You can bear the discomfort until Georgiana Rees leaves. Then you'll run.

With her head spinning and her stomach gyrating in the opposite direction, she tried to stand straight and give the illusion, at least, of control. "No, that's all right. I'll stay." But she wouldn't answer any more questions. "Why don't I make us some coffee?"

That's it, she breathed, distract yourself. When in doubt, play Donna Reed.

Through sheer will, she sent a smile, albeit a brittle one, in Ms. Rees's direction. The woman eyed her like a hawk. In fact, Nettie thought, I'd rather be eyed by a hawk. A hawk would not be in the position to destroy Chase's happiness. A hawk would not tease the past out of Nettie in slow, tortuous nibbles. When hawks went for their pray, they were swift and unequivocal. No pretense.

She took two steps, but her legs felt like tubes of jelly. Breathe. You can relax your body and walk at the same time. She knew it was the truth, but lacked faith that a body reacting as strongly as hers was right now could actually make it all the way to the kitchen. What if Georgiana saw her stumble or start to shake? What if anxiety this extreme really could make a person go absolutely bonkers, and she fell apart in front of the social worker and Chase and even, heaven forbid, Colin?

The dread intensified. She was telling herself all the wrong things. Too many "what if" statements poured more adrenaline into her already sensitive system and within seconds she was afraid she wouldn't be able to walk at all. Without thinking, she grabbed the back of the chair for support.

Chase reacted immediately. Her fiancé had no way of knowing, of course, that there was nothing physically wrong with her, that her body was reacting to a truckload of blame that turned into anxiety. So without another word, he swept her into his arms. There was no pretense in the action; his focus was Nettie.

He was concerned. Even though she was supposed to be helping him, he was concerned.

Brushing aside her protest, Chase murmured to her soothingly as he strode to the bedroom. Guilty and ashamed, she looked into his face, but all she saw was love.

If a heart could swell and break at the same time, hers did.

Gently he laid her on the bed. Gently took her hand and asked if there was anything he could bring her.

"Go back to Georgiana," Nettie told him, taking his hand for a moment. He relaxed at her touch. She could feel it. "I'm fine. I just want to rest awhile." Rest and try not to think, an impossible task.

Chase nodded. "I'll get rid of Georgiana as soon as I can."

It was on the tip of Nettie's tongue to promise she'd turn in a better acting job next time, but it wouldn't be true. She couldn't sit calmly with Georgiana and tell glib lies about motherhood.

Sadly, worried about Chase and Colin and deeply concerned about the part she could play in separating them, Nettie withdrew her hand. "Don't rush her out. Please. Not for me."

Bending forward, he kissed the tip of her nose. "I think we've all had enough for one evening."

When Chase left the room, closing the door behind him, Nettie felt a tiredness so profound, she thought she could sleep for days. She couldn't let herself rest, though. She had to figure out a way to extricate herself from any more of Georigiana's cross-examinations without endangering Chase's case.

A splatter of water hit the exterior wall of the bedroom. Nettie scooted off the bed and went to the window. Pushing aside the curtain, she saw Colin holding the garden hose and turning in circles, spraying everything he could and wrapping himself in a coil of rubber. Give a little boy a chore, and he turned it into an adventure.

She smiled. How could Chase ever let you go?

The thought came unbidden and with it, a tide of emotion that swelled too quickly for her to stem. She had to make sure Colin and Chase stayed together. She *had* to. She could tolerate goodbye…she *would* tolerate goodbye as long as she knew that Chase didn't have to. She had to be able to picture him with his son after they left North Dakota. She could stand being alone again if she knew that Chase wasn't.

"He deserves that," she said, gazing out the window. "He's a good man." She thought of that first night in the jail. And their first kiss when she'd helped him unsaddle King. She remembered how nervous and happy and vulnerable he'd seemed when he told her he had a son.

"Please don't let him be hurt," Nettie whispered to the God she hadn't spoken to much the past few years. She wasn't sure she believed, anymore, in prayers being answered or in a Power that protected... In heaven above. It had hurt to believe almost more than it hurt not to.

She watched Colin. Wound in the hose, he began to struggle with it as if fighting some enemy force. In his imagination, he would always win. But he lived in a world that often changed the rules of the game just when you finally thought you knew how to play.

"Don't get hurt," she whispered. "Don't get hurt." She put a hand on the window, overwhelmed by an urge to call him inside.

He wasn't hers to coddle, and that was a good thing because her fears had made her overly protective. Still, for this brief span of time, there was something she could do.

Quickly, before she wasted any more time, Nettie ran from the bedroom. She smoothed her skirt as she returned to where Georgiana and Chase were still convened, Chase talking and Georgiana still scribbling.

They looked up as she entered. "I'm sorry I rushed out like that," she apologized breathlessly to Georgiana, anxiety unnoticed as she concentrated on winning the other woman over. "A little too much pasta, I think." Smiling as if her illness were already a thing of the past, she patted her belly.

"You certainly look better." Georgiana considered her.

"I am." Nettie ignored Chase's concern as she moved to stand by his chair. "I thought about my answer to your last question, and I'm afraid I may have given the wrong impression."

Georgiana raised a brow, and Nettie knew that nothing but utter sincerity would move the other woman. "I have no immediate desire to have more children," she admitted, and the honesty bolstered her, "precisely because nothing is more sacred to me than motherhood. I know it's the most challenging, most important occupation a woman can undertake. In becoming Colin's mother," she hesitated only briefly, "my focus would be on Colin. He lost his mother. I lost mine, too, when I was still a child. It's inappropriate to discuss more children right now. The one we've got deserves our full attention."

From the corner of her eye, she caught Chase's upturned gaze, though she couldn't see his expression. Georgiana appeared pleased by Nettie's words, but Nettie wasn't through yet. "I also think it's inappropriate to threaten a man with a custody suit when you haven't even met him. Julia's parents are more than welcome to visit—they should visit—but not in a spirit of judgment. Chase and Colin are a brand-new family. They need support, not threats. And they don't need to be put under a microscope. If a few magazine articles are bothering everyone, I can tell you right now that Chase's womanizing days are over. He adores his son. If he didn't...I couldn't adore him."

The words were out. There for everyone to hear, and to remember. Well, it was the truth. Nettie lifted her chin. She'd said what she needed to, and she was glad. Glad and, frankly, proud of herself.

She waited for Georgiana's response. The woman regarded her steadily and with some surprise. Finally she made her copious scribbles.

Nettie glanced at Chase, but met only the top of his head as he watched Georgiana write.

Stabbing a period on the end of a sentence, Georgiana stuffed the yellow legal pad into her oversized handbag and stood. "Thank you. You've both given me a great deal to think about." Chase stood as well. "I'm not supposed to say anything one way or the other regarding a custody case, Mr. Reynolds. However, I'm going to break that rule, because," she shrugged, "because I feel like it. I believe that you are sincere in your intent to be a good father. Your son's grandparents, the Foster-Smiths, are equally sincere in their concern and in their desire to insure the well-being of their grandson. This case will go to court if there's a T left uncrossed."

"And you've found a T?" Chase asked.

Georgiana frowned, musing. "I'm not sure." She included

Nettie, too, in her gaze. "Your willingness to marry for Colin's sake—and I do think that's what's going on here—is admirable. But how much it secures his future happiness, I don't know. And whether it'll persuade the Foster-Smiths to drop the case, I rather doubt. There's still the issue of your moving about so much, who will be at home with this child, where will his home be, etcetera. You have your work cut out for you." She smiled the brusque no-nonsense smile that seemed typical of her.

Chase shook her hand. "I appreciate your candor."

"And wish you could tell me to take a flying leap!" Georgiana's laugh boomed heartily. "Unfortunately, you'll probably be seeing me again." She extended her hand to Nettie for a firm shake and then walked out to her car with Chase.

When he returned, Georgiana's car was already kicking dust down the dirt path. Chase headed for the kitchen. "You want wine?"

"No." Nettie followed him. From the refrigerator, he pulled a bottle of the cabernet that they'd opened at dinner and poured what was left of it into a goblet. "Is Colin still watering?"

"He's winding the hose." Chase took a swallow of wine. "I told him he could play outside until it's dark."

He wasn't looking at her. Like his responses, his movements were spare.

"You're really worried now, aren't you?"

"Shouldn't I be?"

"I think Georgiana likes you. Respects you." Nettie approached the center island, where he stood. "I know it didn't go as well as we'd hoped, but as she said, you'll be seeing her again."

"You think that will help?"

"Don't you?"

"Who knows?" He took another long swallow of wine and set the glass on the counter. A self-mocking curve shaped his lips. "I tend to think I'm pretty clever. I usually get what I want. But this time…" He shook his head. From his contemplation of the Italian tiles, he looked up. His expression was sober, his gaze as focused as a laser. "Why, Nettie?"

She shook her head, unsure of what he was asking.

"When Georgiana wondered if you wanted children of your

own—it occurs to me that was a yes or no question. But it wasn't that simple for you.''

"I explained when I came back into the room—"

Chase shook his head, his narrowed eyes and uncompromising countenance as effective an interruption as if he had spoken. "Not good enough. You knew what was at stake the first time. Even if you'd said no—cleanly—it might have seemed like a normal response.'' He crossed halfway toward her. ''It was your hesitation, your confusion that made her doubt us.''

"I realize that.'' Frustrated, Nettie spread her hands. "I made a mistake. I also fixed it.''

"Why?''

"What do you mean? Chase, I know you're worried and upset, and, yes, you have a right to be. I didn't play my part the way I should have. But I did try to correct it, and if you ask me, I did a pretty good job.''

"Played your part,'' he muttered, jaw hardening. He nodded. "Yes, a 'good *job*' is exactly how I'd put it.''

Nettie put her clenched hands on her hips. "Why are you dissecting my words? Chase, you're nitpicking, and it's not fair. I did my best. She caught me off guard.''

"We're all caught off guard.'' Continuing around the center island, he closed the gap between them. "It occurs to me that we've talked plenty about my inability to commit.'' His voice was soft, deceptively so. "But what about yours? Why do words like *temporary* and *brief* keep coming up, Nettie?''

Calm demeanor or no, Nettie sensed the anger and frustration within him. Surprisingly, it chased away her guilt, leaving *her* frustrated and angry in turn. There was an implied judgment in this cross-examination, and she didn't like it. He had no idea how much courage it had taken to help him with this custody case to begin with.

"We never discussed permanent,'' she reminded him. "Right from the start we said there would be an end to this.''

"*You* said—''

"No.'' She shook her head emphatically. "If you recall, you warned me that you weren't a stick-around kind of guy.''

"And you said that was all right with you.''

"It is.''

"Why?'' Holding her shoulders, seemingly unaware that he

was even doing so, Chase searched her face. "Why is it all right for a man to walk in and out of your life? It's obvious that family means everything to you. I've read your books. I've watched you with Colin. You love kids. You were born to have a family of your own. Colin loves—"

"Stop. Will you please stop!" She tossed up her hands and shook her head. "No, look, you've been "committed" all of what, two weeks? All of a sudden you think that makes you the world authority on family dynamics? Or on what other people need?" Nettie watched her verbal attack fall on Chase like a series of blows, but she felt desperate, desperate to stop him before he finished his sentence, and desperate to end this conversation before he somehow convinced her he was right. It wasn't only her heart at stake, it was her sanity. "I will not let you make me feel guilty for turning out to be exactly who I said I was. I told you I don't want a long-term relationship. I told you I can't give it."

"I don't believe you."

"You don't know me!"

"Then tell me." Chase's grasp tightened on her shoulders. "Dammit! Tell me why I can make you laugh, and I can make you smile. And I can make your eyes flash when we make love, but I can't make you want forever."

A volcano was ready to erupt in Nettie's chest. "Is that what's bothering you? You can't understand how a woman can say no now that you've decided to play family man?" She shook her head. "Well, maybe the idea of family is all novel and appealing to you, but I have been there, and I've done that, and I don't ever, ever, *ever* want to do it again!"

Stunned momentarily, Chase shook his head as if to clear it. "What do you mean, you—"

"No!" Nettie twisted away from him. Eyes filling with tears she refused to let fall, she held his gaze. "You were fun...we were fun together. But that's all. Leave it at that." Her voice fell to a whisper as harsh as a desert wind. "I wanted to help you with Colin. Don't try to turn this into anything else. Please. I can't...I don't love you."

The moment, the very instant the words fell from her lips, Nettie realized the lie she had just told. Like a bolt of lightning, truth shot through her chest—hot and sharp and unmistakable:

She loved Chase Reynolds, she loved his son. Once more life was offering her the chance to need two people fully and completely, with so much of her heart that to lose them would be to lose the part of her that pumped blood, the part that enabled her to breathe.

She hoped God would forgive her for returning the gift, but it didn't fit. Not anymore. There simply wasn't enough of her heart left to break off another piece.

Chase watched her for a long, silent moment. He dug in his pocket, pulled out a small silver box and set it on the counter beside them. "I don't love you, either." He opened the box. Nestled inside the silver cardboard was another box, this one velvet black. "I didn't buy this for you." Without ever taking his eyes off her, he flipped up the lid. A round diamond set in platinum almost as white as the stone and flanked by two trillion-cut sapphires sparkled at Nettie as if it were trying to speak. "I haven't felt like a kid at Christmas every time I imagined you opening this box, and I'm not *angry as hell* right now that something—or someone—in your past means more to you than I ever could." A smile so grim and utterly devoid of humor that it was chilling twisted Chase's lips. "There. We're even now. We've both lied."

Leaving the ring where it was, tucked in a box rather than on the finger for which it had originally been intended, Chase walked from the room, the air of finality as clear as the diamond he had purchased for his intended.

Chapter Eighteen

Two days later, Chase was in New York, involved in what promised to be all-day meetings. Both he and the director of his TV station hoped the caucuses would result in a new career direction, one that would keep him at the station and in the states, or more accurately, in one state—New York. Chase hoped, also, to locate a more kid-friendly apartment. Lilah had agreed to watch Colin while he was away.

Aware of the turbulent and apparently permanent parting between her sister and Chase, Lilah had mercifully chosen to stay at the cottage rather than bring the little boy to the house, but on the afternoon of the second day, she got a call from her agent, alerting her to a plum movie audition back in Los Angeles.

"I booked a plane ticket for the day after next," she told Nettie in a rapid spate of enthusiasm. "I need a manicure and a pedicure before I leave, because there won't be time after I get home. And where am I going to find a decent hairdresser around here who can take me on short notice? I have got to do something about this." She pointed to the top of her head, the bright light in Nettie's second-floor studio illuminating traitorous ash-brown roots that had to be eliminated.

Drying a paintbrush on a rag, Nettie tried to dredge up some empathy for her sister's plight. "Are you going to leave before Chase gets back?"

"Not if he flies in tomorrow night, like he said he would. But if he's delayed…" She shrugged. "Look, I know you're uncomfortable with this, but Colin really enjoys himself over here, and I can't miss this audition, Nettie. I've had a little dry spell, lately. I need the work."

"I know. I don't mind watching him." But Chase had asked Lilah, not her. He was still furious with her. And he had good reason.

It was dead-on accurate to say that fear was the devil that made her want to end their relationship. But Nettie figured that was her business and her right. What depressed her was that she'd promised to help him with his custody case, and she'd blown it. Fear again. It had made her drop the ball after she'd given her word to help.

"Look," Lilah said, misinterpreting the troubled look on her sister's face. "Let's just deal with today…and my dark roots. I'll be home in a few hours, and I'm sure Chase'll be back before I have to fly out of here, so you won't even have to see him if that's what you want. Although I still—"

"It's what he wants, too, Lilah." Chase had made it clear that even the engagement of convenience was over. Georgiana had not been overly impressed by it, anyway.

"—think that you're nuts." Lilah spoke over her sister's comment and then narrowed her eyes. "Fine, so you're both nuts. A perfect match." Scooping her oversized purse up off the floor where she'd dropped it, she flung the bag over her shoulder. "Did Nadine Ritchie ever open a beauty salon in Anamoose, like she kept saying she would?"

"Yes. It's on Main Street. You can't miss it."

"Good. I hope she's not still p.o.'d about my going to the junior prom with Denny Kelter."

"She is."

Lilah rolled her eyes. "Still a twit, but she knows hair. As long as she doesn't deliberately dye me purple I should be okay." She blew Nettie a quick kiss. "I'll see you in a while. I brought Colin's bike over. He wanted to ride it. I told him he could go as far as the Seaforths' place and back." Heading down the upstairs hallway, she spoke while walking backwards. "I think he's hoping you'll read him one of your stories later." She smiled. "He thinks they're about him, you know." Fluttering her fingers, she headed down the stairs.

Lilah disappeared and Nettie sighed. *Nice parting shot, sis.*

Dropping the brush into a can of other clean brushes, she looked at the lone picture left on her bookshelf. Tucker grinned back at her. Wiping her hands and tossing the rag onto her desk, she moved to stand before the photo, running a fingertip along the pewter frame.

"Happy birthday, my big little boy." Softly she tapped the train engineer's hat they'd given Tuck for his birthday. Even at three he'd been thrilled with the striped cap that looked just like the one in his favorite storybook. Along with the hat, Nettie had found a beautiful miniature train, the first of what she had expected to be a growing collection for her locomotive-loving son. Tucker had played with the toy every day, rarely allowing it out of his sight and showing it to anyone who had the patience to affect an interest. He'd had it with him in the car that awful ice-laden day.

Nettie replaced the photo. Next to it on the shelf was the plaster mask of Tucker.

As carefully as if she were handling Limoges, Nettie picked up the heavy mask. Brian had crafted it to look like Tucker was smiling. "Number one in a series," he'd promised as she'd withdrawn the mask from a gift box he'd wrapped for her birthday. She'd loved it then; she loved it now. Gently, she turned the mask over. Tucker Ecklund, Brian had written into the plaster. Thirty Months.

For just a moment, she held the mask close to her heart. It was her most precious keepsake, the only *thing* she could say she truly treasured, a memento of a life measured in months. On the emptiest of afternoons, she could glance at the mask and the expression Brian had captured so well and be instantly transported to the giggle-laced days and cuddle-filled nights of Tuck's babyhood. Just that quickly Nettie could recall all the dear pedestrian dreams she had held for her family. She had never wanted the moon, only a growing collection of sweetly average tomorrows.

Setting the mask back on its stand, Nettie wished briefly that she could resume painting. Working on Tucker's birthday had become a habit, a way to keep from feeling or thinking too much. But Colin was outside, riding his bike, and Lilah was puttering down the driveway in their ancient car, which meant it was time for Nettie to take over.

The first couple of hours' baby-sitting went pretty well, Nettie thought. Colin rode his bike into town while she followed on foot. The sky had gone unseasonably overcast, but the weather was still hot, so they stopped for a cool drink and a snack at the bakery. On the way home, they watched Ina Petty's schnauzer piddle on Lois Johnson's pink plastic flamingo and fed bits of Colin's doughnut to two flickertail squirrels that grabbed the food and chased each other up an American elm.

When they returned to the house, Colin asked if they could go to Nettie's studio to pick out a book to read.

"I like your books," he said as he stomped up the stairs ahead of her.

"Thanks, buddy." She laughed at the huge, roundhouse-style steps he took, clearly playing out some mini-adventure in his mind.

"You choose," she said, leading him to the bookshelf while she went to collect the paint-splotched rags she had used that morning. "My last book was set on a deserted island. Kind of like 'Gilligan's Island.' My sisters and I watched that show all the time when we were kids. We used to make up skits and take turns playing all the characters. Have you ever seen that show? I think they still play it on classic TV."

Nettie turned to see Colin standing on tiptoe, reaching for the life mask of Tucker, a look of pure fascination on his face.

"Oh, Colin, don't!" In a knee-jerk reaction, she rushed to him. "Don't play with that, honey!" She stayed his hand. "It's not a toy."

Colin stepped back in confusion. "What is it?"

"It's called a life mask."

Interest lit Colin's eyes. "A mask? Like the kind you wear on Halloween?"

"No, not like that." Mentally fatigued, Nettie wondered if suggesting a nap would land like a lead balloon. Sighing, she searched for an impersonal explanation. "This isn't the kind of mask you play with. It's a keepsake. Something you put up just to look at. Like collecting baseball cards.''

"You can play with baseball cards."

"Right. Well, there are some things you keep, but don't play with.''

"Why?"

"Because some things would break too easily if you played with them.''

He looked at the mask. "Is it expensive?"

"No. But it's very special to me." Hoping he was ready for a change in topic, she pulled three books off the shelf, two of hers and one by an author from South Dakota, someone whose work was particularly imaginative. With any luck, Colin's interest would be engaged, and she could take a little breather. Beneath fatigue, Nettie felt a mounting restlessness.

"Here," she said, handing Colin the books. "Let's go downstairs and read."

He wriggled close to her on the couch, asking first that she read to him and then choosing to read aloud on his own. Constant motion made his thin body feel warm; the skin on his arms was child-soft, as it would be for a few more years. Focusing on the printed words as Colin read, Nettie couldn't help but notice how good it felt to sit like this at the end of a long day.

Abruptly, in the middle of a page, Colin interrupted himself to announce, "My dad says we're moving to New York soon."

"R...really." So Chase had decided definitely then? Colin's legs fidgeted a little against Nettie's: "You'll like New York, I'm sure," she said, forcing an enthusiasm she didn't feel. "Have you ever been there?"

"No. They got the Statue...the Statue..." Colin frowned. "A statue of a really big lady."

"The Statue of Liberty." Nettie smiled. "You'll like seeing that, I bet."

Colin shrugged. "I like it here," he said in voice that was small and hopeful. "How come we can't stay here?"

Taking a deep breath, praying for words that would soothe a child who had said too many goodbyes in his life already, Nettie put an arm around his shoulders. "Your dad needs to live in the city, because that's where his job is. He wants to take care of you really, really well, and to do that he has to work."

"He could work here. He could be a sheriff, like Sara," Colin obviously thought he'd hit on the perfect solution, "Or... somethin'...like Nick. Then we wouldn't have to move! I like coming here. You smell good and Sara knows how to shoot guns and Lilah says she's goin' to be in a movie someday, and I can go see it for free. And I like helpin' you paint books 'n' plant the flowers. If I go, who'll water the flowers?"

Oh, Colin, Colin, she thought, don't do this. Not now, not today. I don't want to cry until after you've gone.

Taking the book from which he'd been reading, Nettie set it on her own lap and focused on the pictures, turning pages slowly, calming her breathing before she replied. "I'll water them." But she knew that from now on visiting the cottage would elicit a host of memories that could do little more than add to the longing in her soul.

"You can ride in cars that are underground in New York," he said, brightening a bit before remembering, "Sara said she'd teach me to slingshoot."

Tough as Sara was, or pretended to be, Nettie knew her sister had fallen for Colin hook, line and sinker. She even referred to him now as "Little Deputy."

"Maybe there'll be time before you go."

Colin shrugged. Silently, he sat for a moment, looking at his knees.

Nettie's eyes blurred. Images of a dozen future events in Colin's life tried to crowd her mind. And she was there in every vision...she and Chase.

"I love being with you, too," she said, even as she tried to press the yearning aside. Concentrate on the reality. Concentrate on the reality and try to minimize the pain. "But New York is such an exciting place. After you've been there awhile, you'll know so many people and you'll have so much to do, why, I bet you won't have time to think about us much at all!" Cheerful words. Empty words. True for him, probably, over time, but a bald lie for her.

She would think about Colin every day and when she did, she would picture Chase. She would remember what the first stirrings of desire had felt like, how her body had awakened again under his gaze and his touch, and how, despite her best efforts, love had awakened again, too.

Nettie realized that in the off-guard moments when she remembered and pictured him and felt him, she would feel her loneliness afresh, but it would be a pain she could handle. The knowledge that Chase and Colin were alive and well somewhere would help her handle it. And someday…maybe soon…Chase would marry and have more babies and then Nettie would stop thinking about him altogether…well, mostly. There would be no more use of dreaming once he moved on. The only pain she'd have to deal with then would be the one she'd already grown used to: emptiness.

The top of Colin's head invited her to press a soft kiss in his bountiful hair. She kept the touch light and doubted he'd even felt it.

"Looks like it's getting kind of rainy out," she murmured, searching for a diversion. "Want to make cookies with me?" Leaning in, she indulged herself by holding him close in a hug. "When Lilah comes back, we'll have a snack ready for her. She'll probably be hungry after gallivanting around all afternoon."

"What's gavel…gavlan…"

"Gallivanting. It means running around."

Colin nodded. "I'm always hungry after gavlanting."

"Let's do it then," Nettie said, imbuing her voice with enthusiasm. "What kind of cookies?"

He thought about it a moment. "Chocolate chip. 'Cause she's a girl and girls don't get as hungry as boys, but even if you're not hungry, you can eat chocolate chip cookies!"

Nettie laughed. "I believe you're right." Relinquishing her hold on him, she handed Colin the books they'd been reading. "Here. You take those back upstairs, and I'll get all the ingredients out for the cookies."

"Okay." He scooted off the couch.

Outside, the gray sky had begun to sprinkle warm summer rain and echoing in the distance came a muted rumble of thunder. Listening to the storm, Nettie moved to the kitchen to concentrate on the blessedly mundane task of baking.

Butter and eggs from the fridge… Flour and baking soda and brown sugar from the cupboard… She'd stashed a bag of chocolate chips in here somewhere, so Sara couldn't find and empty them into the Cocoa Puffs box, but where…? Ah! Perfect. A whole bag.…

Setting out a mixing bowl and cookie sheet, Nettie pulled a stepladder up to the counter so Colin could reach. It had surprised her somewhat over the past couple of weeks to discover how much Colin enjoyed helping her in the kitchen.

Then again, hot gooey baked goods and spoons and bowls to lick out were persuasive rewards!

Tucker, too, she mused, had loved still-warm cookies and the doughnuts she had made from scratch. His favorite sweet, though, oddly enough, had been cheesecake. He had grinned and cooed over every bite, from his very first. Would he have enjoyed baking with his mom, Nettie wondered? What would he have looked like at age seven, powdered in flour as she taught him to measure ingredients? Nettie's lips curled at the image, but the corresponding pang in her heart made her pull herself up short. Thoughts like that were not helpful to her, not now when she had to remain positive and concentrate on the task at hand.

Turning the radio on, she focused on song lyrics and baking items. She whistled and she hummed, but while she tried to use her head to remain upbeat, her spirit began to feel weighty, a little more and a little more with each passing moment. The time of evening when she took a few minutes to privately commemorate her son's birthday was rapidly approaching, and her body seemed to feel it.

With everything laid out on the counter and the oven preheating, Nettie began to wonder what was keeping Colin.

"Colin, where are you, bud?" she called from the door to the kitchen. "Hey, Colin!"

When there was no answer, she trudged upstairs to see what he was up to. Her body felt heavy and lethargic, too, so maybe she was down with something. As she reached the landing, Nettie noticed dark clouds gathering in the distance and wondered how much longer Lilah would be. The early evening was shifting rapidly from cozy to gloomy.

"Colin?" she called again as she rounded the door to her studio. "Are you in here? I've got everything ready down— Oh, Colin!"

Abruptly, Nettie came to a halt. She stood frozen in the doorway, surveying with awful apprehension the scene before her.

Sitting on his knees, Colin examined the sculpture of Nettie's son. He held a piece of it in each hand, two large chunks. Smaller broken chips lay scattered on the floor around him.

"What have you done?" Nettie's voice rasped. Her limbs felt like stone.

"I wanted to put it on." Colin looked up at her, contrite but unaware of the full import of his actions. "You said it was a mask, but it's waay heavier than masks are s'posed to be."

Nettie felt pressure build inside her.

"I told you not to play with it! Weren't you listening to me?" She knelt in front of him. "I told you it wasn't a toy. It wasn't meant for you!" She heard the sharpness of the words, saw the uncertainty and concern come over Colin's face, but she felt such grief she couldn't stop herself.

"I could fix it prob'ly." Awkwardly, Colin tried to fit the two mask pieces together, like a puzzle. Another tiny chip dropped to the ground.

"No!" Nettie pulled the mask from his hands. "Leave it, just..."

All the breath seemed to go out of her. Sitting on her knees on the hardwood floor, she realized her hands were shaking as she looked at the broken plaster, sick with the feeling that she had somehow been careless or thoughtless. If she'd put it somewhere else, somewhere higher or hidden...

"My dad could get you another, I bet," Colin offered, his confidence returning. "He knows where to get lots of stuff. I'm gonna ask him and then—"

"No!" Nettie raised her eyes to the robust little boy, brimming with childish conviction that what was broken could surely be repaired again. "There are things you can't fix once you break them. That's why you listen to people when they tell you, Colin." She shook her head, unaware of the tears that welled in her eyes. "You...you have to listen!"

Colin stood a moment, uncertainty filling his small body. He had no idea what to do. Clearly he was frightened by Nettie's strong response. Not knowing how to express it, however, his fear turned quickly to anger. "It was just a dumb ugly old mask, anyway," he shot back at her, lower lip trembling, eyes blazing with wounded pride. "You couldn't even wear it!" Before Nettie could say a word or do anything, he tore out of the room.

Nettie wanted to call after him, later she thought she might even have tried, without quite realizing it. She couldn't have made much of a sound, though; tears choked her throat and blurred her vision. Her arms and legs felt boneless. Pain gripped her stomach and for an indeterminate amount of time, she could do no more than sit where she was, caved in on herself, trying desperately not to give in to the pain. If she cried for her baby and Brian, if she ached for the mistakes she had made and could never recall, and for the awful, endless…void…she might never stop.

Taking breaths, she waited until she felt solid again and could stand. Then she got up, still holding the two pieces of plaster. They didn't resemble anything, anymore. Feeling numb, Nettie set what was left of the mask on the shelf.

Just do what's next, she directed herself.

Colin was downstairs, upset and confused. He'd made a mistake, and she'd answered it with another. It was up to her to iron out the clash before Lilah came home. Colin would be gone from her life altogether before she knew it; she couldn't let him leave with anger creating distance between them.

The thought put an uncomfortable urgency in her step. There were so many things in this world you could neither control nor count on, but you could make sure that people knew you loved them before you said goodbye.

Outside, distant thunder had begun its slow, grumbling roll across the evening sky. It had started to rain, too, she noted with vague surprise, though inside the house the air was humid and still.

Nettie expected Colin to be in the living room, sitting in front of the television—his favorite evening spot when no other activities had been mandated—and she took a breath as she hit the base of the stairs, hoping for the right words.

She'd taken only one step into the foyer when she realized there was no sound coming from the TV. The living room was empty. Ditto the dining room and kitchen.

"Colin?" Grimacing in the too-warm kitchen, she glanced at the butter softening to a near melt on the counter and turned the stove down for the time being. "Colin!"

Nettie checked the bathroom, the downstairs coat closet and then ran back up to the bedrooms. Was he hiding? "Colin, I know you're upset, but wherever you are, you need to come out now, so we can talk." Again she investigated all the closets...and under the beds. He was nowhere. Standing with her hands on her hips in the middle of Sara's bedroom, she raised her eyes to the ceiling as thunder rolled closer. "Bike," Nettie murmured. "His bike's outside."

She sped down the stairs a second time, heading this time for the mud porch. They'd leaned his bike against the porch steps. *Be there...be there.*

An impressive crack sounded overhead as Nettie opened the door. Lightning flashed and then sizzled, and the thunder rolled again. He couldn't have ridden anywhere in this; he wouldn't have—

No bike.

"Oh..." Nettie indulged in a cussword that would have done Sara proud. Unmindful of the pouring rain, she ran outside, sandals crunching on the wet gravel driveway. She scanned the distance in all directions, but saw no one, and she shivered suddenly, though not from cold. The rain was warm, the air thick and musky. Summer storms, with their deceptive temperatures and dramatic electrical displays could be the most brutal. Without the bitter cold, there seemed to be less to fear, but lightning and dry summer fields were a combustible duo.

Turning toward the house with the intention of getting her car keys, Nettie realized halfway up the porch steps that Lilah was driving Jezebel.

"All right, think. *Think.*" She thumped her forehead with a loose fist. "Sara!"

Racing up the remainder of the steps, she grabbed the phone and hit Sara's number on the speed dial. The sheriff was out on a call. Swearing again, but determined not to waste precious minutes hesitating, Nettie simply took the next logical action— she changed from sandals to sneakers. If she had to go after Colin on foot, she would. Her shorts and T-shirt would be rain-soaked in minutes, but she had no time to deal with that. She grabbed the thin jacket Colin had brought with him and then, in shoes with no socks, dived back into the storm.

Like a good catastrophist, Nettie's mind treated her to a rapid series of visuals involving flash floods, lightning-struck trees that cracked in two or exploded into flame, metal bike frames as potential lightning conductors—

"Stop it!" she hissed out loud. "Think of Colin. And safety and blankets and warm beds and hot cocoa." She pursued the positive with all the relentless determination of Sister Maria in *The Sound of Music.* A mere instant before she began warbling about raindrops on roses and whiskers on kittens, Nettie had a flash of memory that propelled her jogging feet toward the garage.

Nearly a year ago, Sara had bought a truck from Ernie, an ancient, rust-pocked Ford, which she had stowed in the garage and was gamely trying to restore on her days off. She'd paid a hundred dollars and promised that she'd drive the truck in the annual Pioneer Days Parade with a sign that read Good Eats at Ernie's, but most people thought Ernie'd got the better part of the bargain. Privately, Nettie had considered the heap a waste of good garage space, but right now she felt like kissing Ernie and Sara and maybe even the truck.

Raising the garage door, she searched a rack of hooks for the correct key. Once she had it, she opened a door whose aching hinges made so much noise it seemed possible the panel might fall off altogether. Nonetheless, she climbed into the driver's seat, worked the key into the ignition, and started to pray.

At her sister's request, Nettie had started the truck a couple of times and run through the gears while Sara had stuck her head under the raised hood and listened to the engine. Now as she turned the key, Nettie chanted, "Please work—oh, please work—oh, please work—oh, please work…"

To her undying gratitude, the engine turned over with phlegmy compliance. As the vehicle wheezed its way to life, Nettie wrapped her fingers around the floor-mounted stick shift and stepped on the clutch. Jezebel had similar manual controls, but they handled more smoothly, and that wasn't saying much. Her first attempt to move the vehicle resulted in a giant lurch backwards, a neck-snapping halt as the truck stalled, and the threat of tears—her own—as she tried once more to re-start it.

This time, Nettie managed to back all the way out of the garage and to turn toward the road.

Rain obscured her vision and a sudden wind whistled against

the windows. For once, however, Mother Nature's muscle-flexing served to anger Nettie more than frighten her.

"Work with me," she growled, hunkering over the steering wheel as she searched for something resembling wiper controls. "Howl all you want, but I will bring Colin home safe and sound!"

When she reached the end of the driveway, Nettie realized she had a decision to make: Which direction had Colin taken? Would he have headed back to Nick's or into town? Over to the grammar and middle school? He liked the playground there....

Relax and it'll come to you. As if someone were standing inside her head, the words arrived to calm her racing mind. Nick's. It made the most sense that Colin would have pedaled home.

With sweaty palms, a racing heart and a glance at the thundering heavens, Nettie guided the truck onto the road and hoped that she was right.

Chapter Nineteen

Thunder rocked the earth as Nettie arrived at the farm. In the cab of an old truck with no luxuries to insulate it, she experienced every shuddering ka-boom as if she were standing in an orchestra pit next to the kettledrum.

"Please be here, please be here," she prayed as she opened the driver's-side door, ducked her head and raced to the porch. Lightning struck the earth with angry velocity, as if someone were hurling javelins from the sky. Each wicked flash turned the dark gray sky into blinding daylight.

No lights were visible from the front of the cottage nor was Colin's bike anywhere in sight. Nettie pounded on the door, anyway, shouting his name as loudly as she could, but the time and effort were wasted. She'd guessed wrong.

Diving into the shelter of the pickup, she shoved the vehicle into reverse, grinding the gears as she pointed herself toward the road again. It was slow going. Hitting every bump and dip on the unpaved path, she had plenty of time to consider where she ought to search next. If Colin had headed straight into town when he left the house, he would have found shelter by now. He might have headed for the jail, and even if Sara was out on a call, he'd be safe from the storm. If, on the other hand, he'd headed away from the house, in the direction of the school, there would be no relief from the elements at all. The elementary school was closed for summer. The best Colin would be able to do was huddle in a doorway. Unable to bear the mental picture of him alone and unprotected, Nettie turned in the direction of the school when she reached the road. Each rotation of the tires took her farther from town—and from the people she relied on for the strength and resilience she no longer believed she possessed.

As she drove, she had to fight not to feel disoriented by the amazing constancy of the lightning and thunder. Was Colin frightened by electrical storms? she wondered. They had many in Florida. Having lived in North Dakota for most of her life, Nettie was certainly no stranger to storms, but she couldn't remember ever having driven in one this aggressive.

Brian had.

The unbidden thought arrived with all the jagged sharpness of the lightning. Why was it that time washed crispness from good memories, leaving them as muted as if they wore veils, but did little to blunt the edges of less pleasant recollections? Nettie remembered so clearly Brian's insistence on traveling to his parents' house that bleak Christmas three years ago, despite the weather report of unfavorable driving conditions.

Unfavorable doesn't mean impossible, he had argued.

Very unfavorable, she'd argued back. They'd been living in Chicago then, two struggling young art students with a new baby. Brian's parents lived thirty miles outside the city. In the Midwest, harsh winter weather could make thirty miles feel like a cross-country trip. Tucker had been sniffling, Nettie insisted, and shouldn't be out in the cold. Why couldn't they wait until the weekend? There were still four days to go before Christmas....

But Brian had been stubborn that day, calling her a worrywart. The harder she'd fought, the more insistent he had become.

In the end, she had flatly refused to go; he had refused to stay. It was Christmas and his parents wanted to see the baby, and Tucker was excited about going. Rigid with disapproval, Nettie had watched Brian bundle Tuck into his car seat and drive off while the rain turned steadily into snow. *If I stay here,* she'd thought, he won't be gone long. He'll reach the first freeway exit, and then he'll turn back....

But she had guessed wrong, then, too, and Brian and Tucker had been alone in the car when it hit a patch of black ice. She hadn't been there to warn Brian or to tell him she loved him. She hadn't been there to hold her baby.

Gripping the steering wheel too tightly, Nettie told herself to stop—stop remembering, stop thinking, stop everything but what she was doing right this moment. Her racing mind, however, refused to quiet, and she wished with all her might that she had a cell phone so she could call Sara or Lilah, who might know what to do, who might make the *right* decision for this situation. It began to occur to her that she hadn't driven this far by herself—or in a storm at all—for three years. Her hands began to shake.

"I should have gone by the house again after I left Nick's to see if Lilah came home. It wouldn't have taken that long." Hindsight was a curse. "Damn. Damn, damn, damn!"

She was so busy shaking and chiding, that she almost missed it—a boy's new Schwinn mountain bike sticking up from a gully, half in and half out, on the side of the road.

She slammed her feet on the brake and clutch, grateful beyond words when the truck stopped without stalling. In the horizon a grouping of clouds had turned almost black. Nettie spared it only the barest glance before hurtling out of the cab once again. Her heart was in her throat as she approached the gully, and she began calling Colin's name before she hit the shoulder of the road. No answer came; no answer could. Colin lay at the bottom of the ditch, stomach down, his head turned to the side, facing her, one arm beneath his head, like a pillow.

Panic threatened, but not as the feverish, blinding desire to flee Nettie had grown used to. This panic was cold; it froze her heart and her blood. It froze time.

As if she were watching from somewhere outside herself, Nettie felt a vague surprise that she was able to keep moving. Half running, half sliding down the side of the ditch, she dropped to her knees beside Colin's inert body. He looked so tiny lying there alone in a rough, gravel-lined ditch; by contrast Mother Nature's rough howling seemed almost petty and mean.

Struggling under the dark sky and the consecutive, too-bright flashes of light, Nettie checked for injuries. He was breathing evenly, thank God. There were no visible signs of bleeding, external or internal, and his skin was warm.

"Colin," she said firmly, brushing hair from his forehead and bending close to him. "Colin, wake up, buddy. Come on, sweetheart, talk to me."

Nothing.

A rush of emotions squeezed her chest. Anger, frustration and fear made her tremble; determination made her refuse to kowtow to the distress. She couldn't crumble and she couldn't cave in to worry or indecision. She was all Colin had.

Taking his hand, she began to rub it, smoothing her fingers firmly between his knuckles, over his wrist and up his forearm, willing energy into his small body. "I'm sorry that I yelled. Or that I made you feel you weren't as important to me as that mask. Because you are. I think you're wonderful—funny and brave and smart. Your father loves you as much as any man has ever loved a little boy, so you have to be okay Colin. You have to be okay."

As she continued the massage, Nettie looked around, gauging their distance from the road and the steepness of the sides of the gully. She was going to have to carry Colin to the truck, and she knew she would have to take special care with his other arm, which looked as if it might be broken or dislocated.

"I've got to lift you now, buddy," she said as she rose to a crouch. "I'll be as careful as I can." Moving around him, she searched for an angle where she would have better leverage.

She was about to slide an arm under Colin's legs when the first pellets of hail struck the earth. Within seconds, knots of ice were being spit from the sky like hardballs in a batting cage. As the ice hit the truck, it sounded like a machine gun peppering metal.

Colin stirred and whined. "Owww. Stop it!" The sound of a child's complaint had never sounded so dear to Nettie's ears.

"Colin! That's it, wake up, honey. I'm here!"

He turned toward the sound of her voice, but hail struck his face. Immediately, Nettie braced herself over him, forming a protective tent with her own body. Wind propelled the ice with such force that she felt as if she were being struck in the back with fists. She didn't care. All that mattered was that Colin was awake, and he was all right.

He began a litany of mumbled woes, about his aching arm and that he couldn't breathe with her on top of him and that the "rain" was cold. Nettie answered in soothing murmurs, thrilled simply that he was coherent, not even bothering for now to think beyond getting him to the truck as soon as this ice show was over. Then, as abruptly as it had begun, the hailstorm stopped.

There was a moment's blessed, refreshing silence. Relief relaxed and filled Nettie's lungs. But the relief was as brief as it was earnest. She glanced up to a thick sky the mucky black-green shade of a stagnant pond. A second later, she heard it: the sound of a waterfall where no waterfall could possibly be. There wasn't even time to think the word before she heard the roar and saw the furious, spinning funnel.

Oh, my God. "Tornado," she breathed.

It was heading right toward them.

The emergency room of the small Queen of Angels Hospital in Detale, North Dakota, teemed with the kind of activity it rarely saw, save during flu season. Behind the check-in desk, the air hummed with barked instructions and other commotion; in the waiting room, complaints about the wait carried over murmured conversation and competed with the nightly news coming from a television set mounted high on the wall.

In sharp contrast to the bustling at ground level, all was relatively quiet on the second floor, where the patient rooms were located and where one heard mostly the soft sounds of a hospital at night. In fact, for the past hour, the only noise in the O-shaped corridor had been the rhythmic squish-squeak of rubber-soled shoes. Then the elevator doors opened and out hurried a different pair of feet with a decidedly different agenda. Pounding over the floor, unmindful of the Careful When Wet sign, these feet raced a man to the nurses' station, where he hung over the desk and with neither "Hello" nor "How are you?" gave his name and then demanded to know which room his son was in.

Chase was moving again before the room number was completely out of the young nurse's mouth. He didn't stop running until he pushed open the door to room 2012. A pale blue curtain divided the room into halves. In the bed closest to the door, a little boy lay beneath a thin acrylic blanket, his small body seeming to disappear into the large mattress. A bulky cast covered his right arm.

Colin appeared tired but animated as he regaled Lilah with an account of the tornado that "almost got us." She nodded calmly as if she'd heard this information once or twice already this evening.

When Colin saw his father, his face creased in a wide smile. "Dad!"

Chase moved to the bed immediately. He placed his palm lovingly on the top of his son's head, but realized quickly that the limited contact was not nearly enough. Lowering the safety rail, he sat on the bed and carefully took his son into his arms.

"I was in a tornado, Dad!" Colin's voice was muffled against Chase's shirtsleeve.

"I know that." Grateful that his head was lowered, Chase felt tears fill his eyes. He'd been on the plane already, heading back to North Dakota a day early, when the pilot's voice had announced that a tornado had hit central North Dakota. Chase had listened to the news with interest, but detachment, too. For some reason it had not once occurred to him that the people he loved might be affected. He was used to reporting the news, not being touched by it.

"What were you doing out in a tornado, huh?" Chase pulled back just enough to examine his son, to study his face and count his fingers, the mental tallies one might make with a newborn. "You scared me."

Chase had called home immediately upon disembarking the plane, but there'd been no answer. He'd phoned Nettie's house next and spoke to Lilah as she was heading out the door on her way to the hospital. Nettie and Colin had been caught in the tornado. They were at a small hospital in a town called Detale. That was all Lilah knew.

Chase hadn't just been scared at that point, he'd been more frightened than ever before in his life. He turned toward Lilah now and with his eyes asked the question: *Nettie?*

"I wasn't scared at first because I didn't know it was a tornado," Colin said, speaking before Lilah had a chance to respond. "But then Nettie said it was, and she said stay down in the ditch and don't be frightened 'cause she was takin' care of me, and then the wind got so loud I couldn't hear anything, and she laid down right on top of me and squeezed way too tight, but I wasn't mad or anything. And then the wind stopped and she started to laugh and I told her I had to go to the bathroom really bad so she let me go next to the road where cars could've seen and everything, and then we drove here.''

As a nightly news special report, it would have been shy a few pertinent details and overgenerous regarding a couple of others, but Chase figured he caught the gist. Most importantly, Colin said Nettie had started laughing, which had to mean she was okay, right?

Once more he looked at Lilah. ''Where is—''

''All right, everybody.'' Knocking and bumbling her way through the door—using shoulder, elbow, and forearm—Nettie hopped into the room. ''Who wants to be the first to sign my—'' Her eyes widened when she saw Chase. ''You're here.''

''You got crutches! That's cool!'' Colin said as his father rose from the bed. The little boy looked at Nettie with interest, but his energy was obviously flagging.

Moving swiftly to the door, Chase assessed the rest of her quickly, and he frowned deeply as he noticed the tangled hair, small scrapes on her uninjured leg and a cut on her cheek. Dirt streaked her white top.

He wanted to hold her, kiss her, stare at her until he was positive there was no damage other than the obvious and until his heart had stopped pounding.

''That's quite a load you're hauling around,'' Lilah spoke from behind them. ''Here, take my chair.''

Immediately Chase moved away from the door. Of course she'd want to sit down! She needed rest, she needed care.... ''Why are they letting you walk around? Shouldn't you be in a wheelchair?''

''A wheelchair? No, I— Chase! What are you doing?''

As carefully as he could, he scooped her into his arms.

''My crutches!''

''Drop them.''

''I've got them.'' With a smirk, Lilah relieved Nettie of the unwieldy burden. ''Nice service,'' she said as he delivered Nettie with infinite care into the chair. Dramatically, she sighed. "Now why can't I find a man who will treat me like porcelain?"

"Actually," Nettie said quietly, never taking her gaze off Chase, "porcelain is one of the strongest ceramic compounds."

Tenderly he raised a hand and touched her cheek, careful to avoid the abrasion. "My son tells me you were pretty heroic." He shook his head. "I should have been here."

"Well, you didn't know there was going to be a tornado."

"Doesn't matter." Chase frowned. He looked back at Colin. "This is where my family is." Returning his attention to the woman who had protected his son with her own body, he gazed at her as if he'd like to memorize every line, every detail. "When I think of what could have happened, and I wasn't here—"

Nettie touched a hand to his lips, stopping the words. He looked at her in question then gave a brief nod. She was right; this wasn't the right place.

"Colin's going to stay overnight. Did they tell you?" she asked quietly, while Lilah stood near the bed, talking to the rapidly tiring seven-year-old.

"No. I arrived only a minute or two before you came in." Worry, a once-unfamiliar sensation for Chase, crept into his stomach and chest for the umpteenth time since he'd become a dad. "Is everything—"

"He seems to be fine," she hastened to reassure him. "But he was out cold when I found him. He'd fallen off his bike into a ditch. Since Kalamoose is a full hour from here, the doctor thinks it'd be a good idea if he stayed overnight."

Chase expelled a noisy breath. His stomach was starting to roll as if he were on the high seas. Resignedly, he wagged his head. Who knew that the simple act of loving would require Dramamine? "What about you?" he demanded of the brave, gorgeous woman before him. He touched the cast. "Is this a bad break? I don't even know how it happened."

Nettie made a face. "I slipped on my way into the hospital," she muttered.

"Hey, kids," Lilah called softly. "I think the patient could use a little shut-eye. Maybe you two should take the conversation outside for awhile?"

"Nnooo," Colin mumbled plaintively from the bed, though his eyes were already closed. "I'm not sleepy. Ice cream…"

Chase smiled at Nettie, rose and moved to his son's bed. He bent to give Colin a kiss filled with gratitude. Every time he thought about how close he'd come to never knowing his son, it took the breath right out of him. "Rest," he said quietly, stroking Colin's hair. "Tomorrow we'll have a party. Hot dogs and potato chips and so many flavors of ice cream, Baskin-Robbins will be jealous." Before Chase had even finished his sentence, Colin was snoring softly.

Lilah grinned.

"How are *you?*" he asked, touching her elbow.

"Absolutely fine. My hairdo got rained on," she patted the bouncy, blonder-than-before waves, "but I never even saw the funnel. Anyway, I'm heading back to California soon, where the only natural disasters are earthquakes and running out of Kava Kava." She nudged his arm. "Why don't you take my sister to the cafeteria for a cup of their gruesome decaf and a little hospital food? She hasn't had dinner yet."

"What about you?" Nettie said. "Have you eaten?"

"I have a diet bar and a candy bar in my purse. If you two will get going, I can eat the candy bar and pretend I did it by mistake. Here," she handed Nettie the crutches then whispered in her ear, "Interesting newsflash on porcelain—being the strongest compound and all." She winked. "Good luck."

Nettie smiled then waved off all help as she maneuvered herself up. It was tricky going, but she did it. Chase held the door while she preceded him into the hallway. He hovered near her elbow. From the corner of her eye, she saw him reach for her several times as she tottered, but each time he stopped himself, and slowly but surely they made their way to the elevator and down to the first floor. Silently, they disembarked the elevator. The wall directly in front of them had an arrow pointing left for the cafeteria, but when Chase turned that way, Nettie stopped him.

"Not yet," she said. "I want to go someplace else first."

Chased raised a quizzical brow, but followed her without comment. He seemed immersed in thought and spoke little as she led him to a small chapel tucked into a corner of the first floor.

The walls were painted the cool new blue of a morning sky. Pictures of angels and saints hung at various points and though clearly this was a Catholic chapel, a petite statue of the Virgin Mary shared space at the front of the room with a simple cross and the Star of David. Peace and comfort filled the room as if they were entities.

"I like it here," Nettie said, speaking in a respectful hush even though she and Chase were the chapel's only visitors. "I spent a lot of time here when Uncle Harm was sick. I'd sit in that front pew," she nodded, "and I wouldn't think of anything. I wouldn't even pray, really. I'd just be here and feel the stillness."

When she paused, Chase put a hand on her back. "Do you want to sit down?"

Instead of answering, Nettie executed a skipping quarter turn to face him. There was so much to say, and she swallowed hard, unsure of how to begin. The last time they were together, she'd told him she did not love him and never could. On top of her bureau at home, the engagement ring he'd bought for her sat, still in its box, waiting to be returned. Oh, she'd made a series of wrong turns on the road to this moment. And looking at Chase now, Nettie wondered if he'd even want to hear what she had to say.

Fidgeting, she tottered on her crutches. Immediately, Chase put a hand beneath her elbow to steady her. "Come on, let's sit down. I'm afraid you're going to tip over." Carefully he helped her to a pew.

"Thanks," she said as he took her crutches and propped them against the pew in front.

"I haven't thanked you yet. I'm not even sure how." He gazed at her, sober eyes reflecting the depth of his gratitude. "Protecting Colin during that tornado was incredibly brave."

"Brave?" She shook her head. "Oh, no. I don't think I was brave," she admitted, undoubtedly the easiest confession she would attempt this afternoon. "When I first went out in the storm, I was petrified." She shivered again, merely thinking about it. "By the time I realized we were in a tornado, I wasn't thinking at all."

He smiled. "That's what the great heroes say, you know. That at some point they stop thinking and act on instinct."

Great heroes? Nettie grimaced. "I'm not a hero, Chase." She braced herself to deliver the first critical truth of the day. "In fact, it was my fault Colin was in the storm to begin with. I yelled at him because he broke something that was…well, it was special to me. I completely overreacted, though. I wasn't being fair, and I hurt his feelings."

"What did he break?"

She took a breath. "A plaster casting. It was a likeness of my son."

Chase's expression told her she'd blindsided him completely. His brow darkened with so many emotions Nettie couldn't hope to read them all. "Your son?"

Feeling somehow as if she were standing on the edge of a precipice, about to jump, she nodded. "Today is Tucker's birthday. He would have been six."

"Would have been?" The question was raw and reluctant.

"My son died three years ago in a car accident with my husband."

The words emerged more evenly than Nettie would have believed possible. But as she watched Chase quickly attempt to school his features, she saw not only the pain he felt on her behalf but also the pain of not being given this information sooner.

"I don't talk about it often, Chase. Not to anyone."

Beside her on the cushioned pew, Chase clasped his hands behind his neck and shook his head. Two floors above the softly lit chapel, his son lay recovering from an accident already being viewed as a terrific adventure. He looked at Nettie again, dusty and injured from her attempts to help his child, and he wanted to take her in his arms. He wanted to squeeze her way too tightly to remind himself that she was real and that she was fine and that everyone was safe.

When he felt the touch of her fingers, soft and warm, on his hand, he was shocked to feel longing burn behind his eyes. Nettie was watching him with an expression that was earnest and seeking.

"I want to talk about it with you," she said, "if you want to listen."

He nodded, and she began in a voice sometimes halting, sometimes flowing like an undammed stream, to tell the story of the losses she had known, beginning with her parents, ending with her child.

"For the longest time I thought the accident was my fault. If I'd been there in the car, there might have been something I could do. Or if I hadn't fought with Brian before they left…" Briefly she closed her eyes then reopened them and looked directly at Chase. "It sounds so ridiculous when I say it out loud, but I truly believed I should always be able to keep the people I loved safe."

"It doesn't sound ridiculous to me, Nettie. Not anymore." Chase did pull her into his arms then, burying his lips in the dark curls still matted from their wrestle with the wind. "My God, when I think of you alone in that storm with Colin—"

"But we weren't alone." She pulled back to look at him, hoping that what she had to say would somehow make sense to a man who was inherently brave. "I have been terrified of this life. I've been frightened of anything I couldn't control or predict, and my fear became like an armor. I put it on every morning, and all day and all night I let it steer me away from anything I thought could possibly hurt me or someone I loved." She reached around to take one of his hands, looking down at it, smoothing the strong fingers. "Life is small when you live it in fear. There isn't room for anything wild or unpredictable. And that's what love is."

With his free hand, Chase wove through the hair at her nape. "I came back early from New York," he confessed, "because nothing made sense there without you. I got on that plane today promising myself I wouldn't push you. But I'd already decided we'd wait—Colin and I. We'd wait just as long as it took for you to realize you wanted us, too."

When tears came to Nettie's eyes, Chase gently swept them away. "I've never been as scared in my life as I was when I heard you were in that tornado," he muttered fiercely. "Every time I picture the two of you…" Again he pulled her close, enveloping her. "I understand that you're frightened. You have every right to be. But I swear I'll always protect you, Nettie. You and Colin. On my life, I'll protect you."

With her cheek nestled against his chest, Nettie shook her head. "You can't, you know," she said softly and without regret. "No one can protect anyone all the time. But I love that you want to."

Stubbornly, Chase insisted, "I never should have left in the first place. If I hadn't, you wouldn't have been alone. I would have been there today."

"But you were." Nettie arched back to look at him. "You see, that's the whole point. Oh, Chase, no one can make a tornado stop. You can't guarantee we'll always be safe. But you were with us. I felt you, as truly as if you were in that ditch, like a great warm coat had settled over my shoulders. And suddenly I was strong. Holding Colin in my arms and loving him, *feeling* you love me—that seemed more real than anything else in the world." She blinked up at him, this man who had come to rescue her from a life drained by caution. "I don't want to be safe, anymore, Chase. I just want to love you."

Chase stared at the woman in front of him a long time before dropping his arms. Lightly, giving her room to move also, he cupped her face and brought his lips to hers. The kiss they shared began slowly and with relief, like a homecoming, but soon it built to something breathless and risky and wild, ripe with all the danger of desire and all the glorious exuberant promise.

When they pulled away, they were both grinning dazedly.

"I love you."

"I love you."

The avows overlapped each other.

Nettie's brows rose. "No fair," she complained. "I wanted to say it first."

Chase laughed. "You can say it first next time. In fact…" Taking her left hand, he brought it to his lips. "How about if we spend the rest of our lives taking turns?"

"The rest of our lives?" Nettie managed a watery grin. "See, there you go again," she said in a choked whisper. "I wanted to say it first."

For a moment, they simply looked at each other. Then Nettie launched herself at the man she loved and kissed him with every corner of her heart.

High on the morning-blue walls of the hospital chapel, painted angels looked down benevolently as a young woman chose life and love again and a man staked his claim to forever. Anyone watching would have sworn the angels danced for joy.

* * * * *

If you enjoyed what you just read,
then we've got an offer you can't resist!

Take 2 bestselling
love stories FREE!

Plus get a FREE surprise gift!

Clip this page and mail it to Silhouette Reader Service™

IN U.S.A.	**IN CANADA**
3010 Walden Ave.	P.O. Box 609
P.O. Box 1867	Fort Erie, Ontario
Buffalo, N.Y. 14240-1867	L2A 5X3

YES! Please send me 2 free Silhouette Special Edition® novels and my free surprise gift. After receiving them, if I don't wish to receive anymore, I can return the shipping statement marked cancel. If I don't cancel, I will receive 6 brand-new novels every month, before they're available in stores! In the U.S.A., bill me at the bargain price of $3.80 plus 25¢ shipping and handling per book and applicable sales tax, if any*. In Canada, bill me at the bargain price of $4.21 plus 25¢ shipping and handling per book and applicable taxes**. That's the complete price and a savings of at least 10% off the cover prices—what a great deal! I understand that accepting the 2 free books and gift places me under no obligation ever to buy any books. I can always return a shipment and cancel at any time. Even if I never buy another book from Silhouette, the 2 free books and gift are mine to keep forever.

235 SEN DFNN
335 SEN DFNP

Name	(PLEASE PRINT)	
Address	Apt.#	
City	State/Prov.	Zip/Postal Code

* Terms and prices subject to change without notice. Sales tax applicable in N.Y.
** Canadian residents will be charged applicable provincial taxes and GST.
All orders subject to approval. Offer limited to one per household and not valid to current Silhouette Special Edition® subscribers.
® are registered trademarks of Harlequin Enterprises Limited.

Coming in May 2002

**Three Bravo men marry for convenience—
but will they love in leisure? Find out in
Christine Rimmer's *Bravo Family Ties!***

Cash—for stealing a young woman's innocence, and to
give their baby a name, in *The Nine-Month Marriage*

Nate—for the sake of a codicil in his beloved
grandfather's will, in *Marriage by Necessity*

Zach—for the unlucky-in-love rancher's chance to
have a marriage—even of convenience—
with the woman he *really* loves!

BRAVO
FAMILY TIES

Silhouette®

Where love comes alive™